**The yellowbacks... classics of popular fiction**

The yellowjackets or yellowbacks were a great series of bestselling adventure and crime thrillers that had its origins in the mid to late 19th century following on from the 'penny dreadfuls'. They virtually began the mass market revolution of the early 20th century with a clear standard format and imprint/series livery (what would today be called branding). Hodder & Stoughton published the yellowjackets in two main series with series run dates of: 1923-1939 and later 1949-1957.

As the tagline ('where thrillers really began') on the back cover implies, the imprint and series focused on thrillers that were the bestsellers of their time. This current reissue or retro revival if you will, brings back many of these masterpieces, now classics in their own way and extends it further by including key titles from that period that were either great crime or thriller or even general commercial fiction (including sub-genres of noir, horror, gothic, romance, westerns, etc.) influences of their time. There are some perennial favourites and many rarities either lost or not easily available being revived in the current series. Writers and characters ranged from adventure heroes like Bulldog Drummond, Allan Quatermain, Richard Hannay or the Saint through thriller grandmasters Edgar Wallace and E. Phillips Oppenheim, crime and mystery maestros like Patricia Wentworth, GK Chesterton, Agatha Christie and the Detection club, to western and swashbucklers like Zane Grey, Max Brand, Captain Blood and even romance or general fiction classics like Hermina Black, Denise Robins, Marie Corelli or Stella Morton. These were books that had storytelling at their heart and always entertained.

The yellowbacks had both hardback (with varying design elements) and paperback (which built the series look) versions with the latter still carrying the imprint 'yellowjacket'. The current reissues pay tribute to both and use an amalgam of elements from both editions while retaining the complete yellow (or 'mustard-plaster') livery with the author's name in blue beveled type with a 'simulated emboss' effect and a white outer 'outline', and the book title in black. These reissues retain the distinctive size of the original mass market paperback and follow the three main category variations—the thrillers (crime, westerns, mystery, adventure) had blue lettering for the author's name, while Romance and softer general fiction had red; and other categories like humour had green.

For more detail and a full list of titles visit https://www.hachetteindia.com/home/yellowbacks

# CRIME UNLIMITED

## CRIME UNLIMITED

**David Hume** is the pseudonym of J.V. Turner (John Victor Turner). He also wrote as Nicholas Brady. His stint as a crime reporter on *The Daily Herald Newspaper* in Fleet Street gave him access to network of contacts in the underworld. He also had a brother who has a high ranking official in Scotland Yard and this gave him two inside views and he made good use of that knowledge in his thrillers.

# CRIME UNLIMITED

David Hume

*Crime Unlimited*
First published by Collins, London and Robert M. McBride, US in 1933

This Hodder Yellowback edition © Hachette India 2023
(Registered Name: Hachette Book Publishing India Pvt. Ltd.)
An Hachette UK Company www.hachetteindia.com

1

All rights reserved. No part of the publication may be reproduced, stored in a retrieval system (including but not limited to computers, disks, external drives, electronic or digital devices, e-readers, websites), or transmitted in any form or by any means (including but not limited to cyclostyling, photocopying, docutech or other reprographic reproductions, mechanical, recording, electronic, digital versions) without the prior written permission of the publisher, nor be otherwise circulated in any form of binding or cover other than that in which it is published and without a similar condition being imposed on the subsequent purchaser.

The texts in these editions in most cases have been reprinted as is, with minimal editorial changes and by and large no bowdlerizing for political correctness; though in some editions, a few words and phrases considered archaic, or those considered offensive now, along with archaic punctuation may have been modified in places to make the text more accessible to today's readers. The narratives, language, beliefs, social mores and/or cultural depictions, in these volumes are a reflection of their times and must be viewed as such. They may also contain certain cultural, racial and gender prejudices and stereotypes that may be outdated or clearly wrong then and wrong today; but their removal would be tantamount to claiming these prejudices never existed. The Publisher does not endorse or support those depictions or stereotypes; and these books have been made available for a discerning audience that will read it for entertainment value and a chronicle/record of popular fiction of past times.

Cover design by Priya Singh adapted from the original classic yellowjacket by Hodder & Stoughton.

Cover illustration by Ishan Trivedi.

Series note: Some of the books in the series (unless otherwise credited) may have cover or inside illustrations from the original yellowbacks or early editions, and while full restoration has been attempted, some images may be grainy or faded due to the condition of the original material. The end notes or bonus material or blurb details may have been sourced from the public domain or free use publications such as Wikipedia and attribution is hereby made also allowing similar free use reproduction from here. Sources requiring further specific attribution may write in and further detailing and/or corrections shall be made in subsequent printings/editions.

Reprint specifications may be subject to change including but not limited to finishes, paper, colour sections.

ISBN: 978-93-5731-006-2

Hachette Book Publishing India Pvt. Ltd.
4th & 5th Floors, Corporate Centre,
Plot No. 94, Sector 44, Gurugram - 122 003, India

Typeset in Electra LT STD 10/12.5 pt by Manipal Technologies Limited, Manipal

Printed and bound in India by Manipal Technologies Limited, Manipal

# CONTENTS

| | | |
|---|---|---|
| 1 | A Flying Visit | 1 |
| 2 | Conference at the Yard | 7 |
| 3 | Detective Murphy Sweats | 18 |
| 4 | At The Police Court | 25 |
| 5 | An Escape, and an Offer | 35 |
| 6 | Maddick Enlists a Recruit | 47 |
| 7 | The First Job | 53 |
| 8 | Mick Finds an Ally | 64 |
| 9 | The Reception | 77 |
| 10 | Many Things Happen | 88 |
| 11 | And Continue to Happen | 96 |
| 12 | A Talk with Maddick | 107 |
| 13 | On the Great West Road | 114 |
| 14 | Tommy Kane Escapes | 128 |
| 15 | Mick Makes Arrangements | 141 |
| 16 | Conference at the Yard | 149 |
| 17 | Maddick Gives Instructions | 161 |
| 18 | Mick Busies Himself | 170 |
| 19 | The Pall Mall Hold-Up | 179 |
| 20 | The Yard Makes Arrangements | 192 |
| 21 | Maddick Arrives! | 196 |
| 22 | Many Things Happen | 206 |
| 23 | Mick Meets Maddick | 213 |
| 24 | Maddick's Story | 221 |
| 25 | The Rescue | 226 |

# 1

## A FLYING VISIT

It was half-past ten in the morning, and Old Bond Street was awakening with languid ease. A watery sun struggled to thrust its face through the drab clouds.

Two young men sat in a handsome saloon car, parked at the curb's edge in Berkeley Square. The man at the driving seat threw the end of his cigarette out of the window and glanced at his gold wrist watch. Then his finger touched the gear lever as he pressed the self-starter with his left hand.

"Let's go," he said to his companion.

"I'm all set. Shove your foot down, and the best of luck."

The car slid away from the curb with a purr, and the driver swung the wheel to the right. They crawled down Bruton Street, and waited for two or three minutes before they could cut across into Old Bond Street. A hundred yards farther on the car pulled to a stop outside a small shop with barred windows. Across the façade were the words: Curtis Brothers, Limited, Jewellers.

The driver estimated the distance between his car and the one in front of him, looked backwards to survey the road.

"All clear," he said. "Make it snappy."

"Two minutes at the outside."

Mr Nicholas Proddy looked up as the door opened. He smiled. Trade was none too brisk, and an early customer was welcome. With a keen professional eye he summed up the man crossing the floor. He was young—perhaps twenty-four. Might be intending to buy an engagement ring. The blue serge suit was expertly cut, the material excellent. Would probably cost fifteen to eighteen guineas. The white shirt and collar were fashioned in silk. The felt hat was in perfect shape. Proddy was already guessing. Maybe this customer might go up to two or three hundred pounds for what he wanted. And Proddy would see that he got what he wanted. That was his job.

"Good morning, sir," he said, smiling benevolently.

"Good morning," replied the young man. His voice was cultured, the tone firm. "In your window you have a diamond pendant. May I see it?"

"That pendant," said Proddy, "is priced at fourteen thousand pounds."

"Seems a bit stiff, but the least I can tell my fiancee is that I've examined it and decided not to buy it. Get it out for me."

Proddy walked slowly to the window, drew back the heavy shutters, lifted the black velvet cushion, and turned to walk back to the counter. He nearly dropped the cushion as his mouth sagged, and his knees wobbled. His prospective client held an automatic in his hand, and the muzzle, as steady as a brick wall, was pointing at Proddy's heart. For a fraction of a second the two men stared at each other. The young man moved forward with long, quick strides. His left hand whipped the glittering pendant from its bed. Still Proddy gaped.

"If you shout or move, I'll plug you. If you move out of this shop within one minute after I have left, my friend over the road will shoot you. After the minute has passed you can do what the hell you like. If you want to live, remember what I've said. Good morning."

The young man slipped the pendant into his pocket, and placed the gun in his right-hand pocket. But his hand remained with it, and the shopman kept his eyes on the bulge in front of the jacket. The bandit walked backwards to the door. As he placed his left hand on the handle he gave his final warning!

"If you follow me, you're a dead man. My friend never misses."

The door closed, and instantly Proddy pressed the bell under the counter and jumped for the telephone. The one brought an assistant running into the shop, the other informed New Scotland Yard that, for the fourth time in one week, a robbery of the first water had been committed in the West End. While the assistant dashed out of the shop in pursuit of the bandit, Proddy gave the Yard a description of the man and the pendant. A few seconds later the information was wirelessed to all the Flying Squad cars on the Metropolitan patrol.

As the bandit shut the door of the shop the car commenced to glide away from the curb. As it swung round the car in front, the robber clambered into his seat.

"All O.K., Kelly," he said. "Step on it. I've got the sparklers."

The car had vanished into Grafton Street before the assistant arrived on the pavement. There, it leapt into life as the driver pressed on the accelerator, and he took the turning into Albemarle Street on the skid, and a few yards later the huge car swung into Dover Street. Although less than a minute had elapsed since the time of the hold-up the young man had been busy. From the pocket in the door of the car he took a large envelope, lined with thin canvas. On the cover was the address: Ernest Reames, Esq., c/o F. W. Jackson, Esq., 434 Stanhope Street, London, N. First he placed the pendant in a smaller envelope, and then inserted both in the larger one. The car slowed down, and the young man jumped out, strolled with apparent nonchalance to the nearest pillar-box, posted the letter, and returned to the car. Again the driver turned the wheel—this time into Berkeley Street. And there he applied the brakes and stopped the engine. Both men got out.

A few yards away from Piccadilly stood a sports two-seater. They started the engine. As it moved towards the famous thoroughfare they heard the distant clanging of a bell. The Flying Squad was in Old Bond Street!

Both men were smoking and chatting casually as they moved along in the ceaseless file of traffic. Where Albemarle Street and St. James's Street face each other on opposite sides of Piccadilly the traffic was suddenly held up. In the distance a bell was ringing, and a policeman instantly stopped the traffic flow. A saloon car, bearing the letters M.P. in blue above the windscreen, almost struck the pavement edge as it turned out of King Street at a reckless pace. In another second it had crossed Piccadilly on its way to Old Bond Street. At the head of the traffic stream sat the two men in the sports car. The Flying Squad motor had missed them by a couple of feet! As it vanished round the corner of Albemarle Street, and the point policeman waved them on, they smiled at each other.

At Piccadilly Circus they left the car outside the Corner House, walked through the swing doors, looked round at the confectionery for a few seconds, and departed through another door without making a purchase. In Great Windmill Street they hailed a taxi.

"Charing Cross," ordered Kelly.

"Southern or Underground?" inquired the driver.

"Southern."

After a quick drink in the buffet on the platform they left the station and boarded an east-bound omnibus. Kelly bought a ticket to Aldgate, the other man took a penny stage to Ludgate Circus. They parted without a word, without a handshake. There was no friendship between them.

They had never met before that morning. They did not know each other's names. They had merely acted throughout like automata, obeying instructions to the last letter. And neither of them knew by whom the instructions were given!

One man carried in his pocket a typewritten note. It was signed "Maddick," and had been delivered to the man's house by hand. The note read :

"You will find a Delage saloon at the junction of Saville Row and Burlington Street at ten o'clock tomorrow morning. Take it to Berkeley Place. There you will meet a fair young man in a blue suit. Call him Mullens. He will call you Kelly. Drive him to Curtis Brothers, Jewellers, Old Bond Street. Wait for him outside the shop. Afterwards, down Grafton Street, into Albemarle Street, and through to Dover Street. Wait there while Mullens posts an envelope. Then drive into Berkeley Street. There, a few yards from Piccadilly, you will find a two-seater Bentley. Drive that down Piccadilly, abandoning the Delage. Leave the Bentley outside the Corner House in Piccadilly Circus. Take a taxi to Charing Cross Station. Later board an east-bound omnibus, taking a ticket to Aldgate. Mullens will leave you at Ludgate Circus. As soon as you have finished the job destroy this note. Do not under any circumstance discuss this note with Mullens. He has his own instructions."

He had. And they were equally plain.

"At ten-fifteen tomorrow morning you must be in Berkeley Place. There you will see a small, dark man with a Delage car. His name is Kelly. He will drive you to a jeweller's. Ask the man in the shop to show you the diamond pendant from the window. Hold him up with a gun. Take the pendant and return to the car. Post the pendant in the box in Dover Street, using the enclosed envelopes. Kelly has instructions for you thereafter until you leave him at Ludgate Circus. Do not discuss any matters connected with me."

There were two other men who had taken part in the robbery without knowing it. One, at the time when the bandits parted, was drinking beer in a Villier Street public house. He had been within fifty yards of the other two men. On the previous day he had received a note.

"You will find a Delage saloon outside Sir Ernest Whiteman's house in Curzon Street—Number 23a. Take the car and leave it at the junction of Saville Row and Burlington Street. The car must arrive there at five minutes to ten tomorrow morning. Make no mistake. Maddick."

Another man, reading a midday racing paper in a street at the back of Euston Station, had fulfilled his instructions. They were simple:

"You will find a two-seater Bentley car outside 361 Lincoln's Inn Fields. Take it to Berkeley Street, leaving it on the left-hand side a few yards from Piccadilly. The car must be in position by ten-twenty. Make no mistake. Maddick."

Two days later the four men opened their morning post and smiled. Two of them received a bun envelope. There was no note inside, only thirty pounds in notes. They thought the payment adequate for "borrowing" a car for a few minutes.

"Mullens" and "Kelly" were also pleased. The postman brought each of them a small parcel.

"Mullens" received two hundred and fifty pounds in one-pound notes, while "Kelly" spat on his hands for luck at the sight of two hundred pounds.

Maddick, whoever he might be, always paid both well and promptly!

# 2

## CONFERENCE AT THE YARD

Five men sat round an oak desk in an upper office of New Scotland Yard. They did not look happy. The Commissioner of Police for the Metropolis, Sir Wynnard Salter, cupped his fat chin in two well-kept hands and stared sombrely at the men around him. Chief Constable Cross, whose keen features and piercing eyes had been plastered over the picture pages of the Press during many a murder inquiry, drew circles on a blotting pad with irritating frequency.

Chief Detective Inspector Hall, chief of the Flying Squad, stared at the Thames as it slid past the County Hall. He hated conferences almost as heartily as he enjoyed careering round corners on two wheels in the throes of a chase. Another of his squad, Inspector Reeves, sat silent and gloomy. He had been listening to much that was unpleasant.

At the far end of the desk sat Chief Detective Inspector Cardby. He was stout, and his small grey eyes twinkled in a large expanse of red flesh. An enormous neck bulged over the collar of a well-worn blue suit.

"I feel," said Cardby, "like saying that when I die the name Maddick will be found engraved on my heart."

"This is hardly the time for foolery," complained Sir Wynnard. "I've said before, and I'll say again, that you men have had every chance. The position is most humiliating. It was bad enough before the Home Secretary made his statement in the house. But it's infinitely worse now. I don't suppose you'll need reminding that he gave an assurance that the police were satisfied with their investigations, and that Maddick and his crowd would be under arrest within a few days. That was a month ago. Now we are the prize joke of every Tom, Dick and Harry."

"Who authorised the Home Secretary to make that statement?" asked the Chief Constable quietly.

"I did," said the Commissioner. "At that time it seemed inconceivable that you men with all your resources couldn't lay your hands on him."

"There is nothing we could have done that's been left undone," said Hall. "Maddick must have spent years in building up his organisation, and you can't undo the work of years in a few hours."

"That's what you're employed to do."

"But this idea is something quite new," said Cardby. "I don't ever remember anything like it before, and I've been here for twenty-two years. Maddick, whoever he is, has rationalised crime. That's the position in a nutshell. Instead of working in the old style, when isolated men pulled single jobs, and lay low while they spent the money, he's done what Woolworths, Liptons, Imperial Chemical Industries, General Electric and others have done in commerce. You couldn't break any of those organisations very easily. And you won't break down the structure that Maddick has built very readily."

"Are you trying to tell me, Cardby, that we have got to complain that the job is impossible, and let him carry on with his crime?"

"That wasn't my suggestion at all. I don't mean to be impertinent, sir, but I'm wondering whether you wouldn't change your mind about the job if you tackled it from the inside. The knowledge that we've all got after years of work here is practically useless. We've never had a mob before that throws its net as wide as this one. Show me a confidence trick and I'll tell you the person here who can get on with the job. The same applies to forgeries, smash-and-grabs, murders, housebreaking, arson, and the remainder of the crime calendar. What is beating us, in the first place, is that Maddick's crowd runs all of them. He has put the capital C on Crime, and turned it into an industry.

"Another snag—no more easily overcome—is that not one person employed by him knows the full story of any action taken. They do their own bit, but what happens before they arrive on the scene, and after they leave it, is as much a mystery to them as to us. They work as cogs in a machine, and Maddick sees that the machine is always overhauled and well oiled."

"How many men do you think he employs?" asked the Commissioner.

"We've had plenty of guesses," answered the Chief Constable. "The figure must run to a couple of hundred, but may be a lot more."

"And where did he collect them all?"

"If we knew that we'd know a lot more about Maddick. During the past six months we've laid hands on perhaps ten of his men. They know even less about the business than we do. He must have some odd way of recruiting them, but what it may be we don't yet know."

"Do you mean that you haven't got one man here who can get on the inside of that crowd, and act as an informant for you?"

"If we could have done that it would have been arranged long ago. Maddick's crowd gets tipped off by him whenever one of our men comes within a mile of them."

"You think that someone here is acting as an informant?"

"I wouldn't like to say that. But I will say that either Maddick himself or someone associated with him knows so much about the personnel here that we can't worm a man into the mob. I think I am right when I say that every man in this room, with the exception of yourself, has tried that trick. Not one even started to have a chance. And it is always as well to remember that young Caudry went on the job four weeks ago and since then he has not been seen, and we've heard nothing from him. I'm afraid that lad has gone for good."

"We'll see about that later. He may be having the sense to lie low until he gets what he wants."

"It was for that reason that we've raised no hue and cry. The boy may be doing some work under cover. But I doubt it very much. You can't take Maddick very far along the garden path."

"Have you tried getting one of your regular informants to try the job for you?"

"Our regular 'noses' wouldn't do. Maddick knows them as well as he knows the staff here. We have tried a few new ones, as you know, and we can't say that the result was particularly happy. Cardby slung one of his own pets on the job—that little safe breaker, Tim Kennedy. We thought that since he'd never been used by us before, and his name stands high as a safe smasher he might have some luck. He did—bad luck. That's why they were able to take him out of the Thames at Teddington. And we had to keep quiet about that."

"Then," said Hall, "there was the man I tried to slip in— Heimie Krutz, the con man. That was two weeks ago. Since then I haven't seen or heard anything of Heimie. I reckon his body will be the next to come floating up. These tales spread round, sir, and we'll never persuade any other men to try that job. You've only got to mention the name Maddick now, and they fold up like tissue paper. And we'll never get the facts ourselves. Only last week I picked two of them up in Farringdon Street. I talked to them for a couple of hours.

All they had on them were two notes—one each. One read, 'Wear brown trilby hat, brown tie with white spots, and stand outside the Tivoli at the corner leading to Adelphi at three tomorrow.' The other said 'Hire taxi Victoria Station two forty-five tomorrow. Pick up three o'clock at corner of Tivoli and Adelphi man wearing brown trilby hat, and brown tie with white spots. Drive to Russell Square Tube Station. Meet man there with newspaper under arm, smoking pipe and wearing light raincoat. Take instructions from him.' Well, I took both men with me—I recognised them as the taxi passed me.

"We went to Russell Square Tube to pick up the third man. Was he there? He was not. Did the other two know anything other than the instructions contained in their notes? They did not. That's the sort of thing I've had against me for nearly a year. What would you do under those circumstances, sir?"

The Commissioner stroked his cheek.

"Oh," he said, "don't imagine for one moment that I think the job is an easy one. My point is that whether the discovery of Maddick costs another ten lives or whether it costs only one we have got to lay him by the heels. I called you men into this conference in order that I could hear your suggestions. All that I have heard seems to be a series of complaints and excuses proving the impossibility of arresting the worst criminal we've had for a decade. Don't you think it's time that you used the tremendous experience you all possess?"

"I am quite sure," said the Chief Constable, "that no man from here will ever do any good. They are all too well marked. And I am equally certain that no underworld nark will catch Maddick. In the first place, they haven't the brains; in the second place, they would soon become known and then there'd be another murder, and, lastly, they've heard a few rumours of what happened to two men we've already employed. They wouldn't touch the proposition with a barge pole."

"For God's sake!" exclaimed the Commissioner savagely, "is there one of you here who will tell me that there might be some remote chance of catching Maddick? Or should we wind up the C.I.D. of New Scotland Yard, and delegate our duties to the Boy Scouts?"

"I agree with the chief," said Cardby. "I am convinced that you will never settle this crowd by employing a man from here, or from the criminal classes."

"Then that leaves no one?"

"On the contrary. The two sections I have mentioned probably represent about one per cent, of London's population."

"I don't follow you at all, Cardby."

"Then I'll make myself more plain. In my view the only person who can catch Maddick is the person who is connected with neither the Yard nor the underworld."

"Do you mean that we should employ a private detective?"

"No, I do not. If Maddick knows all the men at the Yard he's sure to know all the private men worth employing."

"I've been very patient with you men all morning, but you're taking me beyond the limit, Cardby. What exactly do you mean?"

"I'll lay all my cards on the table, and then you can tell me whether the hand is strong enough to call from. We've all tried our brains on this job and failed. We didn't fail because he was too clever for us. We failed because we were known to him before we started. What I suggest is that we continue with our inquiries as usual—with an even greater display of energy, if you like—and that while we skim the surface we should use as an undercover man a person who is known to neither the detectives or the criminals."

"And where will you find the person who will work without the assistance of the Yard, without the confidence of the crooks, and without any hope of material reward?"

"I have found him," said Chief Inspector Cardby.

The four men bent forward over the table.

"Who is he?" asked the Commissioner.

"My son," replied Cardby.

Big Ben rolled out twelve strokes. The men sat silent.

"You realise that by your suggestion you may be sending your own boy to the grave?" The Commissioner had changed his tone.

"I realise that I will be giving my son a better chance than I ever had in the whole of my life. I know the boy. He will take the chance with both hands. With him it will be hit or bust."

"Wait a minute," said the Chief Constable. "I've known you for twenty years, Cardby, and I've never known you yet to fool about with your work. But what sort of credentials does your lad possess that he can take on such a job?"

"I could tell you within three minutes," said Cardby, and a trace of pride seeped into his voice.

"Before we consider the offer we would certainly want to know something about him," said the Commissioner.

"You shall. He is twenty-two—not old, it's true, but he's had an odd life. That makes a big difference. In the first place he was weaned on crime, and he's wallowed in it ever since. When other boys were looking for birds' nests and collecting stamps he was bombarding me with questions, and reading everything he could lay his hands on. I don't mind telling you that after each awkward case I've had I've always taken the trouble to explain matters to the lad, show him something of the inside work. Apart from what I've told him he's been a terrific reader, and during the past few years has dabbled in things that I've never handled in my life—fingerprints, ballistics, forensic medicine and things of that sort. So from that angle he's fairly well equipped.

"On top of that he's a shade under six feet, and one of the fastest-moving light-heavies I've ever seen. I hope to God he won't need another of his accomplishments—but if he does, the hours he's spent on the rifle ranges and the damage he's done in my garden with an automatic ought to be handy. Anything else any of you would like to know?"

"If he's so keen on police work why didn't he join the Force?" asked Sir Wynnard.

"Because I told him that education is a bigger thing today than it was in my day, and he's had sense enough to realise it. I spent some hundreds on that boy, and when he took his scholarship for Oxford it wasn't for me to stop him. He left there three weeks ago, and intended joining the Force after Easter."

"He'll never persuade the Maddick crowd that he is on the level with them," said the Chief Constable, "unless he can hold his own in their line of business, and I don't suppose you've taught him how to become a criminal, Cardby?"

"He taught himself that part of it. Always was one of his pet ideas that you could catch a man more easily if you knew his job from his point of view. He can drive a car with the next best man, can talk sound stuff about safes, although he's never cracked one, learnt the con tricks years ago, swotted blackmail as a hobby, and can hand out the argot as though he's done a stretch on the Moor. On top of that he isn't likely to lose his head."

"Looks as though he was made for the job," said Hall.

"What I'm wondering about," said Reeves, "is how you're going to get him into the Maddick crowd. That will be the hardest part of it."

"That's what I thought," said Cardby, "but the boy himself helped me out by suggesting a scheme. The only person who can see that it is carried through is the Commissioner himself."

"I'll do anything within reason," said Sir Wynnard.

"Then you can do this, sir. It is our only safe bet, although it's more than drastic. Tomorrow morning at eleven o'clock my son will stroll round Cavendish Place until he sees a car that can be stolen. We'll have to start by turning the lad into a criminal. He'll dash the car along Harley Street, and swing on to the Outer Circle. Inspector Hall can post one of his men at the corner of Cavendish Place, ready to tell the make of the stolen car. That information will be passed to Hall, who will have one of the squad cars waiting outside Regent's Park.

"As soon as my lad comes to the head of Harley Street the squad car will give chase. Don't tell the driver anything of the plan that has been made. The fewer in this secret the better. All I want is that the run should be fast and furious. Make it about the most dramatic chase you've ever had. Something that the evening papers will gobble up and spread all over the front page. It would be all the better if you didn't catch him up until you were in Camden Town. There are a few likely lads in that district who might pass the word to Maddick. Above all, the chase must be the real thing. If you like you can finish with a rough-and-tumble in the middle of the High Street.

"Inspector Hall can indicate to the Press—without saying too much in detail—that the Flying Squad have made an important capture. On the following morning the lad will be brought up at Marylebone Police Station. But before then the Commissioner must have a talk with the magistrate. He will have to be let into the secret. Tell him that he must accede to the police application for a seven days' adjournment. Inspector Hall will go into the box to give evidence of arrest, and the boy will appeal for bail.

"That is really where the most important moments arrive. Hall, in opposing bail, must paint a picture of the lad as one of the most daring motor thieves and brilliant drivers known to the police. He can embroider that in his own way—how the squad has been after him several times and failed. Anything on that line will do. So the lad will go to Brixton for seven days, remanded in custody.

"The most difficult job—to look genuine—will be to release him from the gaol. It isn't long ago since one prisoner walked out from there during the visiting hours. Things could be arranged so that my lad could do the same. After his escape he can hide out in Walworth, Camden Town, Islington, Clapham, Lambeth, or Euston. Then we can leave Maddick to find him. If my view is worth anything it is that Maddick will find him very quickly. Once that has happened everything will depend on the lad. He won't report here until he considers that the time has arrived for a showdown. In the meantime, while he's collecting the information, he may have to help with a few crimes, but that can't be helped. He wouldn't be trusted until he'd pulled a few strokes. Is there any argument to the contrary?"

"It seems that the boy will be taking a terrible risk," said Sir Wynnard. "Otherwise the idea seems all right."

"He knows how to look after himself."

"Suppose he gets caught by the police on the first job he does for Maddick? That would ruin everything."

"That'll be where he convinces me that his theory is right. He says that any good detective should be capable of becoming a good crook."

"So you'll leave him to take pot-luck?"

"Certainly. He'll give a good run for his money?"

"How do we get out of the row that's pending with the owner of the stolen car?"

"The car won't be damaged, and it will be returned to him within half an hour or so. He ought to congratulate the squad."

"You seem to have thought out all the details, Cardby."

"I haven't. The boy has. He's got confidence in the scheme, and that, to me, is the principal consideration."

"I suppose his idea is that after a preliminary canter with the crooks he will join the Force?"

# CONFERENCE AT THE YARD

"Precisely. All he wants to gain by this move is a rapid transfer to the Yard. Padding a beat wouldn't suit him."

"There's just one other point," said Hall. "You want us to make the chase dramatic, Cardby. But if I'm there I'll have Murphy driving, and the chase is apt to finish very quickly. There's nobody in London who can pull away from him. You know that yourself."

"I'm betting on my lad tomorrow. Hall. You'll be given a run for your money. Don't worry about that."

"Then, Cardby," said the Commissioner, "we must adopt the old phrase of desperate causes and desperate remedies. Best of luck to the boy!"

# 3

## DETECTIVE MURPHY SWEATS

The young man walked with an easy swing along Wigmore Street, whistling bars from a latest dance tune. The onlooker might well have visualised him as a young idler with nothing to do and all day in which to do it. A trained observer would have noted that the proportioned figure was never developed in hours of aimless loafing. The wide shoulders spread beneath a firm, powerful neck; the chest was deep and symmetrical; the waist and flanks narrow. Over all spread a neat, dark-grey suit.

What little of the hair showed beneath the felt hat was light brown, the eyes were blue and deep set. The nose had once been regular, but its contour had suffered under the impact of a well-placed fist. The firm lines of the mouth seemed ready to twist into a humorous grin, the chin was clean cut. He paused for a moment to peer into a bookshop window. Then continued his walk. On the other side of the road, lounging against the railings of the house at the corner of Cavendish Square, stood a middle-aged man. Michael, otherwise Mick, Cardby saw the man and smiled. Obviously the Flying Squad man had grown so used to his seat in a car that he had forgotten the art of unostentatious "tailing."

Mick continued his saunter across the mouth of Harley Street, but now his eyes were awakening from their dreaminess.

## DETECTIVE MURPHY SWEATS

One by one he examined the rank of cars. To his right was a taxi-rank. It would be better to take one of the cars farther along the place. Mick knew cars, and this morning he knew what he wanted. Once Murphy got his foot crammed against the floorboard no ordinary car could hold him off. And this had to be a real chase. Young Cardby's lips turned up at the corners, and his eyes twinkled. It certainly would be a chase!

On the corner, at the junction of Chandos Street and Cavendish Place, stood a long, low-bodied, two-seater, jauntily enamelled in cream and black. Mick rubbed his gloved hands together as he walked towards it. Had the owner left the doors unlocked? That was the only remaining question. The youngster crossed from the corner, keeping the car between the house and himself. Then his hand slid out to the chromium-plated door handle. The doors were open.

Things happened speedily. Mick slid into the driving seat, turned the engine switch, pressed his foot on the self-starter, released the hand-brake, shot the gear level forward, and released the clutch with a swiftness that seemed slow. For the movements appeared unhurried.

The engine roared, the car whirled along Chandos Street, gathered speed in the few yards to the sharp corner, and the wheels screamed as they slid into Queen Anne Street. Mick changed gear, slammed his foot on the accelerator, and tore into Harley Street. He wanted to get the feel of the car before the chase began.

Behind him the middle-aged man dashed into a public telephone box.

The engine was picking up every yard as the car zoomed along the straight stretch, and twenty yards from the meeting with Devonshire Street the speedometer showed fifty-five. Now she could be thoroughly warmed up. The lad twisted the wheel left handed and opened the throttle as he tried to make Marylebone High Street. At the foot of the road a stream of cars filed by. Mick had studied his ground to some purpose. The powerful brakes seized the drums, and the car lurched as it swung suddenly into Beaumont Street, round the sharp corner at the end of the road, and cut between two cars to swing to the left-hand side of the High Street. Within another four seconds the two-seater crossed the road, turned left handed, sharply to the right, and cut through York Gate into the Outer Circle.

Mick made his entrance within fifty yards of the promised place. As the car picked up speed, and started round the Outer Circle to the right, another car moved away from the pavement. At the wheel, his lips set, his brows dragged down over his eyes, sat Detective Murphy, the mad-head of the Flying Squad.

The chase was on !

When Mick passed the entrance to the Broad Walk, the engine had settled down to a convincing note—that regular thrum that proves reserve and efficiency. Sixty yards away Murphy glanced at his dashboard to note that the flickering needle had passed the sixty, and was mounting steadily. All he knew was that they had had a "tip-off." The car in front had been stolen. It was Murphy's job to ditch it, even if he was hurt in the process. At his side sat Chief Inspector Hall, thrilling to the thought of a chase, in spite of his anxiety.

Mick took the left-hand turn without decelerating, and the heavy wheel base gave the car a grip as it slid round on a wide sweep. Already motorists were shrieking warnings. Then they became silent. The racing car at the back flashed the M.P. letters and the bell jangled unceasingly. One approaching driver, brave to the extent of foolhardiness, pulled his car half-across the road. Mick flicked his wings as he edged close to the pavement. Three seconds later Murphy cursed his amateur assistant, and wrenched his wheels to the right. The Flying Squad car tipped the edge of the curb, swayed for a few yards, and straightened out again.

The lad was enjoying himself. A glimpse in the mirror showed that Murphy was gaining. But the chase had only just begun. Mick was going to provide his pursuers with something that they would remember until a pension and the calm of a suburban garden brought peace to their declining days. At Chester Gate the two-seater shuddered under the impact of the brakes, nearly swirled away in a skid as the wheel was swung to the right.

"He'll kill himself—the blinding fool," said Murphy, as he also attempted to kill himself by taking the bend at a terrific speed. The policeman on duty outside the station near the gate heard the clangour of the bell, and drew his truncheon. At that moment the two-seater streamed past him. The constable flung his stick—too late. The truncheon struck a rear wheel and rebounded into the road. Before the policeman could decide what had happened the first car had vanished round the corner of William Street, the back wheels waggling, and the squad car tore into view. The constable pointed to the corner, and Murphy shot his foot on the brake, inclined the wheel, and pressed on to the accelerator in a series of sudden motions.

He arrived round the turn in time to see the cream and black car twist into Stanhope Street. Less than half a minute later both drivers, their teeth set, their hands rigid on the steering wheels, were whistling past trams, cars, buses and cyclists on the Hampstead Road. Pedestrians stood agape on the pavements, waiting every second for the resounding crash that would mark the end of the chase. Twice Mick touched the edges of cars as he wormed his way through with an inch or two to spare.

A quarter of a mile up the road a policeman ran into the centre of the tram track and raised both hands against the speeding cars. Young Cardby, frightened for the first time by the thought that he might hit the policeman, jammed his foot on the brakes. The policeman heard the roar as the car slowed, and dropped his hands, advancing towards the motor. He was not supposed to know that Mick had chosen the car for its remarkable acceleration. The lad's foot jammed down hard on the pedal, and the constable realised his mistake too late as the car twisted to the right round a stationary tram and continued along the road. But the pause had been welcome to Murphy, and he was now within twenty yards. Mornington Crescent Station whizzed past on the right.

Then Mick turned left-handed for Camden Town. A hundred yards before he reached the main street he thought that the chase was over—the road was congested with traffic. There was no loophole, unless he took a forlorn chance down one of the side streets to the left. At that moment he was ready to take any chance. Fortunately there was no walker on the pavement—otherwise he couldn't have taken the turn. The car mounted the footpath and missed a wall by inches before returning to the road again.

Another left-hand turn and he was doubling on his tracks. Murphy tore after him down the narrow street, taking chance after chance. At his side Inspector Hall sat silent. Now he could understand Cardby's confidence. Murphy was not the only driver on the road that day.

The squad man knew it too. That was why he gambled against a smash as he had never gambled before. It stung the Irishman's pride to think that he had met an equal. Both engines were humming as they gained the Outer Circle again, and Mick nodded his head with satisfaction as they careered past the Zoo gates. He had gained distance again. Now Murphy was nearly forty yards behind.

There was no knowing when that chase would end. That thought came to young Cardby's mind at the moment when disaster merged in front of him. To his right were enormous houses with quiet drives leading past them. Suddenly the nose of a lorry appeared past the stone pillars of a drive about forty yards ahead. By the time Mick had covered twenty yards the road was completely blocked by a furniture van. He pulled the car to a standstill a few inches from the lorry and jumped out of the car. Four strides and he reached the spiked railings surrounding Regent's Park, By the time he had alighted on the grass the squad car drew to a grinding halt, and three men were jumping out. Murphy was the first over the fence.

In his best days he had been able to cover the quarter mile in a trifle over fifty-one seconds. Unfortunately for him, the man in front had clocked fifty many times. By the time two hundred yards had been covered the Yard man was a hundred yards behind, and his chances of recovering ground appeared remote. Then the chase came to the notice of two park keepers. It was a long time since they had seen four men racing in single file without the justification of shorts and running pumps. They advanced to investigate, spreading out to cut off the approach of the leading runner.

The younger of the keepers bent his head and tore across the grass towards Mick. As a reward for his energy and zeal he was awarded a hand-off that had seen good service on many a rugger pitch. Thereafter his zeal vanished, and he completed two somersaults before sitting on the grass. The older keeper was more sensible. He blew his whistle and ran towards the gate for which Mick was chasing.

Far in the rear Inspector Hall ambled along at a jog-trot. His first wind had gone, and he doubted seriously whether he owned a second. Murphy, red in the face, and heavy in the legs, realised that hours at the wheel of a car was not exactly an effective method of training.

When Mick was fifty yards away from the gate two keepers appeared on a far path, and a policeman, patrolling the Outer Circle, paused on his beat to extract his truncheon and block the entrance. So again the lad had to change his course, and this time he paced along the grass towards the large lake.

By now the chase had grown to resemble a procession, consisting of three detectives, three park attendants and a policeman. Cardby looked towards the road to see whether he could gain an exit. Two cars were pacing him as he ran, their drivers waiting for him to attempt another break. Before him more attendants hurried along the bank of the lake. Hundreds of children left their play to cheer on both sides. It was then that the pursuers crowded in from all sides. Two men jumped from one of the cars on the roadside, leapt the low railings, ran over the grass, and arrived on the concrete path five yards in front of Mick. As he stopped to seek an outlet three keepers appeared on the left, the second car was guarding the exit to the road, and Murphy, Hall, the third detective and the keeper were bringing up the rear.

The lad dropped his hands to his sides helplessly and stopped. He certainly did not want to add to the damage by starting a free for all fight. Murphy grasped him roughly by the shoulder.

For a second the two men stared at each other, their chests rising and falling as they sought to regain their breath.

"It's a fair cop," said Mick. "But I bet you'll remember it."

It seemed that Hall smiled. But that couldn't be right!

# 4

## AT THE POLICE COURT

Mick Cardby was seated on a bench in the corridor adjoining Marylebone Police Court when the message was brought to him.

"Mr Godfrey Olton, the solicitor, is here to take your instructions."

The young man looked up languidly, no sign of surprise on his face.

"Can I see him here?" he asked.

"You can have a talk to him at the end of the corridor."

"Good. Tell him I'm ready any time now."

A few seconds later the door opened at the end of the passage, and a fat, pale-faced man, wearing a winged collar and an enormous black silk knitted tie, came striding along.

"Here's your client, sir," said the gaoler, pointing to Cardby.

"Come over here. I've got instructions to appear for you this morning. What do you want to say about it?"

The two men stood some twelve feet away from the gaoler, whispering.

"Are you trying to fasten a quick one on me?" asked Mick, his eyes steady as he stared at the lawyer.

"Of course not. Why on earth should you think that?"

"Don't get indignant about nothing. It wouldn't be the first time the tecs have tried to pull a fast one. I only wondered how it came about that you want to nose in. Who sent you?"

"I can't give you the name of my client?"

"Tell me another one, mister. The police had their bit of fun yesterday. They gave me a couple of hours, and all they found out wouldn't convict a wasp of carrying a sting. I suppose they thought that I might fall for a stunt like this? You can tell them from me that I wasn't born yesterday. I gave them one run for their money, but they'll have another before I'm through with them."

"You've misunderstood me," protested Olton. "I've got nothing to do with the police at all. I've come along here to defend you."

"Who told you to defend me?"

"If you're going to be so awkward about it I'll soon show you that I'm only acting on instructions. This morning I received this letter at my office. That's all I know about it."

Mick shook his head dubiously and took the envelope. There was a sceptical twist on his lips as he extracted the contents.

The first paper that fell into his hand was a newspaper cutting, obviously taken from a well-known evening paper. Cardby read the story.

AMAZING FLYING SQUAD CHASE.
MAN ARRESTED.
SIXTY MILES AN HOUR THROUGH CROWDED STREETS.
PURSUIT ENDS IN REGENT'S PARK.

"One of the most sensational chases in the history of the Flying Squad was witnessed by hundreds of Londoners this morning. A Scotland Yard car on patrol round the Outer Circle of Regent's Park received information leading them to follow a cream and black two-seater sports car that cut through York Gate at a terrific speed, after passing through Harley Street,

Devonshire Street and Marylebone High Street. Immediately the driver realised that a Flying Squad car had taken up the chase he accelerated."

There followed a pulsating description of the events leading to Mick's capture. No detail was omitted. In the centre of the column was a photograph of Chief Inspector Hall. The reporter, after paying tribute to the driving of Detective Murphy, ended his description with a show of caution.

"It is understood that a man will appear before the magistrate at Marylebone Police Court tomorrow morning in connection with the affair."

The young man then turned his attention to a brief typewritten note. The missive bore neither address or signature. It read :

"Enclosed you will find five pounds in one-pound notes. Please undertake the defence of the man mentioned in this cutting."

"Will you believe me now?" asked Olton.

"Did this thing cause much of a stir?" asked Mick, ignoring the question.

"Good Lord, yes. It was on the front page of all the evening papers yesterday, and they've splashed it in the dailies this morning."

"And you are sure you don't know who sent you this message?"

"If I did I'd tell you."

"Have you ever had any of them before? Don't get nasty, mister. You'd be a bit careful yourself if you were in a jam."

"Yes, to be candid with you, I have had two of them before."

"Just the same sort of thing?"

"No, in the other cases I was given the men's names. In this case I was not given your name. What is it?"

"That's what the police tried to find out for hours yesterday."

"You'll make things look very black against you from the start if you refuse to give your name. What is it?"

"All I can tell you is that my friend, the gaoler, informs me that I'm Number 7. I've been charged with stealing a motor car."

"And did you steal it?"

Cardby placed his elbow on the window sill, looked at the fat man, and smiled.

"Oh, no," he said, "I borrowed it because I thought of buying one like it, and wanted to discover whether it was a fast car. The only reason why I put my foot on it when I saw the squad car was because it peeves me to be passed on the road. Otherwise I'd have waved them on and blown kisses to them."

"Quit fooling, unless you want to take a long rap. Have you ever been down before?"

"I've never been caught before."

"If you'll tell me your name and give me enough to spiel about—youthful escapade, and that sort of stun—I might get you off with three months. But if you go on acting dumb you'll walk into twelve months of the best. Use your head, lad. Tell me some stuff to hand out."

"You can give my name as Pete Borden, of no fixed abode. I just hate staying in one place too long. It's apt to be unhealthy in my line of work. I've got no previous convictions. I took the car for a joke. That ought to be enough to get me bound over."

"I'm not a miracle worker," said Olton. "You can reconcile yourself to the fact that you're going to take a rap. But we might get away with three months. Are you willing to go into the box?"

"No. I don't want any questions fired at me."

"On what line have I got to cross-examine the police witnesses?"

"Please yourself. There isn't much to argue about. They chased me. I had damn bad luck. They caught me. That's the complete story."

"All right, Borden. I'll give your name to the gaoler now so that he can have it shoved down on the charge sheet. You plead ' Not guilty,' and I'll do the best I can for you. You want the case disposed of now, I suppose?"

"Of course, I don't want to be remanded in custody, and they won't give me bail since I've got no fixed abode. Let's get it over."

"Just one tip before I leave you. Be careful what you say. The Press have fallen for this case like actresses for men of title. They'll report every spit and cough while the case is going on. And if you want to have a chance when you come out—since you're sure to go down—don't let them take photographs of you. The court's full of reporters, and there are four or five camera men outside."

"O.K., Olton. I'll look after myself. I always have."

"See you in court," said Olton, vanishing through the doorway.

Mick returned to the gaoler. He sat down on the bench, stuck his hands in his pockets, and stretched his legs.

"You don't look very worried," said the gaoler.

"I'm feeling grand. It's a new one on me to be waiting to go into court. Maybe it doesn't feel so nice when you face the beak, though."

"It all depends how the old man is feeling," said the gaoler. "If he's got gout he's six months worse on sentences than if he's free of it for an hour."

"Let's hope he's feeling like an advertisement of health."

"He isn't. I saw him getting out of the taxi. He hasn't got too much patience at the best of times. I pity you a lot this morning."

"Ah, well. Worse things happen at sea. My lawyer wanted to give my name. I reckon he hands that to your mate inside?"

"Aye, I have nothing to do with that."

"Is that solicitor bloke of mine any good, do you know?"

"Not bad. Doesn't come here as much as he used to. He can tell a good tale if he's got the stuff to talk about."

Suddenly the door commenced to open and shut at the head of the steps leading into the court. The first four prisoners were soon heard and disposed of. Mick shuddered as he noted the brazen ease with which the women, some young and smart, some old and bedraggled, entered the court, took their sentence, and returned.

"This is quick work," said Cardby, as the man inside the court called for Number 5. The young man had been watching the flow of prisoners along the passage.

"They're all regulars here," confided the gaoler. "Almost as much at home here as anywhere else."

Five minutes elapsed, and the elderly man who had just taken a rap of fourteen days' hard labour for being drunk and disorderly for the twenty-third time, stepped down into the corridor, winked ostentatiously at the gaoler, and strolled along to the cells.

"Number 7."

Mick Cardby rose to his feet and followed the beckoning hand. His shoulders drooped a little, and there was a defiant stare in his eyes when he took his place in the dock. He looked round the court as though amused by his surroundings, noted the crowded Press seats, and caught the eye of Chief Inspector Hall. Murphy sat by his side.

The magistrate, a bulky man with a red face and bald head, was writing. The clerk of the court charged Peter Borden with stealing a motor-car from Cavendish Place at 11 a.m. on the 20th inst. While the charge was being read the prisoner turned to nod towards his fat solicitor. Then he turned to the clerk again.

"Do you plead guilty or not guilty?"

The Pressmen held their pencils at the "ready."

"Not guilty," said Cardby emphatically.

"In this case, your worship," announced Olton, "I appear for the prisoner." He waggled his large head for no apparent reason, and sat down again

Chief Inspector Hall advanced to the witness-box. In common with many other policemen he took the oath with a speed that defied the ear. "I-swear-by-Almighty-God-that-the-evidence-I-shall-give, etc." But the formalities had been complied with.

"Chief Detective Inspector Ernest Hall," he announced, as he laid the Bible on the ledge of the witness-box, "New Scotland Yard. At 11 a.m. yesterday, while patrolling the Outer Circle in company with Detective Sergeant Waller and Detective Constable Murphy, I received information as a consequence of which I followed the prisoner as he turned into the Outer Circle. After a chase lasting for half an hour the prisoner was arrested in Regent's Park. Later I cautioned him and charged him with stealing a motor-car. He replied, ' I deny the charge, and reserve my defence'."

The pressmen dropped their pencils gloomily. Nothing could have fallen flatter. Within two minutes the whole thing would be over.

"On that, your worship," said Hall, "I apply for a remand in custody for seven days."

"Do you desire to say anything, Mr Olton?" inquired the magistrate.

"Yes, your worship," replied the fat man, hobbling from his seat. "I am instructed to oppose the application for a remand."

"On what ground?"

"The prisoner, your worship, is making his first appearance in a police court, and his reply to the charge is that he had no intention of stealing the motor-car. Rather was it a youthful escapade on his part. He appreciates now, of course, the rank folly of his act, and desires to apologise to the owner of the car, and to the police, for the trouble that he has caused them. Insofar as the chase is concerned he says that he entered into it in a spirit of daredevilry. There was at no time an intention in his mind to deprive the owner of his car permanently. Under those circumstances, and having regard to the fact that the prisoner has never been previously either convicted or even charged, I feel that the matter is one which your worship could quite well dispose of this morning."

"What have you to say about this, inspector?" asked the magistrate.

Hall bent over the edge of the box with an air of secrecy.

"The police, your worship, are anxious that certain matters should not be dealt with this morning. Inquiries are still being conducted, and it may be that at a later stage additional charges may be preferred against the prisoner. It is strongly felt that this is a case which cannot be dealt with summarily, and certainly it is not a case in which bail should be allowed."

"But the prisoner has never been previously convicted, inspector," said the magistrate.

Hall stood silent for a second as though wondering whether or not to take the plunge. His manner became even more confidential.

"That is true, your worship," he said at last, "but we have reason to regard the prisoner as a dangerous man. For weeks past we have believed him to be one of the most daring and skilful motor drivers in England. Furthermore, it will be maintained at a later stage that his clean record might be due more to his ability as a criminal than to his avoidance of criminal activities. Added to that, your worship, is the fact that he has no fixed address."

"What do you say about that, Mr Olton?"

The solicitor turned to speak to his client. Mick lounged against the dock rail. Apparently the proceedings held very little interest for him.

"You heard what the inspector said, Borden. What's the answer?"

"Only that I deny everything he's said, and insist upon having the case finished here and now."

"My client," asserted Olton, "protests most emphatically against the statements made by the officer. They are, he says, entirely unfounded, and beyond any proof the police could produce. It is my duty to protest against the unpleasant method of innuendo used by the inspector. My client came into this court today fully prepared to face the charge lodged against him. He now hears, for the first time, that further allegations are to be made. It rather seems that the prisoner is to be condemned before he is tried."

"Is it your suggestion," asked the magistrate coldly, "that my custom is to determine the issues before me without hearing evidence?"

"Oh, no, your worship. I was maintaining that the replies given by the inspector were both vague and damning, statements easy to make and impossible of proof. The procedure, as it affects the police, does seem to me to be most unfair."

"Perhaps," interrupted Inspector Hall, "I might explain the position a little further. The prisoner refused to supply us with any information about himself, and it was not until this morning, indeed, that he gave his name. Even now we have had no time in which to discover whether the name by which he is charged is his right name. Furthermore, we have reason to believe that the chase which ended in his arrest yesterday was not the first in which he has been concerned. Only his brilliance as a driver and his daring has saved him on previous occasions. We propose, at a later stage, to deal with certain of those other occasions. In the meantime, your worship, perhaps the prisoner would give evidence. He could then be questioned as to the urgency for complete trial today."

"Does your client wish to give evidence?" inquired the magistrate.

Again Olton held a fleeting conference with Mick.

"No, your worship, the prisoner feels that having regard to the view taken by the police he would prefer to remain out of the box until such time as they are in a position to withdraw the allegations made this morning, and offer him an apology."

A low titter of laughter passed over the court. The magistrate was glum and dour, or, at least, so it appeared to the onlookers.

"I can do no other in this case," he said, "than agree with the application made on behalf of the police. The prisoner will be remanded in custody for seven days."

"Number 8," called the gaoler.

Mick Cardby, half an hour later, was in the prison van, heading for Brixton. His father was hearing the story from Hall. The magistrate was being congratulated by Sir Wynnard Salter, Police Commissioner.

The campaign against Maddick had commenced!

# 5

## AN ESCAPE, AND AN OFFER

Two days later the Chief Constable walked into Chief Inspector Cardby's office. There was a smile on his face.

"It's happened," he said, and sat down on the edge of the desk.

"What?"

"The Governor of Brixton Prison has just been through on the phone to me. Peter Borden has escaped! He must be a very cunning man, Cardby. Did you ever happen to meet him at all?"

"I don't remember the name. But my memory isn't what it was. How was the trick arranged?"

"Just as he suggested himself. He took a leaf from the other man's book, and walked out during the visiting hours. Of course, the walk-out wasn't made too hard for him. It was lucky for him, too, that a car happened to be parked about two hundred yards from the gaol. By now he must be quite a long way from Brixton."

"They ought to have looked after him more carefully. What move do we make here now?"

"I'm going down to the press-room. It isn't often they have the doubtful pleasure of meeting me down there, but I want this story to hit the front pages with a real bang. So I'll tell the tale myself. But the description they'll get won't be all that accuracy would call for. We must give the lad a run for his money."

"All I hope is that some constable doesn't meet him, and pull him in before he can start work. If that happens the whole thing will go west. We daren't risk another escape."

"We'll have to chance that. You told your lad that so long as he didn't cause any real damage he could resist arrest?"

"Yes. If a single policeman tries to take him in, I told him that one crack under the jaw and a fast run wouldn't be objected to."

"Good. It'll be bad luck for the constable, but we can't bother about one sore jaw during the next few days."

The chief's visit to the Press room caused more than a small surprise. The crime men attached to the agencies and newspapers had been supplied with their news through the liaison officer for so long that they had refused to contemplate the existence of any other mouthpiece for the Yard.

"Good morning, all of you," said Cross. "I've got a story for you."

The six men crowded round.

"I'm no newspaper man," said the chief, "so I don't know where to start. You all remember that remand prisoner escaping from Brixton a few weeks ago? He walked out during the visiting hours."

"Yes," came the chorus. Imagine asking six crime reporters whether they remembered a recent London prison break!

"And you all remember that man, Peter Borden, who was remanded in custody for seven days after being charged at Marylebone with the theft of a car?"

"That was the half-hour chase man, wasn't it?" asked a reporter.

"That's the fellow—the one who was arrested in Regent's Park. Well, he's escaped! He walked out today during the visiting hours just as the other man did. Wait a moment, don't start running for the phones. I haven't finished. His absence was discovered after about five minutes, but it has since been discovered that he stole a car standing at the curb about two hundred yards from the prison. The Flying Squad was immediately informed, and they are patrolling for him now, but I'm afraid that with his start he's run to earth.

"I want you to make a real splash of this. We want that man behind the bars again. Now that he has escaped I don't mind telling you that we attached more importance to his arrest than we showed during the court proceedings. He is a resourceful, daring and dangerous criminal. I'll give you something of a description, and then you can get ahead with the story. Age, about twenty-six; height, five feet ten inches; weight, about eleven stone; hair, brown; eyes, grey; last seen wearing dark-grey suit; white stiff collar, white shirt, and silver-spotted tie. He may have headed for Balham, Mitcham, Camber-well, or the East End. Now you can fight for the telephones.

"By the way, don't mention my name in connection with this statement. Just say that you were officially informed. That will be enough. If we hear of any developments we'll let you know. Good morning to you."

The pressmen were using the telephones before the chief had closed the door. He returned to his office whistling a blithesome tune. The whole affair sounded impossible, and it certainly cut across every rule for the conduct of the force. But so far it was working. And that was all that mattered. Maddick didn't observe the rules. So why should New Scotland Yard gag and bind themselves with yards of red tape?

Inspector Cardby pulled at his pipe and read a deposition over three times before he grasped its meaning. His mind was elsewhere. It was following his lad, stigmatised as a criminal, hounded by the police, holding both arms open to danger. Then he thought of his wife. She knew nothing of the plan. Her

Michael, she was sure, was holiday-making in Lucerne before following in his father's footsteps. That was the inestimable benefit of these cheap tours, she thought.

\* \* \* \* \* \* \* \*

Mick Cardby was breathing more freely as he turned the corner from the prison and strolled along the main road. His eyes sparkled as he saw a car parked against the pavement. It didn't look as though that was there by accident. That opinion was more than confirmed when he discovered that there was no one within fifty yards, and the engine of the car was running. Four minutes later he turned left at Kennington Horns and proceeded along Westminster Bridge Road. Farther along he took the right-hand turn into Lambeth Lower Marsh. Then he left the car at the corner of the street and walked along towards Waterloo Road. At Frazier Street he left the wider road, walked until he arrived at the junction with Oakley Street, and finally arrived in Tanswell Street. There he knocked at the door of 78a.

A blowsy woman with untidy hair and a dirty frock opened the door.

"'Ello, Mister Wall," she said, "you're soon back."

"A day early, Mrs Chapman." He walked inside. "Anybody been for me, or any post?"

"Nothin' and nobody," announced the woman, and she vanished along the linoleum-covered hall to the kitchen at the rear. Mick walked up the stairs to the top floor. There he opened the door at the end of the passage and walked into his bedroom. It could scarcely be called luxurious. A pair of cheap imitation lace curtains that had once been white screened the dirt-smudged window. In one corner of the room stood a single iron bedstead, surmounted by a hideous crimson overlay, originally decorated with some unidentifiable species of ornate bird, but now worn into threadbare patches.

## AN ESCAPE, AND AN OFFER

By the side of the bed a three feet by two mat covered the bare boards. A cane chair, with several broken strands in the centre of the seat, stood against the wall. On the far side of the room a cheap wash-hand stand supported a cracked bowl and a damaged jug. At the side of the door was an unpolished oak cupboard, occasionally referred to by Mrs Chapman as "the wardrobe."

Mick had become the temporary owner of the room ten days previously for the modest sum of twelve shillings a week. He had left it only half an hour before his appearance in Cavendish Place.

The dark-grey suit was soon in the cupboard — together with the hat, shoes, collar, shirt, tie, socks and a gold wrist watch. When he next appeared downstairs he wore a blue suit, cut with wide lapels, an accentuated waist, and a slightly undue width of trouser. His shirt and collar were blue ribbed with a wide, black stripe. In his knitted tie he wore an imitation pearl pin. The patent-leather shoes were too pointed in the toe-cap, and the socks, checked in black and silver, were a trifle too ornamental. A thin watch chain ran from one waistcoat pocket to another. One end was attached to a thin dress watch, the other to a medallion. In his pocket were many letters, all addressed to Mr Stan Wall, 78a Tanswell Street, Waterloo, S.E. All were in different handwriting; all had been written by Mick himself. He was taking no chances.

He knocked on the kitchen door.

"If anybody calls for me, missus," he said, "you can tell 'em that I'll be back in an hour. I've got to see a man about a dog." His broad wink made the woman smile. She had met his sort before. In fact, she had already decided that her boarder had probably vanished for two days to do a "country job." But times were hard, and beggars can't be choosers. And, to add to that, her husband, "Midnight" Chapman, had just arrived on the Moor for the third time. So he wouldn't be able to maintain her for another four years. It did seem a shame, thought Mrs Chapman, once known as "Coughdrop Beattie," that "Midnight" should have done that "bust" at Esher without stopping to find out that the squeak had been put in.

"All right, dearie," she said, adhering to the formula of an earlier profession in an anxiety to be amiable.

Mick knew the lay of the land. He had not stayed with Mrs Chapman for seven days for nothing. He strode along the pavements until he reached a public house in a narrow side street.

"Good morning, stranger," said the shifty-eyed landlord as Mick came through the swing doors of the saloon bar. Three men and two women stood against the counter, lodging their elbows on the polished mahogany in the manner born. One of the tawdry women and two of the men nodded to the lad. The others stared at him suspiciously.

Mick knew three of them. He had had them checked up at the Yard. The small man, dressed in the flashy brown suit, was Ed Connors, fresh back from the Moor after a lagging. Before his nerve gave out there were few better "peter" men in the Metropolis. He could play on a safe as others can plan on a pianola. He'd have to be content now with a few quid for playing bo-peep round the corners while someone else got on with the job inside.

At his elbow stood Taxi Long. He had made a profitable business, until the police found him out, by cruising along with an empty taxi near the scene of a smash and grab until the bandits threw their loot through the open window of his cab. That game was now played out, and Taxi Long worked as driver with a few smash and grab specialists from the Walworth side.

Beside him stood a woman, her eyes thickly made up, her lips daubed with crimson, her cheek-bones fiery under the coating of rouge. It was difficult to guess her age. Somewhere between twenty-five and thirty-five. She wore a cheap fur coat,

# AN ESCAPE, AND AN OFFER

the art silk stockings were twisted, the patent-leather shoes had begun to tip off on the edges of the high heels. As she held a glass of stout in her hand she showed two rings, both too good to be true.

This was "Miss Ellen." She was taking a holiday — hence the daubs of make-up and the shabby attempt to achieve smartness. In her working hours she strutted round better-class houses as a domestic servant taking the lay of the land for her "friends." Her disappearance from the ranks of the employed usually signalised another robbery.

The other man and woman Mick did not know.

"Bitter, mister," said young Cardby. He turned to Connors. "Are you having one?'

"Don't mind," replied the ex-peterman without enthusiasm.

"And your friends?"

"Better ask 'em."

"If they can't speak up for themselves I'm saying nothing." Mick slid his hand into his inside pocket and dropped a pound note on the counter. The other occupants of the bar emptied their glasses and slid them across the counter.

"Been away?" inquired the landlord.

Mick realised instantly that these people were not ready to accept him as one of themselves. Otherwise, such a question would never have been asked. There is no rule more rigidly kept among the criminal classes than the simple one: If I want to tell you anything I will; if I don't tell you, keep your mouth shut.

"Getting curious, mister?" He asked the question casually as he raised his glass from the counter.

"No, just thought you hadn't been around for a day or two."

"Anybody been making inquiries about me?"

"Nope. Hanging out round here?"

"I've bedded down at the back for a bit. Good luck, folks."

"Reckon to stay long?" asked Connors.

"Listen, mates, I came in here for a comfortable drink—not to be stifled with all these questions. If you want to suit me—get on with your drinks, and close your mouths over the glasses. If you wanna fall out with me—just ask some more questions."

"No offence," said Connors.

"There's been a break-out at Brixton," said Taxi Long, apropos of nothing.

"Oh," commented the landlord casually. "Anyone from round these parts?"

"That Pete Borden bloke that pulled the stroke in Cavendish Place and got brought in from Regent's Park."

"He must be a real swell at the job," said Connors. "Any of you happen to know him at all?"

Mick stood with his back to the bar and gazed at an advertisement on the far wall. If the people in the room had been speaking without reserve they couldn't have handed the information to him more plainly. One of them, at any rate, had recognised him!

Suddenly a mental picture flashed before him— he saw the passage leading to the court at Marylebone. He saw the procession of women as they filed in and out of the dock. Then he remembered. The woman at his side whom he had not recognised had been one of the prisoners!

All were looking at him curiously. The landlord, wiping glasses at the sink behind the bar, was squinting in his direction. Mick turned round and yawned, picked up his glass and took another drink. His eyes caught a glimpse of the woman to his left. He moved his head round and smiled at her.

"I've been trying to place you somewhere, sister, ever since I came through the door. Where've we met?"

The woman placed her glass on a side table and turned to him. Her eyes were puffy, her complexion unhealthy.

"You seem to have a pretty bad memory," she said.

"It's handy sometimes, my dear." Mick was thinking as he spoke. What was his best line? The position was difficult. "Maybe there are things you've wanted to forget, eh, my dear?"

"Plenty of 'em. As a rule I can keep my mouth shut. It pays in the end. But it isn't very long since we met."

"Not years, at any rate. I don't remember your name, though. Mine's Stan Wall."

"And mine," said the woman with slow deliberation, "is Greta Garbo."

"Then we're quits, Miss Garbo. Now we seem to know each other."

"I wasn't expecting to meet you again quite so soon."

"No? You never can tell what's going to happen in this world."

"Perhaps not. Feeling nice and cheerful this morning?"

"Feel like ten men, my dear."

"I hope your luck holds out."

"Thank you. I hope we don't meet again in the same place for at least another twenty years."

The men stood without a move. By now the conversation had spread the facts before them as though the pages of a book had been turned.

"Have one with me," said Connors, "and the best of luck."

Nothing further was said until the glasses were filled. Every person in the room was feeling his or her way. Mick grinned at them cheerfully.

"All the best," he said. The youngster wasn't used to drink. So he had taken the precaution of swallowing a tablespoonful of oil from a sardine tin before leaving the bedroom. This much, at any rate, he had learnt from his father. "Makes the booze float," the old man had said.

"Working?" asked Ed Connors.

"Already? Give me a chance!"

They all laughed. The publican joined in.

"After what I've heard about you," continued Connors, "I thought maybe you're one of those nonstop blokes who go from job to job."

Mick tipped the bowler hat to the back of his head and smiled at the company.

"Which is better, Connors—to earn five pounds a week for a year, or to pick up two hundred and fifty in a day?"

"It's no good coming that stuff round here, Wall. The days when you could collect the heavy dough have gone. Now if you pull a stroke and get thirty or forty quid out of it you aren't unlucky."

Cardby sighed and reached for his glass.

"It depends," he remarked slowly, and to the room in general, "upon whether you know what you're doing. I knew a man once—no names, no pack drill—who could pull as nice a job in his own line as you'd ever see. But he was never cut out for anything bigger. He finished up by getting too ambitious. He dropped his own game and started another. He's been on the Moor for a few years now. He'll do no good when he comes back. If you're a thirty pound a stroke man—stick to it, and don't stare at the clouds until someone says, 'Come with me.' That's the way most of the boys get at the finish."

"Well," said Connors deliberately, "take the case of the man who pinches cars. What does he get out of it by the time he's shopped 'em?"

"The man who pinches cars for the purpose of selling 'em ought to be in an asylum. That's the biggest boob's job in creation. They ought to get a stretch and the cat for being mugs enough to try it."

"I know folks who do it," said Long, staring hard at Cardby.

"Then you know someone with a few bob in their fist and a nice rap coming very soon."

## AN ESCAPE, AND AN OFFER

Suddenly silence flooded the saloon bar. Mick waited for the first one to speak. He knew what was running through their minds. Connors was the first.

"Listen to me for a minute, Borden."

Mick bent forward, grasped the peterman by the lapel of his coat, and shook him as a terrier might shake a rat.

"Lay off that funny stuff," he said, his face and Connors' face separated by a mere few inches. "I've plastered men on the walls for speaking out of their turn. You go your way, Connors, and leave me to look after myself. The next time you make a mistake like that I'll be liable to hit you first and warn you afterwards. And if any friends of yours" —he looked round at the men and women— "are walking round with similar ideas in their heads they'd be well advised to forget 'em. I'm all right as a friend. I hope none of you find out what I'm like when I fall out. We'll have another drink, Connors, and then you can get outta here. Men like you are worse than a 'nose'. They're paid for what they say. You say your little piece because your tongue runs away with your head. Good health, and may your memory grow less."

They drank in silence. "Miss Ellen" emptied her stout rapidly and left the bar. The other woman followed her. Mick watched their sudden exits with interest.

"Reckon the girl friends thought there was going to be a rough house," he remarked easily.

"Looks that way," said Long. "Have one with me for the road."

"Sure, I will. I hope you boys are going to take what I said sensibly. I'm telling you now that if anyone of you puts the squeal in on me you'll be for it, even if I have to wait a few years on the Moor before I can get at you."

"We're not squealers here," said the landlord.

"If we were we'd all of us soon be in a fine mess," added Ed.

"If we didn't trust each other we couldn't get a living," helped Taxi Long.

"Stow your tongues," said the third man, speaking for the first time since Mick entered the bar. "You shoot like a crowd o' bleating kids. Wall's right, Connors. Your mouth'll land you into trouble before long. You'd better put some stitches in it. My name, mate, is Delaney, otherwise known —since we're both on the up and up—as 'Alibi' Delaney."

"Thank God I've found somebody with a bit of sense. Next time you're with these two, Alibi, tell 'em what happens to naughty boys who talk out of school. So long, folks. See you again soon."

Delaney opened the swing doors for him, and Mick felt a piece of paper thrust into his hand. He walked slowly towards Tanswell Street. As he turned the first corner "Miss Ellen" slipped out of sight too late to be unobserved.

Back in his bedroom he unwrapped the dirty note. It was quite brief. "Will call see you seven to-night."

# 6

## MADDICK ENLISTS A RECRUIT

Mick was lying on the bed when Mrs Chapman knocked at the door and informed him that the "gentleman you was expecting is 'ere."

Delaney poked his head round the door.

"Hallo, Stan," he said. Then he shut the door. The landlady bent her eye to the keyhole. Immediately the door was flung open again. Alibi grabbed her by the shoulder, gave her a violent push that landed her at the head of the stairs.

"Scram!" he said. "And don't come up here again."

Mick handed him a cigarette, and they sat on the bed together.

"What's the big idea?" asked Cardby.

"I just wanted to have a talk to you. Seen the evening papers?"

"No, been sleeping. Anything interesting?"

"They're full of this prison break. Seems that the police want Pete Borden very badly. If he sticks by himself he'll get caught within twenty-four hours."

"Maybe he doesn't think so."

"Maybe he does. That lad has got brains, and he won't have to use all he's got to know that he can't lie low for long without a helping hand. It'd be just too bad if he was taken back to Brixton."

"I don't suppose he'd enjoy it very much, Alibi."

"What do you suppose a man in that fix might do about it?"

"Hard to say. He may have half a dozen hideouts he can run to. It wouldn't be easy then to follow him from one to the other. Maybe he's got a job in mind that he intends to pull before he does anything else. Maybe he wouldn't tell anyone what he intends to do until they put their cards on the table and called with the hand exposed."

"You think he's the sort of bloke who would talk on the straight, but wouldn't like running round circles?"

"From what I've heard of him he sounds that way to me."

"All right, Borden, we'll talk. I've come to see you because a certain gent is beginning to take an interest in you. What's more to the point, is that this certain gent can hand out a helping mitt better than any man in London. Once you get under his wing you can sit back and smile. He's ready, on terms, to do a bit for you."

"Stow it, Alibi. I thought this was going to be a straight talk. What's all this stuff about the certain gent? If that's your idea of a straight talk, we're wasting each other's time. You might as well go, and I'll have another spot of shuteye."

"Don't get hasty, lad. We've both got to be a bit careful. My boss thinks he can use you; he is ready to help you, but first of all he wants to know a bit about you. He's a shrewd 'un, the boss is, and he ain't the kind to buy pigs in pokes."

"I haven't said yet that I'm up for sale, have I?"

"It'd pay you to loosen up and tell me a bit about yourself."

"Listen to me, Alibi. So far I've got along by myself. And, believe me, I've handled some big coin. Why should I start with somebody else when I can pull my strokes single-handed and have the rake-on all to myself? You answer that one before we start family histories."

"I'll soon answer that one, Borden. You have to find your own jobs, don't you?"

"Surely. The police don't hand them on to me."

"And when you've got the stuff you have to shop it yourself?"

"And I know some damn good fences, Alibi."

"I dare say. But wouldn't it make things easier for you if someone else picked your jobs for you, made all the arrangements, provided you with an organisation, gave the cars to you, and reliable men to work with, and then, at the end of all that, fenced the stuff for you, and posted your rake-off to you? Doesn't that sound better than solo work?"

"There are one or two ' ifs' about that I'd want to think over. In the first place, what sort of a rake-off would I get?"

"How can I tell you that unless I know what sort of a job you were on? It might be anything."

"Hold your horses for a minute, Alibi. If this boss of yours has to pay men to help me, men to get the cars for me, men to find roe, men to work out the job, profit for the fence, and a heavy share for himself—where do I come in? Don't forget that I've never split with anyone."

"You'd be able to handle better stuff than you do now."

"How do you know what sort of stuff I've been handling? I told you a minute ago that I've had my hands on the heavy metal."

"My boss doesn't call coin heavy till it runs into the thousands."

"I've heard that tale before somewhere. You manage a job like that once in a lifetime, Alibi."

"We manage 'em at the rate of one a week."

"There ain't that much money in England. Who is this boss of yours?"

"Take your time, Pete. Got any other complaints?"

"Yes. So far I've always relied on myself. I don't reckon I could get used to relying on anybody else working with me."

"All the boss's men are good."

"Not one of 'em ever been on the Moor?"

"Maybe one or two of them have had a trip."

"Then they can't all be good. The good 'uns don't visit the Moor."

"Don't ride the high horse, Pete. The proposition I'm shoving in front of you would be jumped at by scores I know. It's the best chance I've ever known a youngster to have. That chase of yours with the Squad must have tickled him. It ain't like him to take sudden fancies."

"All right, get down to the brass tacks. Who is your boss?"

"He's known by the name of Maddick."

"Who is he? I've heard of that bloke and often wondered about him."

"So have hundreds of others. It isn't good for the health to ask questions about him. I've worked for him for more'n a year, and he's always played straight with me. I don't know any more about him now than I did the day I joined up with his mob. And I don't want to know any more about it. We had one bloke once who was curious."

"What happened to him?"

"It's hard to say," replied Delaney, with a hard smile, "but some think that he fell into the Thames just above Teddington."

"And you think I'm going to join with Maddick when you sit there and tell me that folks who work for him might slip into the river?"

"But you'd have sense enough to do your jobs, collect the cash and keep your mouth shut, wouldn't you? So long as you can see and hear and be blind, deaf and dumb, you can live to be an old man."

"Who told you to come round trying to collect me?"

"I got a note a few minutes after you pulled your breakaway telling me to look around for you. I reckon the same note was

## MADDICK ENLISTS A RECRUIT

sent round to all the boys. If I hadn't found you one of the others would."

"Sounds as though your boss gets mostly what he wants."

"You can take it from me, Pete, that what he doesn't know isn't worth knowing. That man's got informants that'd make the police green with envy if they knew anything about them."

"What sort of protection does he give you?"

"He reckons that his arrangements are so good that there should be no slip, and every man should be able to stand on his own feet and keep out of trouble. But if it isn't your fault he'll shove up bail for you, and get you the best lawyers in England to defend you. It's nothing to him to pay a couple of hundred guineas for a K. C. if the job has been a big one. He won't leave you in the lurch."

"Sounds a bit more interesting. What am I supposed to say?"

"The boss won't take you on until he knows something about you. Just give me an idea, and I'll do the rest."

"He won't find me on the police books until this last business. There's two good reasons for that. First is that I haven't been grabbed before. The second is that I've pulled a lot of my stuff abroad. I only came back from the Riviera three weeks ago. Always single-handed, mark you. I did a job in Mentone before I left that gave me a roll big enough to last for six months. And I'm a fast spender."

"What were you going to do with that car you pinched?"

"I don't mind telling you now since I'm not going to have another shot at it. I was going to extract some coin from a joint at Camden Town. I knew there'd be about four hundred there, and there's only three men in the shop."

Alibi looked at him with heightened interest.

"And you were going there to collect all on your lonesome?"

"Sure. Why not? Single-handed always makes a cleaner job."

"My God! No wonder Maddick wants to get hold of you."

"Now, Alibi, let's talk business for a minute. I'm not the sort of bloke to talk hot air. These are the terms under which I'll join your crowd. One, I will not handle any small stuff. The first time I get handed a third-rate stroke I quit. I'm not in this game for the good of my health, and the sooner Maddick knows that the better. Second, if I get pulled in, Maddick has got to provide me with a mouthpiece, and a damn good one at that. Third, while the police are looking for me he's got to see that I'm tucked away somewhere peaceful until I'm wanted. Fourth, I'm not going to take instructions from anyone other than him about any job I pull. That's to save anybody putting the squeak on me. And that's about the lot."

"You've got a hell of a nerve, Pete. Folks don't dictate terms to Maddick. He dictates 'em, and they accept them. But I'll see that you get a fair deal. Now, there's only one thing left. What's your best line?"

"Anything, except murder, if there's plenty of dough in it. I'm not going to meet the hangman for Maddick and twice his money. But I'll do anything else. The bigger it is the better I like it. So far, I've done a spot of black, handled slush,[1] managed a few hold-ups, tried the con game without much luck, and wangled a few safes. There's plenty more I can do if the job's big enough to be tempting."

"You certainly haven't neglected your education, Pete."

"I started young, Alibi. I don't intend to spend all my time on the run. When the middle-aged spread starts to push my waistcoat out I want to be sitting pretty and forgetting where my dough came from."

"That about settles it, Pete. I'll look you up in the morning about eleven, and tell you how the land lies. You'd better stop indoors tonight. They're running round with a fine comb looking for you."

"I should worry," said Pete. "Good night, and the best of luck. Give my love to the boss."

---

[1] Counterfeit currency.

# 7

## THE FIRST JOB

Mick sat on the edge of the bed reading the two morning newspapers brought by Mrs Chapman. Apparently he had first been seen boarding an omnibus in Blackfriars. This seemed to conflict with the theory of the elderly lady who, at the same time, had dropped her shopping basket with surprise in Lewisham High Street at the vision of the escaper driving south at "a most tremendous pace." After that he had been sighted by a postman in Hammersmith, a girl typist taking lunch in Wimbledon, a greengrocer on his round at Kensal Green, and a small boy playing in the street at Bethnal Green.

Below these reports appeared the sober information that the police were conducting inquiries which they felt sure would lead to the arrest of Peter Borden within a few hours. The car in which he had escaped had been found in Lambeth, but the theory held by Scotland Yard was that the prisoner, being a cunning man, had abandoned the motor at that spot as a blind before seeking a refuge in a totally different part of London.

One of the papers carried an impression of the escaped man made by an artist who saw him in the police court. Mick didn't realise before how much he resembled many well-known film stars; nor that his hair cascaded from forehead to crown in a succession of elegant waves.

For two hours after rising, the youngster had been pacing the bedroom, congratulating himself on his early initiation into the Maddick circle, considering ways and means of turning his enlistment to account. It was typical of him that the risks involved had occupied no place in his considerations. It would be time enough to think about those when they arrived. Inactivity bored him, and he was glad when Alibi Delaney poked his head round the bedroom door.

"Hallo, Pete, how're you feeling?"

"Just about ready for anything. What's the big news?"

"The boss says you can make a start."

"That's quick work, Alibi. When did you find this out?"

"I passed the word to him last night—told him what you'd got to say. He thinks you're aiming for the moon a bit, but doesn't seem to mind that very much. At any rate, he'll give you a start—you've got a job for today, but it's a very cushy one."

"Good. It beats me, Alibi, how you pass on your information to Maddick and take your instructions from him when you don't know who he is or where he lives. What's the big scheme?"

"You'll find out before you've finished, but you won't discover who the boss is. I can tell you that much. And if you do find out who he is the knowledge won't do you any good. Dead men, you know, don't often do themselves much good."

"Can that stuff. If you think you're scaring me, you can tell your boss that a hundred of his sort wouldn't even spoil a meal for me."

"Take my tip, Pete, and stop thinking things like that. But if you can't help thinking about them, for the sake of your health stop talking about them. Now we'll get down to the job."

"Don't land me on one that takes me into a police station."

"This one's a gift. In a way, Pete, it's a good one for you to start on. It'll show you better than anything the way Maddick arranges things for anyone who gets knocked off. One of his blokes is strolling into the dock at the Old Bailey in the morning, and if we can't square things he'll go down for three or five years. Maddick's made all the arrangements, and all you have to do is follow the instructions.

"Here's the lay of things. We've been handling slush lately— ten bobs and quids. Where they were printed doesn't matter to you. That was all fixed up. But a while ago we had a bit of bad luck. One of the boys got knocked off, and he had about forty pounds in dud notes on him. He's got an unpleasant record at the back of him, and if they find him guilty of passing those notes he'll take a stiff jolt. On top of that—and this is Maddick's prime consideration—the other men handling the slush will get frozen feet and throw in the job. So we have got to fix things a bit!"

"Tough job, isn't it, trying to rescue a man from the Old Bailey?" The question was asked casually.

Delaney swung round and peered closely at the young man.

"Good God!" he said. "If you're not the coolest thing that walks on two legs. Fancy thinking that we wanted you to pull a stroke like that! Do you really mean that you'd try it?"

"I wouldn't try it tomorrow morning, but if I had the time to work things out a bit I can't see why it shouldn't be done."

"I'll pass that on to Maddick," said Alibi with a laugh; "It'll tickle him to death. Now, just listen to me for a couple of minutes. We've got a smart firm of solicitors for this bloke— Arch Redfern his name is—and Maddick has put down the heavy coin for a top liner to defend him in court. Conway Addison, the K.C., is doing the spot of mouthing. They've got something of a defence to work on, but we want a stronger line. That's where you come in."

"Tell me the job, and I'll do it."

"That's the spirit, boy. The story, in brief, is that Redfern was given the notes at the races. Any amount of dud notes are handed over to the bookies, and back again to the punters. So that's the defence. But we've got to have some corroborative evidence. That's your job.

"In the Borough, at 486, you'll find the offices of Andrew Purvis, the bookmaker. Just jot down the name and address. Now, he's a pal of ours, and will do us a turn if he can. Here's a photograph of Redfern. Show it to him, and tell him that Redfern has been betting regularly with him on the course. On March 26th—that's the day on which the cops collected Redfern—it happened that Purvis paid him nearly sixty pounds in one-pound and ten-shilling notes. Then the K.C. will ask one or two questions, and these will be the answers to them:

"'Look at those notes, Mr Purvis. Can you tell me whether they are the notes you paid to the prisoner on the day of his arrest?'

"Answer! ' I cannot say that these are the identical notes, but as the prisoner left me a short time before his arrest I assume that he received these notes from me.'

" 'You realise, Mr Purvis, that these notes are forgeries?'

"Answer: 'It may well be that they are. In common with all other bookmakers who work on the courses, I have had the misfortune to handle a large number of forged notes. On occasions I have found myself at the end of a heavy day with as much as two hundred pounds worth. Perhaps I may add that the racecourses of this country are recognised by those specialising in this form of crime as one of the main markets for forged notes.'

" 'So that if the defendant had these forged notes in his possession at the time of his arrest, and he pleaded that he had received them from you, you would not contradict him?'

"Answer : 'Certainly not. It is most probable.'

"There you have the whole story, Pete, and we reckon that we can get an acquittal on it. Now do your stuff."

"Damned ingenious," said the young man admiringly. "Is this one of your ideas?"

"No, came straight from Maddick himself. The boss has got a genius for working these things out. I only work the alibis for the boys—that's where I got my name from. Wait a minute, and then I'll be through with the instructions. When you have talked to Purvis and drummed the whole story into his head, take him along to the solicitors, Newall and Gibbs, of 45a Chancery Lane. He can make his statement there and have it properly drawn up. After that go over with him to the chambers of Addison, the counsel, and see that he's got it all straight. Maybe Addison will want to rehearse Purvis a bit, and you'll have to be there in case Purvis starts to draw away from his tale. Once the K.C. has got everything O.K., you can come back here, and you'll find me waiting for you."

"What about the solicitors and the counsel? Do they know anything about this phoney evidence?"

"Good God, no! You must tell them that by accident you've just bumped into Purvis, and thought that maybe his story would be helpful to the prisoner. That's why you must go with him— in case he gives the show away if he's alone."

"Why don't you do the job yourself? You know Purvis."

"There are three good reasons. The first is that I haven't been given the job. The second is that I've got one of my own. The third is that I don't want Purvis to be asked in the box whether he has seen me lately. Carry on with the job now. You ought to be back here by one o'clock."

"Suppose Purvis wants to know what he'll get for the evidence?"

"Tell him that he's always been treated fair, and this time, as always before, Maddick is paying on results."

Cardby slipped the bowler hat on his head, tipped the brim to a jaunty angle, stared into the mirror while he readjusted his tie, and descended the stairs with Delaney. At the foot of the stairs Alibi stopped and lit a cigarette.

"Carry on," he said. "I'll give you a three-minute start. We don't want to be seen together."

Mick nodded and strolled into the street.

Alibi walked along the passage and opened the kitchen door.

"What do you know, Beattie?" he inquired.

"Can't find out nothin'. He's dead cute."

"Got any money?"

"Paid me a month in advance. Doesn't seem short."

"You don't seem to be doing much for your money, Beattie."

"You've only give me a quid so far, Alibi."

"Here's another. Think he's done many jobs?"

"'Ard to say. They ain't like they was in my young days. It's come to a fine thing when ordinary 'ouse busters walk round like peers of the realm. What's 'is line?"

"Anything to everything—according to what he says."

"Empty cans make the most sound."

"He's no empty can, Beattie. Either that boy has got me beaten to the wide or he's one of the smartest men on the crook I've ever met."

"I know," said the blowzy woman, with a sigh, "poor Midnight used to think that. He doesn't now."

"You can't compare this lad with Midnight," said Delaney brutally. "Your man had nothing but a couple of jemmies, and an idea that there was something worth pinching in every house. His day's gone, Beattie. We don't want jemmies now. We want brains. That's what Midnight never had, and he's paying for it now."

The woman heard the comments without changing features.

"I suppose you're right," she said, "although my man did some pretty stuff in his young days."

"The prettiest thing he ever did was to leave his fingerprints on that electric lamp bulb at Purley when I pulled that stroke with him. Keep your peepers open, Beattie. There won't be any more of these quids coming forward while you stay dumb."

"I'll do my best, Alibi, but 'e's an 'andful for an old woman."

Mick walked to the Borough, and soon found the bookie's offices. An office boy took his name into an inner room before beckoning him forward. Cardby passed through the gate into a small office at the back. The carpet, desk and every fitting showed the horrible effect upon a room when wealth is expended without taste.

Andrew Purvis completely filled the ornate armchair. His jowl sagged on his collar, the cigar was held in wide, loose lips. Little piggy eyes were bedded in crimson flesh and the man's huge bulk strained under a blue serge suit. Without rising he waved a pudgy hand towards a nearby chair, puffed at his smoke, and waited for Mick to speak.

"I've come from Maddick," said Cardby simply.

Purvis studied the diamond ring on his finger before sending another cloud of smoke to the ceiling.

"Who is Maddick?" Still the bookmaker averted his glance from Mick.

"You know as much about that as I do, Purvis. I was sent by Alibi Delaney. Now tell me that you don't know him."

"Seem to have heard of him. What's all the trouble?"

"We want you to give us a hand—only a small matter."

"That's what I'm told every time anyone of you fellows walks in."

"This won't cause you any sleepless nights. Have you read anything in the paper about Arch Redfern?"

"Um. Wasn't he dragged in for passing dud notes?"

"Right first guess. He's up at the Old Bailey tomorrow. And we want you to give us a hand."

"Let's hear the idea, and then I'll think it over."

In five minutes Mick had explained the whole position. Purvis lit another cigar, and slid the box towards Mick. The youngster shook his head, but he accepted a whisky, flooding the glass with soda.

"Yeah," said the bookie, stifling a yawn. "I'll do that—provided it's worth my while. What sort of cut do I get?"

"Maddick is paying on results. You know he's fair enough, Purvis."

"All right. I'll trust him. Let's get a cab and finish the job."

On the way to the solicitors Purvis groaned and moaned about the parlous times through which members of his fraternity were passing. Cardby, by the time the cab stopped, had begun to wonder when the diamond ring would arrive in "Uncle's," and the cigars would give way to the lowly Woodbine. They clambered up the winding stone steps to the office, Purvis puffing and cursing each time he put a foot down.

"I want to speak to the gentleman responsible for the defence of Redfern at the Old Bailey tomorrow," Cardby told the clerk.

Before long they arrived in the office of Montague Newall. The solicitor was tall, bald headed, pale and thin. His black coat draped round his shoulders as though it hung from a coat hanger.

"The Redfern case," he said, slipping a bundle of papers on the desk. "What do you want to see me about?"

"I am a friend of Redfern's," said Mick, "and this morning this gentleman, Mr Andrew Purvis, told me something that should materially assist the defence. Tell your story, Mr Purvis."

The fat man rattled off his version of the forged notes with a glibness thoroughly convincing.

"Most important, most important," said Newall at the end of the recital. "We'll have your statement properly drawn up." He pushed the bell. "I take it that you are prepared to offer that statement in evidence tomorrow?"

"Certainly, if you think it will help."

When the bookmaker had signed the statement Mick spoke again.

# THE FIRST JOB

"In order that there can be no doubt about the strength of this evidence I have been instructed to take Mr Purvis, and the statement, to Mr Conway Addison."

"That would be—eh—a little unprofessional, Mr Wall."

"Surely it will be all right if you accompany us?"

"H'm. Very well, we'll walk over there now."

Again Purvis cursed as they mounted the wooden stairs round the tortuous curves of a temple staircase. They were fortunate. Mr Conway Addison was not only in his office, but was prepared to see them.

The K.C. sat behind a pile of documents. On the right and left of his desk were open volumes of law reports. Addison was elderly and withered. Mick guessed his age at seventy, and realised that he might easily have underestimated. The dark eyes seemed oddly alert in the face of yellow skin. The man's lips were pale. In height only little more than five feet, it did not seem that he could have weighed eight stone. Quite insignificant, except for the lustre of his eyes, the fluttering, bird-like movement of his hands.

He played with a piece of tape while Newall told his story.

"That makes a very big difference," he said at length. There was a surprising depth in his voice, a resonance out of keeping with his meagre frame. "Perhaps, if you'll hand me the statement, I might go over the evidence with Mr Purvis."

For ten minutes the bookmaker was coached as thoroughly as a backward boy about to sit for an examination. At length Addison sat back in his chair and looked from one man to the other, then towards young Cardby.

"I wonder," he said, speaking as though alone, "what the prosecuting counsel will do with him. We must work that out. Suppose, Mr Purvis, just for a moment, that I am appearing for the Crown, and you have just completed your evidence in chief. Try to answer me just as though you are standing in the box before the judge and jury. Do you follow me?"

"Yes, I know what you mean, sir."

"Have you often discovered these forged notes at the end of the day?"

"Quite frequently, although they come in patches."

"When you discover that you have in your bag notes that are not genuine, what do you do with them?"

"I take them back to the course on the following day, and hope that the people who get them back are the folks who handed them to me."

There was dead silence in the room. When Addison spoke again there was a grim smile round his thin lips, and his voice was crisp and clear.

"So that you, yourself, utter those notes, well knowing them to be forgeries?"

Purvis loosened his collar and opened his mouth.

"God!" he said. "I walked into that one."

"The further comment," remarked Addison, "is that on such evidence you should be in the dock with Redfern."

"What am I supposed to say?" asked the harassed bookmaker.

"I think," said Cardby, "that there is one way out of it. I would say that I didn't examine the individual notes at the end of the day—I simply counted them. There were occasions when notes handed in by me had been rejected by the bank. They were then either destroyed or passed on to the police. The same course was adopted when a punter on the course found out that I had handed him forged notes. It was no part of my duty as a bookmaker to scrutinise all notes handed to me and paid out by me. The ordinary course of business on the race track is too swift to permit of any examination."

"I'm sorry," said Addison, "that you are not taking the stand yourself to give this evidence. You'd better memorise that answer, Purvis. It seems to fit the questions very well. That's all, gentlemen, if you will excuse me. I have a lot of work to do. I will meet you in court."

Cardby arrived at his lodgings shortly before one o'clock. Alibi was sitting on the bed reading the morning papers.

"All clear," reported the youngster. "Purvis knows his stuff."

"Good. Then you can start to collect your clothes. We've got some digs for you that should be more healthy than these. The police are tightening up round here, and we don't want you to be caught before you've started. I'll get a taxi while you pack your duds."

# 8

## MICK FINDS AN ALLY

The taxi was waiting at the door. The youngster commenced to walk towards the kitchen, but Alibi stopped him.

"Don't bother about your landlady. I've squared everything with her. Keep in the corner of the cab and don't look out of the window unless you want to meet the Governor at Brixton."

Cardby looked over the shoulder of the driver as they passed over Westminster Bridge. He had not heard Delaney give the direction. The cab turned on to the Embankment and passed New Scotland Yard. Mick jerked his thumb in the direction of the building and grinned.

"They'd like to know that I was within fifty yards of 'em," he said.

"Pipe low," growled Delaney. "Men are apt to laugh a bit too soon sometimes, and it's a bad habit."

They turned into Northumberland Avenue, along Haymarket and Regent Street. Then the driver swung into Great Marlborough Street and proceeded past the police court.

"Have you arranged this ride to make me feel nervous?" asked Cardby.

But before he got a reply the taxi crossed Oxford Street and drew to a stop in Titchfield Street. Delaney paid the driver and knocked at the door of a small, dirty house, while Mick lifted

## MICK FINDS AN ALLY

his bag from the car. The door was opened by a henna-haired blonde.

"Here we are," announced Alibi. "Meet your new boarder, Mr Wall. This is Mrs Weeldon. Let's get inside."

"How are you, dearie?" asked the landlady.

Mick shivered internally. This was worse, infinitely worse than the bedraggled Mrs Chapman. The woman eyed him closely. The inspection was mutual. She saw a well-set up young man with a pleasant face, and clothes too extravagantly cut. He saw a woman of thirty with pencilled eyebrows, a pert nose with wide nostrils, carmined lips that parted to show teeth white, but uneven, and a figure suffering from the ravages of reduction. The woman had an air of smartness that did not altogether disguise traces of common origin.

"So, so, and you, my dear?" Mick was playing his trumps to the last trick. "Let's have a look at my next resting-place."

Mrs Weeldon smiled, and led the way to the second floor. On the stairs going up they passed another woman—red-lipped, bold-eyed, slim-hipped, another edition of the landlady.

"Here you are then," said the landlady, swinging the door back. The room was certainly better than the one he had just forsaken. A blue carpet covered the floor, the walls were papered in coral, and the furnishings were more ample and more comfortable. In one corner stood a divan, by its side was a small table, and in front of the gas fire were two easy chairs upholstered in blue cloth.

"How will this suit you, dearie?" inquired Mrs Weeldon.

"Looks good to me. Hallo, I see you've got a telephone in the room."

"Yes," said the woman, with a smirk, "there are extensions in most of the bedrooms. Some of my boarders want them for one thing—and some want them for others." She stopped while Alibi laughed at the implied obscenity. "You might find yours handy, Mr Wall."

"He will," said Delaney. "There's no sense in having a phone unless it's private. I'll be ringing you in a few hours' time, Stan. So long."

The man turned and left the room abruptly. Mick was embarrassed. The woman was eyeing him curiously.

"What brought you this way, dearie?" she asked.

"Felt like a change of air, Mrs Weeldon."

"Oh, don't keep calling me Mrs Weeldon or I'll think we're not going to be friendly. My front name's Mona, so I shan't forgive you a second time. Change of air you've come for? Does the West End suit you?"

"Anywhere suits me so long as the going is good. What made Delaney beat for the road so suddenly, Mona?"

"He's funny that way. But he means well. What sort of hours do you keep—tell me, by the way, what's your name?"

"Plain Stan. What hours do I keep? That depends. Sometimes I just don't keep them at all —I spend them right and left. After that I stay in the house and save up some more. At the moment I've finished spending 'em. Now I'm going to start saving."

"So you'll be in this room nearly all the time?"

"Right with the first guess."

"I envy you folks who have no work to do. It must be nice."

"Why, what do you do for a living?" The question was put bluntly.

"I run this place, and that's enough work for one person."

"If all your folks give you as little trouble as me you'll have an easy time of it. By the way, how do you get numbers on this telephone?"

"Just ring through, and if the phone downstairs in my room isn't being used, you're right on to the exchange."

"Which means that whatever I say over the telephone can be heard by any person in the house owning an extension?"

"We don't bother about what people say in this house, dearie."

"That's lucky for all of you, Mona, because the first time I find anyone listening in on the line when I'm talking they're never going to forget it. You might remind all of them about that, and remember it yourself. Just one other thing. Where's the key to this door?"

"It's never had a key as far as I know."

"Has it ever had a bolt as far as you know?"

"No, we just trust each other here. We're like a big family."

"I see. Well, the door is going to have a key and a bolt, or I'm moving. I don't aim to join this happy family of yours, Mona."

"I'll fix you up with those. You sound as though you're on the run."

Cardby walked towards the window and looked down into the street.

"A little girl like you, Mona," he said at last, "should know a lot and say nothing. Otherwise, you'll end your days selling matches in Piccadilly, or maybe worse. What I do here is no concern of yours. What you do doesn't matter two hoots to me. Get that key and bolt."

The landlady flounced out of the room, and Mick started to place his clothes in the wardrobe and in the drawers of the dressing table.

As he returned towards the window another thought occurred to him, and he dragged one of the easy chairs to the door, tilting the back until it lodged beneath the handle. Then he walked over to the telephone and cautiously raised the receiver. Immediately he recognised the voice of the landlady.

"Yes, I'll look after that. Nothing will come from here, you can be sure. He says he'll spend all the time in his room."

"Let me know," came a man's voice, "if he goes out."

"Right. Glen is over the road. He'll tail him wherever he goes."

"That'll do then. Keep your mouth shut and your eyes open."

The bell clanged slightly as the receiver was replaced. Mick slid his earpiece back on to the clip and moved the chair from the door. Before he could stride across the room there came a knock at the door. A second later the landlady entered with a key in her hand.

"I don't know whether this one will fit the door," she said.

"I wouldn't mind betting that it does."

Cardby was right. The woman smiled at him.

"You're a cute little fellow, aren't you, Stan?"

"No, not a bit. It only seemed to me that in this sort of house it would be funny if there weren't keys to the doors."

"I can see you haven't got much to learn, Stan. Watch your step, or one of these days you'll be getting too cute."

"My boss," said Cardby slowly, "likes 'em cute, doesn't he?"

"I don't know what you mean," said Mona, raising her heavily-painted eyelids to indicate surprise.

"I thought you said you wanted to be friendly, my dear. What's the good of beating round the bush with friends?"

"I don't aim to lose a good job by forgetting I'm dumb."

"Nor me. But we might as well know where we are."

"I know. That's why I stay dumb. I'd rather know where I am than where I used to be. You're a nice boy, Stan, but you won't stay nice for long if you can't learn to keep the air off your tongue."

"Wise girl. Got any grub about the place?"

"Come down and have lunch with me. I'm all alone."

"Suits me fine. Lead the way. Here, before I forget, what am I to pay you for hanging out here?"

Mona placed her hands on her hips and laughed.

"That's a good one, Stan. What on earth gave you the idea that you'd got to pay me anything? You own this joint as much as I do."

Mick heard the answer without any show of surprise.

"There you are," he said, "you tell me to act dumb, and the very first time I take your advice you laugh at me."

## MICK FINDS AN ALLY

"You certainly pulled my leg that time," she answered.

Mick was young, healthy and hungry. But he did not enjoy his lunch. The woman's painted face, her attempts at familiarity, her efforts to turn each comment into a *double entendre*, took the edge off his appetite. He was glad to arrive back in his own room, having incurred Mona's displeasure by his refusal to spend the remainder of the afternoon with her.

At five o'clock Delaney rang up.

"All O.K., Pete?"

"Splendid. Any news?"

"Yes. I want you to take a walk this evening. At eight o'clock start from your place along to the left until you come to Upper Marylebone Street. Turn to the right, and then take the first turn to the left into Charlton Street. Walk along until you come to the junction with Carburton Street. Somewhere near the corner at about ten-past seven you'll see a man wearing a black double-breasted overcoat. If he says to you 'Could you help an ex-officer?' take his evening paper from him. Gummed to page three you'll find some stuff for yourself. Don't say anything to the man, and, above all, don't change from the clothes you were wearing when I left you. All clear?"

"Yes, that's plain enough, Alibi. Suppose I'm tailed?"

"It would only be one of our men to see that nothing happened to you. Just carry on and take no notice."

"Suits me. Cheerio, Alibi. See you soon."

Later Mick sent out for an evening paper. He found that the search for him had already been relegated to an inside page. In another day or two the public would have given up their search. And Cardby feared the public more than he feared the police.

Promptly at seven he started his walk. Before he had gone twenty yards he observed that a man had crossed the road from Mortimer Street and was keeping pace with him at a discreet distance. Mick did not turn round again. It wouldn't do to show that he was uneasy.

He followed Delaney's directions exactly. At the corner of Charlton Street and Carburton Street stood a tall man in a black overcoat. Immediately he noticed Mick approaching he walked across Cleveland Street and into Fitzroy Square. The youngster caught him up half-way round the square.

"Could you help an ex-officer?" inquired the man.

Cardby looked at him, nodded, took the paper from under his arm, and vanished into the darkness. He continued to walk, grateful for the opportunity of taking some exercise. Soon he left Tottenham Court Road and Gower Street behind him. Then he commenced to speed his way through the many streets surrounding the British Museum. For ten minutes he turned and twisted. Finally, he walked into a public house, called for a drink and sat down. He was the only person in the bar. The landlord, after a feeble attempt at conversation, retired from the fray and picked up the evening paper. Mick sat for nearly half an hour, reading the paper. For most of the time his eyes were on page three. He read the message over four or five times. The note was typewritten on a piece of paper some fourteen inches by eight, and the paper had been gummed to the newspaper sheet.

Mick ordered another drink, and read the instructions for the last time. His brain was racing in an effort to find a solution. He read:

"Tomorrow evening Lady Mead will give reception, 352 Brook Street. Guests number three hundred. Announced she will wear Sonnenshein necklace. Guest announced, walk across hall thirty feet long. Lord and Lady Mead receive them at head of five stairs. Guests then pass along twenty-foot corridor to reception room. To right of host and hostess is low window, five feet above lead roof. Window will be open. Early tomorrow you will receive card inviting Count and Countess

Metri to reception. Meet lady eight-thirty tomorrow night outside 32 Bruton Street. She will wear blue dress and fur wrap and sit inside Daimler car. Ask her way to South Audley Street. If she replies 'Second on left,' get into car. She has further instructions."

Small beads of sweat formed on the young man's face. His first plunge was to be no mean effort. He walked through to the lavatory, tore the note from the page, placed it in his pocket, and left the paper behind him. Then he emptied his drink, and continued his walk. He had completely lost his follower. As he strolled along Holborn his thoughts were everywhere. What should he do?

Obviously the stage had been set for the theft of the necklace. If he proceeded with his instructions without informing the police it was almost certain that the robbery would be successful. Maddick did not fail. On the other hand, if he passed on his information to the police and the robbery failed, suspicion would instantly rest upon him, and that would end his connection with the Maddick gang, even if it did not end his interest in life. So that all the preliminary work would be undone, the police might prevent a theft and capture a few underlings, but the organisation headed by Maddick would still exist.

Mick decided to take the risk and talk the matter over with his father. Where could he find a "safe" telephone? Then he remembered a friend of his in St. Martin's Lane and turned back to find the flat.

His friend was at home, and Mick bustled him out of the room while he used the telephone, giving the number of his father's private house.

"Is that you, Dad?" asked Mick. ". . . Good. Listen to me. I don't want to waste time. I've enlisted with Maddick and am living in Titchfield Street with a Mrs Weeldon. Tomorrow night they are going to steal Lady Mead's necklace when she gives her reception in Brook Street. I am on the job, attending the reception as Count Metri. That's all I know. How the job is to be done I don't know. Listen, Dad. If you stop this job I'll be suspected and kicked out of the crowd. That would mean the end of the idea before I learnt anything. But if you take no action that necklace is going for a million. I can't think of a way out. What do you say?"

"Very awkward, Mick. You'll have to leave it to me to think of the best way out. Just go along with your arrangements as though you've said nothing to me. I'll have someone at the reception."

"For God's sake don't send one of your men. They know them all."

"Don't worry about that, Mick. I'll send someone they won't know."

"Have I got to carry out whatever instructions they give me?"

"Certainly—unless they tell you to shoot someone. Anything else you know?"

"Nothing. I don't suppose I'll be able to ring you up again."

"It's too risky to try, Mick. Unless it's absolutely necessary don't get in touch with me again. In any case, I'll be out of the Yard most of tomorrow. I've got a job on at the Old Bailey."

"Doesn't happen to be a forgery job against one Arch Redfern?"

"That's the case. What do you know about it?"

"Nothing, Dad, except that the man will be acquitted. Good night."

"Thanks for the pleasant news, Mick. All the best."

At nine o'clock young Cardby was back in his room. Mona sat on the bed.

"Are you trying to cause trouble?" she asked. "Alibi has been on the phone for you every five minutes for the last hour. Where've you been?"

"What does he want me for?"

"Hell, Stan, don't you know that we wouldn't let you walk round loose without a tail on you? We haven't known you so long that we're full of confidence. The tail rang up to say that he'd lost you, and I had to report to Alibi. Since then he's been going nearly mad about it. You'd better not do that again. It isn't likely to be healthy a second time. If Maddick heard that you had slipped the tail tonight it would be a neat tombstone and no flowers for you. There's the phone again."

Mick lifted the receiver. Delaney's voice was loud and angry.

"What the hell game do you think you're playing, fellow? Where've you been, what have you been doing, why'd you lose our man?"

"Cheese it," said Cardby roughly, and with some menace in his tone. "Who the hell do you think you're talking to, Delaney? You're not buying me, you know, you're only borrowing me. Any more talk like that and I'll hit you for six the next time I see you. Calm yourself down, big boy, before you get into trouble. Now talk sensible."

"Don't start thinking you can pull that rough stuff on me."

"Come round here and see whether I'm joking. Or give me your address and I'll be with you right away. Talking big doesn't suit you, Alibi."

"You're heading straight for trouble."

"I've been in trouble all my life, so a bit more won't make any sort of difference. Neither you nor anybody else is going to upset me."

"All right, can the argument and we'll get down to tacks. Why did you lose our tail?"

"For two reasons. One was that I forgot he was at the back of me. The other was that he couldn't walk fast enough. Next time you want to provide me with a keeper don't give me a senile cripple."

"Where did you go to?"

"Two pubs—one near the British Museum, one in Holborn."

"See anyone you knew?"

"Yes. Had a talk with a friend of mine. Met him in St. Martin's Lane."

"Who is he?"

"I'm not telling you his name, and if I explained his business to you I don't think you'd understand it. He works a game better than yours."

"What's his line then?"

"Providing dubious collateral security for people with overdrafts."

"What did you see him about?"

"Wouldn't you see a man when you'd got forty quid to collect?"

"All right, Pete. I hope for the sake of your health that you're playing on the level. I'll be round to see you in the morning."

Mona lit a cigarette and beckoned to the divan at her side.

"You certainly do tell them where to get off, Stan. I never heard any man stand up to Alibi like that before. Have you ever seen him beating anybody up?"

"No, but it must be amusing. I'm tired, kid."

"Oh, don't get rid of me so soon, Stan. I thought we'd have a chat."

"I'm a bad talker when I'm sleepy, Mona."

"Not the world's perfect little gentleman, are you? Good night, damn you!"

"Good night, you perfect little lady. Happy dreams."

By the time Mrs Weeldon arrived in her own room, flushed and angry, Chief Inspector Cardby had completed two calls and was on his way to a third. Obviously his work so far had pleased him. His fat face was wrinkled in a smile, and he hummed as he sat in the speeding taxi. The cab pulled up outside a small house in Chiswick. Cardby paid the cabby and dropped the brass knocker.

## MICK FINDS AN ALLY

The door was opened by a middle-aged woman, tidily dressed in black.

"Good evening, Inspector Cardby," she said. "He's in the front room."

"He" happened to be the lady's husband, Cardby's closest friend, and Detective-Sergeant Gribble, of New Scotland Yard. For seven years they had worked together. Oddly dissimilar in appearance, and in mind, they were recognised by the men at the Yard as a singularly effective combination. Gribble sat before the fire, the wireless blaring into his ear. In his hand was a bundle of papers. He was studying the depositions for the last time before giving evidence at the Old Bailey.

Gribble was tall and slender, his face pale and thin. His hands, as usual, protruded some six or eight inches beyond the short sleeves, and his upper lip was covered, or almost covered, by a black moustache that stopped almost before it began to start. Added to his physical characteristics was an air of overwhelming grief.

"Don't tell me you've got a job for me," he said, dropping his papers on a side table and turning off the wireless.

"Now then, misery, wait until your troubles arrive. But you can bet I haven't come here on a social call because I'm fond of you. There are moments, Gribble, when you persuade people into the belief that you possess sense. I've come here tonight under that illusion."

"Have you heard from Mick?" inquired Gribble.

"I have. Everything is going according to plan, and he told me on the phone that he does his first job for them tomorrow night. That's why I came to see you. He is attending Lady Mead's reception as Count Metri. Her diamond necklace is going to be pinched. How, he doesn't know. The point is, Gribble, that we dare not stop the robbery, or Mick will be kicked out of the Maddick crowd before he gets his hands on the goods."

"Then what are you going to do?"

"Don't worry yourself about the robbery. I've seen to that. We'll let them go ahead with it in their own way. What I am anxious to do is to place someone there among the guests who can keep a weather eye on things for us, and tell the tale later. I don't want them to take any part in the proceedings. All they'll have to do is to stand and watch. We must get the description of the occurrence, and of the people involved, from someone who is concentrating on that alone. If we trust to the evidence of the ordinary guests we'll get ten different stories, and won't know which to trust.

"So far that's plain enough. The next thing is that we dare not send a man from the Yard—any more than any of our men could have taken on the job that Mick has got now. That's what I came to see you about. What shall we do? I want someone there of real intelligence, keen observation, acute memory and appearance to pass among the guests with self-confidence. Now, speak, my oracle."

"It shouldn't be difficult. Your son is there on behalf of Maddick. What could possibly be better than to send my daughter, Mavis to hold a watching brief on behalf of the Yard?"

"That's exactly what I had in my mind when I came to see you. This, my lad, is developing into quite a family affair. Got a drink in the house? We'll quaff to the health of Cardby and Gribble, Limited, suppliers of agents to New Scotland Yard."

# 9

## THE RECEPTION

Mick paced the room restlessly on the following morning. The inactivity was wearying him. The attentions of Mona were cloying. The absence of any real information about Maddick was worrying him. There were seconds of despondency when the youngster commenced to think that Maddick had built such a structure of subterfuge round himself that identification was impossible.

Shortly before lunch Alibi appeared. He had forgotten his ill temper of the previous evening.

"A little present for you," he said, holding out an envelope.

"Where did you get this from?"

"Ask no questions and you'll hear no lies. Open it."

Inside was an invitation card to the Mead reception issued to Count and Countess Metri. Also, there were five one-pound notes.

"I thought," said Mick, "that Maddick only paid on results."

"He does, Pete. Arch Redfern was acquitted at the Old Bailey half an hour ago. The judge told the jury that having regard to the evidence given by Purvis it would be very dangerous to convict. They threw the case out of court. That's why you collected your five."

"But how did you get hold of it if the case was only thrown out half an hour ago?"

"Because I've had that money in my pocket since yesterday morning, waiting for the verdict before gave it to you."

"But the envelope was stuck down. Do you mean that this card was given to you in an open envelope?"

"I can see you don't know much about Maddick. The man who gave me that envelope had instructions to get that fiver from me, insert it in the envelope, gum down the flap, and hand the envelope to me. I haven't any idea what's written on that card, and I don't want to know anything about it. My only job was to see that you had it. Your only job is to carry out your instructions. Step across the way, and we'll have a drink."

"Do you think it's safe, Alibi?"

"Yes, I think so. The hue and cry has died down. This morning there was a little paragraph in my paper saying that you hadn't been caught yet, but you had been seen in Liverpool, and the police there were making inquiries. Slip your hat on and we'll walk."

"If we're going out, I want you to do a small job for me. We'll take a cab, and you can drop me at some pub on the way to Waterloo. Then take this ticket to the cloak-room at the station, and get my suitcase out. There are some togs in it that I'll need tonight, and I dare not go for them myself. Would you mind?"

"Not a bit. We'll take Mona with us. It'll be a change for her."

"That's a good idea."

Mick knew exactly what the suggestion meant. Alibi did not intend to leave him alone. While he went to Waterloo station, Mona could sit at Mick's elbow. That is precisely what happened. Half an hour later they returned to the house.

Cardby unpacked his evening suit and some linen. While he was in the midst of unpacking he turned to Delaney.

"I don't mind you opening my case and examining the contents, Alibi. I don't even mind you going through my pockets. Perhaps you've earned your living by doing it for so long that you can't drop the habit. All I have to request is that you should replace the articles as you found them. You're a damnably untidy packer. Mona, send these trousers out and have them creased for me."

It was eight-fifteen when young Cardby took a last look in the wardrobe mirror and decided that all was as it should be. The bow was faultless, the suit of perfect cut, the overcoat swathed him as though he had been poured into it. The silk scarf completed the ensemble. At the end of the hall he paused to place his hat at the requisite angle. Then he stepped into the street and walked leisurely towards his meeting place. This was the sort of adventure Mick had frequently dreamed about. It surprised him to find that now he was on his way his elation was subdued, his nerves under steady control, excitement non-existent.

Crossing Regent Street he strolled down Conduit Street, and a little later he glanced casually at the numbers. It was eight twenty-five. He was five doors away from Number 35 when a large Daimler turned round from Berkeley Square and pulled to a stop a few yards in front of him. Mick waited until he was at the side of the car before he slipped a cigarette case from his pocket, and twisted his head as he struck the match. There was one person in the car. From the glow of a street lamp Mick caught a glimpse of a light fur wrap. He threw the match down and stepped towards the lowered window.

"Excuse me, madam," he said, "but could you inform me which way I take to South Audley Street?"

"Certainly. Take the second on the left."

The voice was vibrant and musical, low pitched, slightly husky in an attractive key, it was perfectly modulated, the words clear.

Mick placed his hand on the handle, gave a twist, and entered the saloon. The occupant moved slightly to the left. Immediately the young man sank back into the deep upholstery the car moved away.

The chauffeur, without receiving any further instructions, turned into Berkeley Street, swung right-handed into Piccadilly, and slowed down to ten miles an hour as he proceeded towards Hyde Park.

"We have ample time," said the woman. "My name tonight is Eleanora."

"And mine, Eleanora, is Andrea. As you say, we have ample time. Suppose we use some of it. First of all, might I see your face?"

"Is that part of your instructions?"

"No, it had been overlooked. It occurred to me that if you retain that fur collar against your cheek until we arrive at the reception I will be in the awkward position of escorting a wife I have never seen, and whom I might not recognise among the guests. Imagine my embarrassment if I had to request the host or hostess to identify my wife for me!"

The woman laughed softly and dropped the collar of her wrap. In some curious way Mick had anticipated that the woman's beauty of voice would be equalled by a facial beauty, but he had not contemplated that each feature would so elude criticism as to make his mouth open in a confusion of admiration and astonishment.

The dark hair rose from a high, white forehead in large waves, smoothed out over the arch of the crown, and dived in a black sweep into the nape of her neck. The eyes, dark brown and luminous, were large and set well apart. Her mouth was boat-shaped, the perfect contour of the lips slightly accentuated by application of lipstick. Mick caught a glimpse of the white, rounded chest rising above the low-cut blue gown, he noted the faultless curve of the neck, the firm contour of the chin. Then the woman raised the wrap once more to her face.

"Are you quite satisfied?" she asked.

"Entirely, Eleanora. You look as though the reception should be given in your honour."

# THE RECEPTION

"That's clumsy, Andrea. In any case, if the reception isn't being given in my honour it's being given for our convenience."

"Quite true. What time do you intend us to arrive in Brook Street?"

"Nine o'clock. The driver has his instructions. Now you can have yours. What anyone else does makes no difference to you. Remember that. All you have to do is to carry out your instructions in detail and make no attempt either to fall short of them or to go beyond them. We must get that quite clear before we go any further."

"What other people do does not concern me at all."

"That's sensible. After we have been introduced, we pass through to the reception room. We will sit as near the entrance to the passage as possible. Lord and Lady Mead will be at the far end of the passage. At some time in the neighborhood of nine-thirty all the lights in the house will go out. Immediately that happens place yourself at the entrance to the passage and stop anyone either coming or going. Try to do it without attracting attention. Then, when the lights go up, we can be distraught with the rest of the people, and plead that we, too, tried to gain access to the passage and were stopped by some person at the entrance. There's bound to be a lot of trouble after that, and it may happen that we won't be able to get away. But if you can see any chance at all slip out of the house. I will look after myself. That's all."

Mick offered his case, and they both lit cigarettes.

"Sounds to me like a very comfortable evening," he said.

"You've got the easiest part of the job."

"What about yourself, Eleanora?"

The woman looked at him haughtily and scornfully.

"My work this evening," she replied, "is to add a little colour to your masquerade as Count Metri; to help you over social stools when you find that you're in difficulties, and to provide you with a companion in order that you won't arouse suspicion by walking around alone."

"You have forgotten another of your tasks, my dear Eleanora."

"Don't call me that name. This is a business transaction, not a piece of sentimental nonsense between two maudlin fools. What is it that I have forgotten?"

"Why, you have forgotten that you are also employed to keep a most careful eye on me, and see that I don't interfere with the carefully-made arrangements in any way."

"It is as well that you realise that. It makes my job easier. I only hope that you don't cause me any trouble."

"What would be the penalty for such a tragedy?"

"Another tragedy. I would advise Maddick to dispose of your body. And he often agrees with what I say. You might find it useful to remember that. It's better to be an intelligent person than an interesting corpse."

"What an entertaining companion you are, Eleanora! I really must thank you for the efficient way in which you've cheered me up."

"Let me tell you, whoever you are, that I'm not doing this for fun, and any humour from you isn't well received. This necklace is worth more than forty thousand pounds, and my cut of that will keep me for a few months. What you get doesn't concern me. It is ten minutes to nine. You'd be well advised to pull yourself together a little, and remember that if you make one bad move during the next half-hour a job that's been arranged for nearly five weeks will peter out. And that's something that Maddick would never forgive."

"You can lead me to the slaughter whenever you like. I'm neither trembling with fear nor buoyed by booze. Just let me get one thing clear before we part. I am to look after myself from the moment I leave the house, and you will go your own way?"

# THE RECEPTION

"That is what I told you before."

"Has it occurred to you that every shred of suspicion in the house will be on your shoulders if I vanish and leave you alone in that reception room?"

"I am well able to look after myself. I repeat, again, since apparently you don't understand me, that once the lights go up you can adopt whatever course you think best without considering me for a moment."

"That will suit me. Once those lights go up, Eleanora, we're both going to need all the luck we can lay our hands on."

"Getting cold feet?" asked the woman contemptuously.

"No, and if they're cold when those lights go up they'll soon be warm by the time I've finished running."

"All right, Andrea, now talk about something else. We're in Brook Street."

The Daimler slowed down to a snail's pace as it drew in at the rear of a file of cars. One by one the occupants were alighting farther down the street where a blaze of light under a canopy revealed the crimson carpet extending from the steps of a handsome house down to the edge of the curb. Doors were being opened by a tall man attired in uniform.

Six or seven minutes later the Daimler had advanced, yard by yard, until it stood outside the door of the house. Mick saw the brilliantly-lighted hall, the backs of their predecessors as they vanished inside, and then the door of their car was swung open. A second later young Cardby, holding the woman tenderly by the arm, was mounting the carpet-covered steps. Now it was too late to turn back!

In the handsome entrance they parted company, bestowing upon each other a winsome smile. Those who noted their entrance had cause to consider that the best-looking couple of the evening had arrived. Mick deposited his hat, coat and scarf. It was not until he turned to go that the thought of his departure occurred to him. Those clothes, if he intended to take them with him, would make things very difficult. He turned to the manservant.

"Please leave my clothes handy on the corner, will you? I may have to leave for a few minutes a little later."

"Most certainly, sir."

Young Cardby glanced at his reflection in the mirror, and sauntered towards the hall, seating himself at a corner recess. A few minutes later Eleanora appeared. The woman's beauty shone even more than before. He gazed in admiration at her billowy blue gown. To him it represented the final word in good taste and luxurious clothing. To the creator it meant a pale-blue silk net with a bouffant skirt, overlaying the shimmer of a blue taffeta underskirt. The ladies who noted Eleanora's progress might have helped with the description by adding that double ruchings of taffeta bordered the cross-over fichu, and reappeared again on the deep hem of the skirt. All of which would have meant nothing to the young man as he rose from his seat to meet his "wife."

Together they sat down, witnesses of the slow procession that filed through the central door to the steps where Lord and Lady Mead were smiling upon all comers with smug and easy grace. The host and hostess were well known as celebrity hunters. It apparently satisfied them if among their three hundred guests they discovered half a dozen valuable scalps. All the famous who visit London know before long that an invitation to the house in Brook Street is one of the penalties lying in wait for the famous.

Eventually their turn arrived, and they left their seats. Mick felt cool and confident; his companion might well have been the guest of honour, if one could judge from the languid grace with which she crossed the polished floor.

Mick handed over his card. Then he heard a voice boom in his ear:

"The Count and Countess Galleone Metri."

## THE RECEPTION

Facing them stood an elderly couple. The host was stout, rubicund, and cheerful. He had made his money by canning "Mead's Fruit for British People." He had obtained his title by offering something further than oracular support to one of the well-known political parties. His wife was grey-haired, sharp-featured, and quick in speech. She had mounted arm in arm with her husband from the joint ownership of a shop in the north to the acquisition of a title. Now, still together, they were riding the waves of society, sometimes drenched, sometimes smothered in spray, but never totally submerged.

Cardby and his companion moved towards them slowly, with grace. As he reached the foot of the stairs he noted for the first time the blaze of diamonds encircling Lady Mead's neck. Well, she wouldn't have those for much longer. He stood back while Eleanora performed her part in the feats of etiquette; soon they were wending their way along the passage to the reception. On the way he noticed the two windows, one on each side of the corridor. The host and hostess were not more than two feet away from them. It was going to be an easy job.

"Let us sit in that corner, darling," said Mick, nodding towards an empty settee against the wall in an angle at the side of the entrance to the passage. Voices hummed in the room like the drone of a giant bee. Friend had found friend, group had joined group. Occasionally they caught fragments of conversations as it drifted by.

". . . At Cap Antibes—we were there just before Easter, you know . . ."

". . . Said he wouldn't, and you know what Monty is when once he . . ."

". . . The most delightful old man. We were thoroughly entranced, my . . ."

". . . You shouldn't have missed it, darling. It was just too, too . . ."

"Tell me," said Eleanora, after glancing round the room, "after looking at these people and listening to them for a while, can you tell me why they're enjoying themselves?"

There was no one within ten feet, and the noise in the room was enough to deaden her low voice.

"I don't suppose there's a single person here who could tell you that. They're here for all sorts of reasons, I expect."

Eleanora smiled sardonically and stared into his eyes. Mick blinked.

"That's right," she said. "Some are here because the amusement, such as it is, is cheap; others because they are under an obligation to Mead and dare not refuse; some because there is a slim chance that Lady Mead, by accident, has inveigled someone passably interesting into coming; some young men are here because their lady loves have been dragged along by aspiring mothers; some are here because Nuzzi, the violinist, is going to crack their ears later with some of his futurist stuff, and it is their duty to attend wherever he plays in order that they can class themselves among the supporters of the modernist movement. Poor boobs! And I suppose the remainder are gossip writers who have dropped in to have a look round before they pass on to some place that's less stodgy and much more interesting."

Mick realised that the woman was talking to create an impression—not upon him, but upon the many curious people who occasionally turned to glance at them.

"Pitiful, isn't it?" said Cardby. "Makes me feel at times as though I would like to renounce my title and throw in my lot with the working men."

Eleanora laughed softly. Her eyes were sparkling. Mick noted, for the first time, the thin platinum wedding ring and dazzling diamond ring on the second finger of her left hand. She moved the hand nearer to him, and as she moved the lights played on the diamond.

"I well remember the day I bought those for you," said Mick, looking into her eyes. "What happy days those were!"

"Weren't they?" Eleanora's tone was dreamy. "And do you remember the trouble when father wouldn't give his consent?"

"How well I recall that night when he turned me from the castle door, Eleanora! And I had to obtain the written instruction of Mussolini to hand to your sour-faced boob of a parent before he'd say 'Yes.' Those were trying times, my dear. Many times my memory goes back to that first night at Naples, and I think of the moon pouring silver streamers over the film of your hair, and I think of the kiss you gave me."

"Was that the same one that you gave back to me later, Andrea?"

"Exactly, Eleanora. Do you remember those days at Capri?"

"Who could forget? You were so sweet to me in those days."

"I might well be. I didn't know then that you'd got no money. You led me properly along the proverbial garden path. Oh, Eleanora!"

"It wasn't my fault that father's margarine works failed. I think—"

But whatever she thought was never communicated to Mick. For at that moment the lights failed, and heavy darkness, complete and absolute, shrouded the room. A scream sounded from the direction of the passage. Then the reception room was filled with screams. Mick slid away.

# 10

## MANY THINGS HAPPEN

Cardby was the first to reach the foot of the three steps leading to the passage. For almost a minute he was alone. People in the room were still trying to get their bearings. The transposition from brilliant light to impenetrable darkness had left them as helpless as small babies. From the far end of the passage came a sob.

"Loose me, damn you," shouted someone. At the far side of the reception room a woman screamed hysterically it was the signal for another outbreak of shrieks. Then another voice boomed in the room.

"She's fainted. Get some water."

The optimist did not stop to explain how the water was to be obtained. Still no one came near the stairs. Above the clamour came a sharp, loud spoken command:

"Keep your heads. There's nothing wrong. The lights have fused. They'll be on again in a minute."

Then someone brushed against Mick on their way up the stairs. He stretched out his hands and felt the smooth surface of a man's jacket.

"Stay where you are for a minute," said Cardby. "Wait until the lights go up before you start blundering about. You'll hurt someone."

"What the hell is happening?" asked the man, struggling to evade the young man's grasp.

"Don't be such a fool, man. Set the women a good example, and see that you don't knock any of them about running round in the dark."

"But I want some water. My wife has fainted."

"You'll find some at the other side of the room. Keep to the wall as you go round. Then you won't hurt anyone."

There was a shuffle of feet as the man departed. Almost immediately someone crashed into Mick's back and he fell forward on to the stairs, the other person on top of him.

Cardby twisted from underneath and swung the man round.

"What do you think you're doing, you damned fool?"

"Who screamed in the corridor?" panted the man. Mick's knee was embedded in his chest. "I heard a woman scream out there."

"I know. And I've heard a couple of score of them scream in here. All that's happened is that the lights have fused, and you're not helping anyone by adding to the panic. Get back into the room and see if you can calm some of those women. In a minute they'll be stampeding, and then somebody'll be hurt."

Cardby lifted his knee and took his hands from the man's shoulders.

"My necklace has gone," screamed Lady Mead.

"What do you mean?" bellowed her husband, forgetting his veneer of refinement in the agony of a contemplated loss.

Two people made a rush for the stairs. Mick stopped them.

"Wait until the lights go up," he snarled. "Are you such boobs that you can't see that you're adding to the trouble instead of stopping it? Go and quieten some of those women."

Barely a minute afterwards another shadowy form brushed past the youngster, and he shot out a strong hand, clutching savagely. His fingers wrapped round a bare arm. The newcomer was a woman!

"All right, madam," said Mick softly, "don't get alarmed."

"I'm not alarmed, thank you. I want to see what's happening in this passage. Please let me go."

There was nothing of hysteria in the voice of this newcomer. She had used the same tone that one might employ when ordering soup in a restaurant. Cardby was in a difficulty. He dare not plead that nothing had happened, could not bring himself to restrain the woman by force, and it was impossible to plead with her not to become nervous since she was apparently quite collected.

His problem was solved for him. The lights flared. The sudden blaze robbed everyone of vision for a second. During that moment Mick stepped away from the stairs, standing near the alcove. As the jumping figures before his eyes steadied down he looked towards the passage.

On the first step stood a girl of nineteen or twenty. Her blue eyes were fixed on Mick with an unwavering stare. He smiled. There was no response. The girl's pretty features had set in a hard cast. The small mouth was firm, although the severity of her appearance was offset slightly by the presence of two dimples that cupped the firm flesh at the ends of her lips.

Cardby darted forward towards the steps.

"Excuse me," he said to the girl as he brushed past. She followed him until he reached the side of Lord and Lady Mead.

"Did I hear you calling that you had lost something?" he asked.

"Yes," said Lord Mead. "My wife has had her diamond necklace stolen."

"What happened?"

"I don't really know. When the lights went out someone grasped my wrists from behind, and at the same time another person snatched my wife's necklace."

By this time a flood of people arrived in the passage from the reception room. All were in a state of excitement. Mick took a plunge. The girl's unwavering stare embarrassed him.

"Someone must have come through that window," he said suddenly, pointing behind Lady Mead. The window was half-open—so also was the window on the host's side of the passage. "And that's where the man stood who held your hands."

The guests gaped at the windows. Still the young girl stared at Mick. He sensed that some questions were on their way, and decided to advance the answers without waiting for the queries.

"That must have been how it was done," he said. "It certainly wasn't done by anyone in the reception room. I can swear to that. The very second I heard you shout, Lady Mead, that your necklace had been stolen I rushed to the foot of the steps and refused to let anyone pass until the lights went up again. Two or three people did try to get by— they said they wanted to help you, but I wouldn't let them leave the room. I thought it was safer to keep them where they were."

"That's quite true," said one of the men, "because I tried to get past and couldn't."

"I'm sure you did everything for the best," said Lady Mead. "The best thing we can do now is to send for the police."

At that moment a manservant appeared in the passage.

"My lord," he announced, "the lights were put out deliberately. The switch-box downstairs has been tampered with. The fuse wasn't caused by accident."

Again the guests gaped. Feet moved restlessly. It seemed that no person knew what to do. Mick knew quite well what he wanted to do—dash for his hat, coat and scarf. But that was impossible. Each time he turned his glance from the host and hostess he met the eyes of the young girl. She, at any rate, did not believe a word he said.

"Excuse me," said the young man, "I must go and find my wife."

The crowd parted while he walked back to the reception room. Many people unable to gain entrance to the corridor were standing round in small groups.

But Eleanora had vanished!

"Hell," said Mick to himself, "now I'm for the high jump."

Still considering ways and means of escape, he turned towards the steps again. To rescue his clothes he had to pass through the throng in the passage and leave the house in the presence of all of them. It was then that he looked up and saw that the girl was standing on the top step, again watching his movements.

"With that jinx around," he thought, "I'll never get out of here without handcuffs on."

"Did you find your wife?" she asked.

"She appears to have slid away somewhere for the moment."

"That's quite right," announced the girl, her eyes steady, her tone level, "she did slide away. As a matter of fact, as the lights went up she vanished through the far doorway. Curious habit for a guest to leave without bidding either host or hostess good night, more curious still to depart from a reception through the domestic quarters."

"My wife," said Mick, "is sufficiently eccentric to do anything."

"So eccentric that she will leave her husband without any indication that she contemplates departure?"

"Even to that extent, madam."

"I hope," said the girl, and now her tones were more incisive, "that she took no more away from this house than she arrived with."

"I am quite sure that she did."

"I had that impression myself. At least you're honest."

"Why shouldn't I be? Of course, my wife departed with something she did not possess on arrival—the fixed conviction that the guests here this evening were much too uninteresting to justify a long stay. She has the courage of her convictions and, that being so, did what many here would like to do and dare not—leave the house."

"A most unusual woman. Is she fond of diamonds?"

Young Cardby stared at the girl. The lines of his mouth hardened.

"If you're trying to be humorous the effort is a failure. If you're trying to be insulting you have succeeded. In either case it might be advisable for you to consider that I don't know who you are, what you are, or where you come from—and it only remains for me to say that I am not in the least interested. Forgive me."

Mick edged past her on the steps and walked towards the group in the passage. The girl followed at his heels.

"Did you find your wife?" inquired Lord Mead, realising that, although a robbery had been committed, a certain responsibility still rested on him to ensure that the night's entertainment did not fail.

"No, I did not," replied Mick, "but she must be somewhere around. I was merely worried for the moment as I feared that the sudden darkness and confusion might have made her feel ill."

"In that case," said the host, "I will send round for her immediately. Summers, here one moment. Call round for—for—I'm so sorry, my memory for names isn't what it used to be."

"Countess Galleone Metri," asserted Mick.

Thereafter things happened with a speed that took the young man's breath away. As he gave the name a tall, dark-haired man on the outskirts of the crowd moved forward and stared at Cardby. Mick felt the imminence of trouble, the vision of it flooded his brain. He was right.

"Do you say, then," asked the man, "that your wife is the Countess Galleone Metri?"

"Most certainly I do," responded the youngster indignantly.

"In that event," said the man, and his thin lips curled into a sneer as he spoke, "you are my cousin, and I escorted you to your wedding. How funny that I should think we have never met before!"

"It does seem odd that your imagination should be so vivid."

The men and women looked from one to the other. It would have been easy to hear the drop of the proverbial pin.

"*Che la facesse di menzogna rea.*"

Cardby knew that he was cornered. So did the other man.

"How curious that there should exist a Count Galleone Metri who can't understand Ariosto in the original. Perhaps it would help you if I supplied you with the English version. 'As plainly manifested it was a lie.' Rather an appropriate quotation, I think."

Three or four men grouped themselves round the young man. It seemed that Mick's last chance had gone.

"You hear what this man says?" asked Lord Mead severely.

Then another of the guests moved forward. He was tall and well built, about forty years of age, and carried an atmosphere of officialdom with him. He waved the group of men back and silenced Lord Mead.

"You're caught," he said to Mick, "and so is Clare, so you might as well come along without causing further trouble."

"What's all this about?" inquired Lord Mead, passing a trembling hand over his wrinkled forehead.

"It only means, my lord, that you need trouble no further about the matter. This man is ' Flash' Larkin and the woman he came here with tonight is known as 'Peeress Polly.' They work this sort of game regularly. Fortunately, we received information that something of the sort would happen to-night. This man stole the necklace, and handed it to his accomplice when the lights went out.

"She made her way through the servants' quarters—an arrangement that had been made by her weeks ago. But this time her luck didn't hold out. We had two men waiting outside the door for her. She is now at Vine Street police station— and so is the necklace. We will want both of you to come along to the station as soon as possible. Come along, Larkin. Perhaps, my lord, you'll send one of the servants for his clothes."

A man departed to collect the clothes, and there was complete silence in the passage as the crowd waited.

The girl who had followed Mick for ten minutes elbowed her way through the crowd until she stood by the side of the tall man.

"Excuse me," she said, "but if you are going to take this man away I think it's only right that we should know who you are."

"I agree with you entirely," said the man tolerantly. "I am Detective-Sergeant Gribble, of New Scotland Yard."

"In that case," replied the girl, "we will wait until the police arrive to arrest both of you. You are no more Detective-Sergeant Gribble than this man is Count Metri."

"Don't be so stupid, girl. Why on earth do you say that?"

"Because," responded the woman slowly and deliberately, "I happen to be the daughter of Detective-Sergeant Gribble, and it would be a funny child that did not know its own father!"

# 11

## AND CONTINUE TO HAPPEN

There followed a second that dragged into seeming hours. Mick looked at his would-be rescuer, at the girl, at Lord Mead, and then glanced towards the windows. Two men were flung heavily to the floor as he jumped towards the left-hand window, another man fell as the pseudo detective plunged to the right.

Mick dived through the open space, landed on his knees on the flat lead roof, and ran towards the end of the short stretch. Below him, ten feet below, were the area steps. He calculated the distance, swung over the ledge, balanced himself as he gripped the guttering, and then dropped. His feet landed on different steps, and he fell backwards, striking his head against a side wall. Stars soared before his eyes, and vanished to give place to the area steps. In four strides the youngster reached the square landing, and as he mounted the gate three men in evening dress raced round the corner.

They were not more than ten feet away when he dropped to the pavement. Furthermore, they had not suffered the misfortune of a collision with a brick wall. Mick shot away from the gate as though pacing from the holes at the start of a hundred yards sprint. In fifty yards he gained a few feet. His head was working with his feet. Which way should he turn? He grinned at the incongruity of thought as he recalled his words to Eleanora—"If I have cold feet when the lights go down they'll be warm by the time I've finished running."

He crossed New Bond Street and turned into Hanover Square. By now a policeman had joined in the chase. But Mick had established a lead of seven or eight yards. He decided that his only chance was to venture the crossing of Regent Street and seek refuge in a chase through the maze of streets lying to the east. Luck favoured him. Only a few stragglers were about as he flashed across Regent Street and passed down Argyll Place.

During the next five minutes his pursuers dropped away one by one as he twisted and turned through Carnaby Street into Beak Streak, then into Bridle Lane, from there to Brewer Street, and through Lexington Street and Broad Street into Berwick Street. Then he walked across Oxford Street, trotted down Wells Street and Eastcastle Street and so arrived at Titchfield Street.

For the first time he was glad to see Mona. Out of breath, he sat on a seat in the hall and panted.

"Where are your clothes, Stan?" she asked.

"At Vine Street by now," he said a moment later, when his breathing was regaining normalcy. "God, I feel as though I've done a five-mile cross-country run. Have I got a bump on the back of my head, Mona?"

"Yes, but it's no bigger than a pigeon's egg."

"It feels more like an ostrich egg to me. Get me a drink, Mona."

Mick took the whisky and soda gratefully. For the first time in his life he felt the need of a stimulant. As he drank he thought. Someone would be blamed for the bungle that was made at Mead's. Of that he was certain. The best thing to do was to take the bull by the horns.

"Get Alibi on the phone for me," he said to the woman. "I'll take the call in your room—with you outside the door while I take it."

Delaney was apparently in high spirits.

"Hallo, my lad, what's the big news?"

"Plenty." Nick was terse, his tone savage. "Just listen to me for two minutes, Delaney, and you'll get an earful. Did you put the squeak in on me tonight?"

"Good God, no, Pete."

"Well, it looks to me as though somebody did, and if I find them, even if it's M. himself, I'll swing for them."

"Take your time, lad, don't get excited. What's happened?"

"I can't tell you, Alibi, since you know nothing about the job. But things happened tonight that must be told to somebody. Either someone squealed or the arrangements were damned awful. Say, Alibi, tell me how I can have a word with Maddick. He ought to know what's happened—and the sooner he knows the better."

"H'm. I can't do that, because I don't know how to get hold of him myself. But I can find out, I think, and if you're sure that it's so all-fired important I'll see what can be done. Hang around and I'll give you a ring in a few minutes."

Mick sat back in the chair and lit a cigarette. His mind had now turned to something else—the vision of the girl at the reception. What a staggerer to find the melancholy Gribble with a daughter like her! She might have placed him in an awkward fix, she had done her best to give him a night at Vine Street, she certainly had been nasty-tongued, she most emphatically was not in the same street as Eleanora as a beauty—but Mick very much wanted to meet her again under more propitious circumstances.

"You look lonesome, dearie," said Mona, opening the door. "Have the rats been getting at you?"

"Nope. I've just been telling Alibi a few home truths."

"You seem to spend most of your time arguing with Delaney. It's a waste of time, kiddo. That man's only job is to say 'Yes' and 'No' to all that his boss says. He's a nobody—although I shouldn't say so."

"Well, Mona, aren't we all?"

"I suppose we are. I'm glad I'm no nearer to the boss. If I ever had to meet him I'd be scared stiff."

Cardby dare not say what he would feel like if called upon to meet the "boss." The vision was too good to be true. He had sense enough to note that Mona was in a philosophic and reminiscent mood.

"There are times," he said, staring at the ceiling and apparently speaking to himself, "when I wonder how much M. is worth."

"Call it a million, and don't think about it any more, Stan. It gives me a pain in the stomach to think of anyone earning more than twenty pounds a week. At the rate he's going on he'll be worth ten million in ten years' time."

"What a racket, Mona. Blackmail, forgery, smash and grab, arson, plain robbery, drug peddling, murder, con tricks, bucket shops, long firm frauds, bribery, slush printing—and all in the one firm!"

"You've forgotten vice and torture," added the woman.

"Got a lot of places like this?" asked Cardby.

"Any amount, Stan. This is one of the little ones."

"Do any torturing on the grand scale?"

"When he wants information, and someone doesn't want to part, he gets quite cute. I read somewhere once that the Spanish used to be hot at that game. I reckon Maddick was born after his day. He could have taught them tricks that would have turned their spines into icicles. Ever hear what he did to that man from the Oxford Street Safe Deposit?"

"No, something pretty ingenious, I guess."

"Oh, it was ingenious enough. The poor devil wouldn't hand over the safe combination. Maddick took him into the country for an evening's rural air. When the body was found at Sonning the feet were blistered and scarred from burns, all the nails had been dragged from his fingers and toes, every knuckle of his right hand was broken, his knee-caps had been split, and it must have seemed a pleasant end to him when they held his head under a tap of boiling water."

Mick swallowed his revulsion and appeared casual.

"You'll have to be careful, Mona, to see that something like that doesn't happen to you one day."

"It won't happen to me. Whatever M. says I agree with. That's the way to keep out of trouble. I had enough of him with my husband."

"Another spot of bother?"

"Slightly. He played a fast one on M. and was sent to do a job in the country. The squeak was put in, and he's gone down for five years. M., of course, was the squealer."

"It's a risky game working for him, Mona."

"You've said it, Stan. If I were in your place— but then, you say that you can look after yourself, so I'll leave you to it."

The telephone bell rang.

"Delaney here. Is that you, Pete? Good. Listen. I've put out the feelers and fixed things up for you. I passed on the word that it's really very important, and I hope for your sake that it is. All I can tell you is this. You've got to change your clothes and go along to Hobart Place, just off Eaton Square, near Victoria Station. Ring twice on the third bell from the top outside the door of 34a. You'll see the name A. A. Wheeler on the door-plate. When the ring is answered say that you have come to see Mrs Wheeler. That's all I can tell you. See you in the morning. Don't forget to change your clothes. Cheerio."

Mick replaced the receiver with mixed feelings. This sounded too good to be true. Had Maddick found him out? Was this arrangement one by which he was led like a lamb to the slaughter? Would it be safe to visit Hobart Place without leaving some indication of the visit for his father? Cardby decided that his only chance lay in boldness. Now that he had gone so far he might as well be hanged for a sheep as a lamb.

"Going places?" asked Mona when he rose from the chair.

"Yes, my dear. If I don't come back in a hurry you can add me to the list you were talking about."

The woman's face blanched under the coat of colouring.

"Are you going to see the boss?"

"Ask no questions and you'll hear no lies, Mona."

"God help you, if you are. He'd never let you live if you once knew who he was."

Cardby quickly changed, and ten minutes after replacing the receiver he was ready for the road again. In his coat pocket was a Steyr automatic, the clip full of bullets.

At the foot of the stairs Mona waited for him.

"Best of luck to you, Stan, and I hope you don't need it."

"Don't lose your beauty sleep over me, my dear. If I don't come back, at least you'll be able to say that I've had a good run for my money."

The youngster hailed a taxi and was soon riding towards — what? He dismissed the cab in Grosvenor Place and walked the remaining few yards. His head was throbbing from the effects of his fall. But his step was jaunty, his face set in determined lines.

He struck a match when he reached the house and lit a cigarette while his eye ran down the long list of brass plates. Delaney had not told him wrongly. The third plate from the top bore the name A. A. Wheeler. Mick prodded the bell.

His heart was beginning to pound against his ribs, and he drew a deep puff of smoke. After this affair — if there was any after for him — life as a police constable would seem very dull.

The heavy door swung back, and two people stared at each other. It was difficult to assume which of the two was the more surprised.

The trim maid in uniform was Miss Ellen! The rouge and lipstick had gone. Now her face was sallow. Her eyes grew larger as she stared at the caller. Mick grinned cheerfully. It seemed years since they had parted company in the Lambeth public house.

"I have called to see Mrs Wheeler, Ellen. How are you?"

"You want to see Mrs Wheeler?" The girl spoke as though he had asked to see the King and the Cabinet. "Does she know that you're coming?"

"The first thing you should do, Ellen, is to let me get through the door. It's bad form to leave callers on the doorstep. That's better. Yes, she is expecting me. Just tell her that Mr Wall is here, will you?"

"You'd better follow me." The girl led the way to a small lift, slammed the gates after them, and pressed the button for the third floor. She spoke again as they ascended. "What brings you here?"

"You'd be surprised, my dear. How long have you had this job?"

"Since this morning."

"Like it?"

"Nothing to do. I'm fed up already."

She opened the gates and walked ahead along the carpet-covered passage. Then she opened a door and showed Mick into a handsomely-furnished drawing-room.

"Sit down for a minute, and I'll tell Mrs Wheeler that you're here."

Cardby did not sit down. Instead, he paced the room, examining its contents. But there was nothing personal to be discovered. No books, no papers— nothing but the elegant furniture and fittings. He sank into a heavy upholstered damask chair a moment before Miss Ellen returned.

"Come this way, sir." Her air was that of the perfect domestic. It seemed a far cry from her stout-drinking days at Lambeth.

Cardby followed in her wake along the passage. At the end the maid swung open a door, announced "Mr Wall," and departed. Mick, feeling more confident now that the adventure had begun, strode into the room.

Before the fireplace, her lips opened in a smile, stood Eleanora!

"Good evening, Andrea," she said, inclining her head with sarcastic humility. "I feared that my husband might have become lost."

"He certainly lost his wife."

"Sit down and make yourself at home. Have a drink?"

"Not for the moment, thanks. You know, of course, why I have come?"

"Certainly. You will be able to talk to him in a few minutes."

"Good. There's quite a lot I want him to hear."

"I hope, for your sake, that there isn't quite a lot that he wants you to hear. That would be much more awkward, wouldn't it?"

"How can I say? I'm not in the least nervous about anything that I've done. Have you been home long?"

"You jump to conclusions very quickly, my dear Andrea. What made you think that I am at home?"

"Just a few odd things, Eleanora. You don't usually wear a dressing-gown in a stranger's house, you don't usually offer drinks that don't belong to you, you are known to the maid as the mistress of the house—there may be other small points."

"Your thinking apparatus doesn't seem to be affected by excitement."

"Excitement, my dear Eleanora? What excitement?"

"Blasé youth. I suppose that in a moment you'll tell me that you've really had a most boring evening?"

"It was hardly that, but I've certainly had a most distressing evening. You remember me telling you that if I vanished and left you at the reception you'd be the centre of suspicion?"

"Yes, I remember that quite well."

"Then you realised, of course, that the obverse would apply, and that in the event of your disappearance I would be the suspected party?"

"That question's too obvious to need an answer."

"Would you mind telling me how you thought, or imagined, I was going to extricate myself from lat position?"

"I never even gave it a thought. I was not sufficiently interested. I had my instructions, and I adhered to them. What happened to you after that was no concern of mine."

"Thank you, Eleanora. Naturally, you knew all the time you were talking to me that you had made four arrangements, and that the very second the lights failed you vanished?"

"Most certainly. If you aren't competent to look after yourself the time has come for you to take yourself for a walk and get lost—permanently. You're no use to us if you can't think one stride front of the next man."

"Now, let me get down to brass tacks for a moment. Did you, or did you not, know that a meal had been put in?"

It was the woman's turn to appear surprised, she moved nearer to the young man and looked at him closely. Mick stood the examination without any sign of embarrassment.

"Do you really mean that someone squealed?" she asked.

"It looks uncommonly like it to me. That's why I wanted to have a word with M. I won't be satisfied until I hear a lot more about it."

"Oh! And who are you that you should have to be satisfied?"

"That question can be answered very simply. I'm merely a young man who is prepared to work well so long as he knows that the people he is working with are on the level. If I can't be assured tonight that the affair at Mead's was a pure accident, I hand in my cards and take another job—and this time I'll go back to my own job of working single-handed. I can trust myself not to squeal, but I have my doubts about some other people."

"So you think that as soon as you tire of our company you can pick up your hat and walk away?"

"Hardly that. But I imagine M. to be a person of real intelligence. That should mean that he would have sense enough to realise that a man who is dissatisfied is a man you are better off without."

"It is possible that M. might think the same— although you may not be thinking of the same type of separation. Tell me, is it your idea that I informed the police about the affair?"

"I am not prepared to say that. I am prepared to say, though, that if you knew that the squeak had been put in you couldn't have arranged things better. I'll go further and say this: If M. or anyone in the crowd had wanted me placed in a cell tonight they could scarcely have made more effective arrangements."

The woman moved still closer. Her hand slid to his shoulder.

"Don't start the trouble before you have to meet it," she said, patting his arm. Her hand moved down his side and closed over his pocket. "And please hand that gun over to me. Little boys shouldn't be allowed to carry things like that in their pockets."

"I'm sorry to disappoint you, Eleanora," he said; "but I've become used to carrying one, and I fear that I'll catch cold if I leave it off."

"In that case I must insist that you hand the gun me."

"It grieves me to fail a lady. I, also, am insistent."

"And so am I," came a male voice from the other end of the room. The man who had passed as Gribble at the reception stepped from behind the blue velvet curtains. In his right hand was a .38 Colt. The muzzle pointed to Mick's chest.

"Take that gun away from him," ordered the man. Cardby smiled as the woman slipped the automatic from his pocket.

"It seems," he said easily, "that we are holding quite a family party."

"If you don't act more sensibly," said the man, "we'll be holding an inquest without a coroner. You'll be the corpse, and the verdict will be that you died to stop your own tongue wagging."

"And very nicely phrased, my friend. If you'll put that cannon away and look a trifle more amiable, I'd like to thank you for trying to help me out of the jam to-night."

"I only did what I was told to do."

"Were you at that affair all the way through?"

"I got there before you, and left with you."

"In that case you can tell me whether I am wrong in thinking that someone squealed. What do you say?"

"For the moment I'm saying nothing about it."

"God, this is a real house of silence. What about M.? When do I have this talk to him?"

"Immediately," said Eleanora. "You see that door in the corner? Go in there. You'll find a telephone. M. is already on the line. We'll wait."

# 12

## A TALK WITH MADDICK

Cardby sensed the grimness in the woman's tone when she said "We'll wait." The man still held the revolver in his hand. The girl crossed over to the settee and settled down among the cushions. Mick walked over to the blue-painted door, his nerves tensed ready for an emergency. But there was nothing to fear.

The room was about six feet square. There was a rug on the floor, and a mahogany table and armchair completed the furnishing. On the table was a telephone. Mick raised the receiver slowly. What would happen?

Immediately the receiver was against his ear a voice came over the wire.

"Hallo, Borden. This is Maddick. Whatya want?"

Cardby blinked his eyes. The voice was low-pitched, the drawl nasal, the accent definitely American! God, had the racketeers started operating in England?

"I want to have a word with you about that job tonight."

"Go right ahead, and when you've finished there are two or three words I've saved up for you. Make it snappy."

"I will. This was the first job I've pulled for you. And I'm certain that someone squealed. I had all the luck in the world to get away. I wanted to tell you that I don't aim to place myself in a jam like that a second time."

"Strong words, big boy. How comes this idea of the squeal?"

"The woman I went with walked out on me and left me to hold the baby. That was enough to start with to put me in the cell. To add to that there were relatives present of the man I was impersonating. That doesn't sound to me as though things were too well arranged—unless the police were told. It would have suited them to have an identification squad handy. Then your man was told to give the name of Gribble—the very one out of thousands he should not have picked. On top of that Gribble's daughter was there acting for the Yard. Honest, it looks to me as though someone was trying to put me away."

"Is it your idea that I tried to frame you?"

"I'm not saying that you arranged it. I am saying that everything points to one of your folks squealing to the police."

"Suppose, Borden, it was suggested that you were the one who handed out the spiel to the bulls? What would you say about that?"

"Only that such an idea might come from a lunatic or a drunken man. Did it happen to be suggested to you why I wanted to be caught only a few hours after I've managed a getaway?"

"That break of yours might have been arranged so that you could pull a double-cross on me, Borden."

"I know. I might have escaped to act in the films, or play a tin-whistle outside Scotland Yard. But I didn't. Let's get this straight. I want to be as plain as I can. If you can convince me that all that happened tonight was accidental I'm game to have another try. But if the troubles came about through me being framed, I'm no good to you. Is that quite clear?"

"You've got a gosh-darned nerve, Borden, to sit there and tell me what I've got to do. One of these minutes I'll be telling you where to get off. Let's start by asking why you were heeled when you came tonight?"

"Heeled? I don't know what you're talking about."

"Been in the States much?"

"No, only one trip for about a fortnight. It isn't my meat over there."

"Then that explains why you don't understand me. Why did you pack that gun to come round here?"

"I didn't pack it specially to come here. I always carry one. Sort of makes me feel comfortable."

"Don't lie to me, Borden. You didn't have a gat with you when you went to that reception."

"Would you mind telling the lady that she's wrong. I know she dabbed the tail-pockets of my coat. I know she didn't find one. One of these days you should try a draw from a tail-pocket. It isn't the fastest thing on earth. It may interest the lady to know that in my hip-pocket I carried the gun she now has. It may also interest her to know that, just to stop people frisking me easily, I wear my hip-pocket on the left instead of the right."

"Let me tell you, Borden, that you interest me. You're not dumb like most of them. Just tell me in your own way exactly what happened tonight. Don't get high-falutin' about it. Just make it snappy."

Mick told the story concisely, leaving no matter untouched. Maddick's next words, when he had finished, made his jaw sag, and a feeling of coldness ran from the top of his spine to his feet.

"I guess we'll have no more trouble from that Gribble dame, Borden. When skirts like that start running after me I just teach 'em one lesson they never forget, because they never remember it. We'll take her for a ride. That'll be another of them moved. Would you like the job?"

Cardby had to think that one over. If he said "No" the job would be given to another man, and he would know nothing about it—would not be able to warn the girl in time. But if he said "Yes" they'd soon find out that he didn't intend to harm the girl. That would end his bluff.

"If I thought she tried to fasten that job on me tonight I wouldn't mind the job."

"All right, big boy. I'll think it over and let you know. You can have the first cut if she's going to be bumped off."

"I want you to play square with me, and let me know whether what happened tonight is likely to happen again."

"If this sort of thing is gonna happen again there'll be trouble for everybody—including you. There's a few other things I wanna say to you, Borden. I heard all that was said in the other room, and I don't think they come any harder than you do in a tight corner. That's not a pat on the back. It's just a fact. You're the sort of man I can use this week—and if you do your stuff O.K. you can pack up and sit in easy street, looking pretty with a fat roll for the rest of your fife. Does that sound good to you?"

"Just like sweet music. What's the stroke?"

"Don't ask questions out of your turn. When I wanna tell you the dope I will. All you need know now is that I am to make one real clean-up. It won't be a job for small men. This stroke is no good unless I have the big-timers in on it. You've got the makings of a big-timer. Just stay where you are, and you'll be hearing from me pretty pronto."

"You haven't told me yet whether I was framed."

"I can't tell you whether you were or not. But I can hand you this good and true—the squeal was put in all right. When I find out who shot the works there'll be another death in this country."

"Are you certain that the police were told?"

"Hell, am I certain that I'm sitting here? Let me tell you something that you can close your mouth over. The necklace that Mead dame wore tonight was a wrong 'un! I've given it the once over, and it's worth about four quid. I'll say someone squealed! Good night, Borden."

Mick rose to his feet with a feeling of bewilderment. He had expected that event would follow event with speed once he had been enlisted in the army of Maddick. But the succession of events was more hectic than he had anticipated. Already, within a week, he had been chased by the police, charged in a court, walked out of a gaol, fraternised with crooks, joined Maddick, defrauded a judge and jury at the Old Bailey, changed his name three times, and his lodgings once, participated in a barefaced robbery, been found out, chased again after diving on to a roof, and spoken to Maddick himself. It seemed to Mick that there was not much else he could do.

Then he thought again and remembered Maddick's words. In fact, there was quite a lot that he could do yet. Already, within the last five minutes, he had been offered the job of murdering Miss Gribble and assisting in a big job. The latter thought brought another consideration to his mind—having regard to the man's normal sphere of roguery, remembering that he arranged the robbery of a forty thousand pound necklace as a sideline, that his activities embraced crimes involving thousands and thousands of pounds, what sort of job had he in mind that he himself would regard as both big and important— so big that Mick could retire on his share of it, so important that only big-timers were wanted to handle it? Cardby gave it up without attempting to find a solution. He opened the door and stepped into the other room.

He noticed immediately that the man no longer held the revolver. The girl rose from the settee and handed the automatic to him. A quick change had taken place during his talk with Maddick. Had they heard what was said? Had Maddick already given a message to them before he could leave the telephone room. Certainly they were both quite amiable.

The young man slipped the magazine from the butt of the Steyr and examined the clip. The bullets were intact.

"You're a suspicious sort of fellow," said Eleanora.

"It pays in the long run. Think how awkward it would be if you stuck this gun into someone's ribs and found that it wasn't loaded."

"Where are you hanging out?" inquired the man.

"Somewhere between here and heaven."

"Don't tell me if you don't want to."

"Don't worry—I won't tell you. If you want to know, ask M. By the way, just to make things a little easier you might tell me your name, or some name that I can call you."

The man fingered his bristly moustache and hesitated.

"Go on," said the woman, "he's all right now."

"I suppose he is," remarked the man dubiously. "You can call me Clan."

Instantly the young man's brain flashed into action, his memory struggled to uncover some recollection. Then he remembered.

"What's that—short for Clanwilliam, Clancy, or does it show that you're from Scotland?" He waited eagerly for the reply.

"Short for Clancy, but that doesn't matter."

It mattered very much to Mick. The last occasion upon which the young detective, Caudry, had been seen was in the buffet at Victoria Station with a man named Clancy—and the description certainly fitted this man.

"Right, Clan, I hope the next time I get into a jam I'll have you at my side to help me out again. That was a brainwave of yours tonight, and it would have come off nine times out of ten. We just had bad luck, and that's all there is about it."

"I know I took the skin off my knees when I landed on that damned roof, and they hurt like hell now."

"We're quits. I bashed the back of my head into the area wall. It seems to me that you were better off than either of us, Eleanora. And mentioning that name reminds me that it's too big a mouthful to be convenient. What's your name when you're not the Countess Galleone Metri?"

"It has a curious habit of varying from time to time. The baptismal name is Kathleen, but it's been changed so often since that if anyone calls me Kathleen I ignore them, thinking that they've mistaken me for someone else. At the moment you can call me Mariel. I found the name in a magazine last week and adopted it because I like it."

"Now we know each other, don't we?"

"Hardly. I'm not going around calling you by a comic opera name like Andrea. Haven't you a handle a little more commonplace?"

"Pete is one of the names I'm known by. You can use that one."

"That'll do. Have a drink before you go?"

"Not for me, thanks. I'm tired and I want to go to bed. Good night."

The maid escorted him to the front door, frightened to speak now that the young man was on terms of proved intimacy with those living in the house. The night was fine, a white moon scudding through filmy layers of cloud. Mick decided to walk home. It was fortunate for him that he did!

As he reached the corner of Oxford Circus he heard his name called from the doorway of a shop. He stopped and turned to find Mona beckoning.

"Get a taxi right away," she said. "The police have raided our place, and they've got two men waiting for you to return. They came about ten minutes after you'd gone—five of 'em. Pretended it was an ordinary raid on that sort of house, but kept asking for you. I came out to look for you. The other boys are watching all corners to Titchfield Street."

"Thank you, Mona, I'll get a cab."

# 13

## ON THE GREAT WEST ROAD

"Where do you want to go?" asked Mick when he had attracted the notice of a taxi-man.

"65c New Street, off St. Martin's Lane."

"You'd better tell me some more about this, Mona," said Cardby when the cab started. "What did they say when they arrived?"

"They showed me a warrant, and started to search the house."

"That looks like trouble for you."

"No, I don't think so. I had a real stroke of luck. There was only one man on the premises, and he happened to be the girl's husband. The girls had all gone to the opening of a new club in Carnaby Street. It didn't take me long to see that they were not very interested in me, or the house, or the way in which it was conducted. They wanted to know who you were, what you looked like, what you did for a living, how long you had been staying with me. Then they turned out all the drawers in your room and went through your pockets."

"They wouldn't find anything. What did you tell them?"

"I said that you gave your name to me as Stanley Wall, that you told me you were on holiday from Birmingham where you worked as a clerk, that you arrived *three* days ago—remember that— and you had received neither post nor callers. They asked me where you had gone to, and I told them that you left the house just after *nine o'clock, wearing an ordinary lounge suit,* and you said you'd be back when you'd had a look round. After they'd looked round they left the men behind to wait for you. I sat with them for a bit and then excused myself while I went on with my work in the kitchen. I slipped through the back door, gave the word to the boys to look for you, and came along here, thinking that you might come this way. That's all."

"You seem to have done very well, Mona. Tell me, where are we heading for now?"

"Another place run by Maddick, but not on the same lines as mine. This place is kept for the men only—mostly those who've got a job soon, and want to be on the spot so that they can look round before they pull the stroke. You'll find all sorts there, Stan."

"That'll suit me better than your place, Mona, although you've done me a good turn. Who told you to take me there?"

"I telephoned a friend of mine down the street asking what I should do with you. Three or four minutes later he rang up to say that he had spoken to M. and you were to go to New Street."

"Who did you ring up, Mona?"

"Same one I always report to—Regency. But I got him at home on the Hampstead number."

"Lucky he was in, Mona."

"He's always either there or at his place in Regent Street. It's more than his job's worth to be at neither one or the other."

The taxi stopped outside the house in New Street. The front was dismal and dirty.

The door was opened by a young man in a neat and expensive blue serge suit. He was dapper and well groomed, a typical young man about town. But his eyes were sharp and venomous. "Killer eyes," Mick called them.

"This is Pete Strange," said the woman, "and this, Pete, is Andy."

Cardby sighed. How many more times was his name to be changed? He was beginning to lose count.

Andy scrutinised him from head to foot. Mick found the perusal insulting. But he said nothing.

"You two had better come inside," he said at last.

They entered an overfurnished sitting-room. Andy closed the door behind them and sat facing Cardby.

"You've heard all about it?" inquired Mona.

"Yes. I had a call ten minutes ago. What started you on the run?"

"Ask Maddick," replied Mick, "and if he says that it's part of your job to know these things I'll tell you."

Andy's dark eyes narrowed. Somewhere in his veins was foreign blood.

"Let me put you right," he said, his voice low and toneless. "You may be a hell of a smart fellow, you may think you're sitting on top of the world, but in this house my word goes. And when I ask questions I get answers. I'm apt to get nasty when folks get fresh with me, and when I say nasty I don't mean a nursery rough and tumble. I mean trouble, spelt with capital letters."

"Is that so? In that case, Andy, your other guests are going to have an amusing time. You see, I don't take anything I don't like sitting down. It just goes against my grain. If we fall out, and I hope we won't, you'll be too busy thinking of other things to spell trouble or any other word. Where's my room?"

"Just one minute—before we start talking about rooms." Andy rose from his seat and placed his hand in his coat pocket. Mona touched him on the arm and led him into the passage. Mick sat whistling.

"Leave this man alone, Andy, and be sensible," said Mona. "If you start a row with him you'll start something that you can't stop. This lad has put the fear of God into Delaney, talks to him as though he's dirt, and then gets Delaney eating out of his hand. And one other thing, Andy, that might save your skin if you remember it. Tonight this lad, Pete, walked out to meet Maddick, expecting trouble, in the same easy way that you'd light a cigarette. Think those things over, Andy, and then see that your sense doesn't let your body get hurt."

Andy was impressed. His eyes opened as he listened to Mona.

"What's his line, Mona?" he asked.

"I'm not sure," she replied, "but you can take it from me that he is one of the boss's top-line men. Be careful with him. M. has got an eye on him, and if anything goes wrong you'll be for it."

"Come and have a look at your room, Pete," called Andy. And in this way peace was established between them.

His new quarters were comfortable without being luxurious.

"No telephone, Andy?"

"It's not safe here. We've got one in a private room at the back downstairs, and you can use that whenever you want it."

Young Cardby used the telephone, quite unexpectedly, at half-past eight on the following morning. Andy popped his head round the bedroom door.

"You're wanted on the phone right away. Hang on for a minute and I'll get my dressing-gown for you."

Mick, of course, only possessed the clothes which he had worn on his visit to Hobart Place. He slipped the dressing-gown on and was shown the private room.

"Is that you, Pete?" inquired a strange voice. "A car will be left outside your house in half an hour's time. Take it. Drive through Kensington, Hammersmith, and Turnham Green until you come on to the Great North Road. Keep your speed at twenty miles an hour, and drive along that road for thirty-five minutes. A green two-seater will pass you. Accelerate until you draw level with it. Pull close in, and the driver, if all is clear, will throw a parcel into the back of your car. Slow down and turn back for London without attracting attention. Stop outside Olympia. A man wearing plus fours will instruct you. Is that all clear?"

"Splendid, thank you."

Cardby returned to his bedroom, dressed hurriedly, and insisted upon having his eggs and bacon in the sitting-room. Andy thought his visitor slightly eccentric. He didn't know that Mick wanted to see the driver arrive with the car. At nine o'clock to the minute Cardby finished his breakfast and the car arrived.

The driver was Taxi Long! The car was a cheap four-seater tourer—brother to thousands of others. Long vanished immediately the hand-brake was applied. Mick sought Andy and gave him a ten-shilling note.

"Send one of the lads out to buy a scarf for me— one of the gaudy woollen sort I want. I haven't got a coat with me, and it would look funny driving on a cold morning without a scarf or coat."

A few minutes later Mick swung the yellow and black scarf round his throat, and depressed the clutch. He was starting his third job.

He had been driving for rather more than an hour when he sighted the green two-seater through his mirror. The other car was not hurrying—travelling at not more than thirty-five miles an hour. The driver, swathed in a leather coat, sounded his horn and swung past Mick, turning to wave his glove as he advanced. Mick had never seen the man before. His name was Kelly, and this trip was a joy-ride after his excursion in Old Bond Street a few days previously.

Cardby pressed down on the accelerator and watched the needle as it climbed past the forty and rose to almost fifty. On either side of them were fields, and only an occasional car passed. A mile farther on Mick sounded the horn, and was waved on. He looked through the mirror. There was nothing behind him. The road in front was clear for two hundred yards until it swerved round a bend.

As he passed the green car a parcel, wrapped in brown paper, and about the size of a boot box, appeared in Kelly's hand, and was dropped into the back of the tourer. Mick slowed down, and the two-seater tore ahead again. By the time the bend was reached the green car was sixty yards ahead, and three minutes later it had disappeared.

A little farther along the road Mick swung towards a gateway, reversed, and headed towards town again. At ten-past eleven he slowed down and stopped outside Olympia. A young man in brown plus-fours stepped from the centre of the pavement and stretched out his hand demonstratively.

"Hallo, old man," he said. "Fancy seeing you here. What about one?"

"Suits me," replied Mick "but what do I do with the bus?"

"Shove it in the park round the corner and I'll wait for you." He lowered his voice. "And bring the parcel with you."

Two minutes later the men were standing at the bar of a neighbouring public house. They talked for a while of motor-cars and football. Mick held the parcel under his arm. Eventually they found a corner seat well away from the bar.

The young man in plus-fours picked up a midday racing paper, and bent his head over the list of runners.

"Take that parcel," he said, "to Crosby House, Regent Street. It's a few doors away from Liberty's. You'll find the Regent Income Tax Agency on the third floor. Ask there for Mr Clason, and hand the parcel to him." He raised his voice. "I reckon that Merlin can give an easy five pounds to Socrates now they meet over the longer distance. What do you say?"

"It looks like a safe bet. Can I drop you on the road? I must be moving."

"No, it doesn't matter, thanks. I'm going the other way."

They parted company outside the public house, and it was not until Mick reached Piccadilly that he remembered something the young man had not told him—what should be done with the car? All the way from his meeting with the green two-seater his thoughts had centred on the thought of the parcel and its contents. Should he open the wrapping? Now he decided to kill two birds with one stone.

He drove the car into a large and famous garage near Piccadilly Circus, left a fictitious name, and walked through towards the repair shop at the back as though in search of someone. Under his arm was the brown paper parcel. On his left was a lavatory, and Mick walked in. He studied the way in which the paper had been turned, the position of the string, and the nature of the knots before he proceeded to unfasten the parcel. Inside was a tin box with an air-tight lid. The youngster levered the lid from the box and peeped inside.

Two minutes later the box was again secure under the paper, strings and knots being exactly as they were before he touched them. The merest glance showed him what he was carrying.

He strode along towards Crosby House with about twenty-five ounces of cocaine under his arm.

Taking the lift to the third floor, he rapped on the small window labelled "Inquiries." A girl slid the window up.

"I want to see Mr Clason, please."

"He's engaged for the moment, but will you step this way?"

Mick followed the girl into a small waiting-room. There were two other men in the room, one carrying a brief-size case under his arm, the other nursing an attache case. Both were middle-aged, and apparently business men.

"And your name?" inquired the girl, as she turned to walk out.

"Mr Peter Strange."

Minutes dragged by. Cardby listened to the wearisome conversation of the two men. They talked of income tax, and nothing but income tax. It began to appear that he would not be away for another hour. Suddenly the girl appeared, and both men looked towards her expectantly. But she pointed to Mick, and bent her finger to beckon him.

"This way, Mr Strange."

The young man followed her through a general office in which some seven or eight clerks were working. At the far end of the room was a door with the upper half consisting of frosted glass. On it was painted "T. E. Clason, Director."

A stout man, attired in the conventional black coat and vest and striped trousers, sat in a swivel chair before a large and ornate desk. His face was plump and red, his hands white and carefully manicured.

"Good morning, Mr Strange," he said. "I see that you have brought all the documents. Are they in order?"

"So far as I know, Mr Clason. Will you take them now?"

"Yes, and we'll go into matters as soon as we can. By the way, I find you were overcharged on the previous occasion. Permit me to make the necessary adjustment."

The necessary adjustment was two five-pound notes. Cardby nodded his thanks and slid them into his inside pocket.

"Is there anything further you would like to know before I go?"

Clason rapped the desk with his thumbs for a second. Meanwhile, he pursed his lips and stared at the visitor.

"I think," he said, "that we will look these papers over in my inner office in case there is any point I want to raise."

He walked over to the door at the side of the fireplace and ushered Cardby into another room. The reason for the second office was obvious. There were no windows in the room, the inside of the door was baize lined to deaden the noise, and a telephone stood on the table. In the far corner stood a large safe.

"Could you open that one?" asked Clason, apropos of nothing, nodding towards the safe. Mick walked over and examined it. There were two combinations—a numeral and a letter.

"I wouldn't try it without an oxo-acetylene torch and plenty of gas," he said, "and even then it would be a long job. It'd be an hour before you could cut the locks out, and if you tried to finger it open you wouldn't get the tumblers falling right for maybe four or five hours. It's a very useful safe, Mr Clason."

"I'll say it is. But that isn't what I wanted to talk about. First of all, excuse me while I have a look at this parcel."

Mick studied the safe for another two or three minutes.

"All O.K.," announced Clason. "Now sit down in that chair, Strange, and we'll have a bit of talk. You've never been here before, have you?"

"Never heard of you until this morning."

"Well, just forget me when you've left until you have to see me again. If ever you want to get into touch with M. telephone me either here or at Hampstead 79475. That's my home number. Always remember that—it might get you out of a jam one of these days. If ever you have anything of vital importance let me know. You can always be sure that the quickest way to M. is through me. Just one other thing. If you hear any of the others refer to Regency you'll know that's me. Quite clear?"

"Absolutely." Mick was bubbling with elation. This was certainly a jump towards the fountain head. A move from Maddick. It was certain that by now he was a trusted member.

"That's good. Now, I've got some instructions for you. I'm thinking that between now and this time tomorrow you're going to have the busiest time of your life. Both the jobs you're going on are tough, more than tough, although the second is much worse than the first. You don't mind taking a chance, do you?"

"I told M., and I'll tell you, that the only thing I stop at is murder, and that may be the only reason why I stop at that is because I've never had cause to do one."

"That's the way I like to hear young men talk," purred Clason. He was certainly a surprising type to hold a brief for murderers. His voice, educated and suave, would have fitted a women's doctor; his prosperous appearance and ruddy health would have suited a golfing stockbroker. "Ever heard of Tommy Kane?"

"Tommy Kane? The name seems a bit familiar, but I can't just hit on it. Let me think. What's his line?"

"Tommy Kane was Maddick's best man. That's who Tommy Kane was." The man could not have spoken with more awe had he referred to a sportsman as the Lindrum of billiards, the Bobby Jones of golf, the Gordon Richards of the saddle, and the Alex James of the football field.

"You keep saying ' was.' Is he dead?"

"No, but unless something is done soon he might as well be as far as the boss is concerned. I'm not really surprised that you haven't heard about him since the police have kept it so quiet. The best thing I can do—since we've got to trust each other —is to tell you what happened.

"Tommy Kane is the best safe-man I've ever heard of. He opened this one here in an hour and ten minutes with his bare hands—just taking the tumblers as they fell. He's drawn more money for M. than any other ten men. He was never given a job that he couldn't do. And to be able to say that at the end of eighteen months is saying something. A week ago we fixed everything for a real job—one that would have made a clean-up of more than a hundred thousand.

"The safe was at the offices of the Tamberley Loan Club, and we knew they'd got over a hundred thousand to pay out to their members on the next day. We had a clerk in the office for a month and got a pretty good description of the safe. Tommy was told about it, and said he could open it in under an hour if we got the equipment for him. Well, we spent about seven hundred on his stuff, and he had the best outfit any peterman could work with. Then we arranged all the details.

"Their offices are past Tufnell Park towards Highgate Station. We fixed up to give the night watchman a sleeping cap, and everything was set. Two of the boys went there with Tommy. He was the first out of the car. As soon as he reached the pavement three plain-clothes men who'd hidden in the offices ran out from the front door. The men in the car drove away and left Tommy to look after himself. Tommy was arrested. The other two have not been found. If they want to live it ought to be their nightly prayer that the police catch them before M. does. Ten thousand of their sort aren't worth one Tommy Kane.

"The police wanted to keep things quiet so that they'd have a chance of getting the other two men, and, perhaps, of getting at those who'd arranged it. So instead of bringing Tommy into Highgate Police Court in the ordinary way during the morning, they put him in the box after lunch when the court was empty, and the Press, thinking the court had risen, had gone. They remanded him until this afternoon.

"Tommy Kane is not going to go down again, Strange. We're going to get him out of it this afternoon! It might sound impossible to you—but that's only because you don't know M. as well as we do. He says that Tommy has got to be taken from the police. And what he says goes. You've got to give a hand with that job, Strange. Have you got anything to say before I carry on?"

"Nothing, except that a job like that makes me nervous. Don't in any way misunderstand me, Mr Clason. All I mean is this. I've worked single-handed all my life, and I just hate having to rely on other people. Last night, through working with others, I was nearly grabbed. You can take it from me that it isn't pleasant to work on a tough job with folks you don't know. That's all I mean."

"There'll be nothing to worry about this time, Strange. The very best men we've got will be on this job with you. Every single one of them can be trusted. Just think it over and let me know whether you are ready to join them."

"Sure, I'll be there with them. I only thought I'd mention that I don't like that kind of job. You tell me what I have to do, and I'll see that it's done. I can't say more than that, can I?"

"I'm sure you can't. I see now why Maddick is so fond of you. There's got to be nothing spilt between the cup and the lip on this job, so listen to what I've got to say.

"The police are taking no chances of him being released, so they're bringing him to the court by himself. We've found out that the Black Maria will arrive at Highgate Court at two o'clock, and the court sits at quarter-past. The van will slow down outside the court to take the turn. We've got men following that van, and when it slows they're going to drop guns on the driver and the man with him. Another car will draw to the back of the van, and Tommy, who knows that we're going to hold 'em up, will have to make his own break. He's plenty strong enough to look after whoever is with him, and they won't be watching him much since they'll know they've arrived at the end of the journey.

"As soon as Tommy gets into the other car the driver will turn round down the hill, and then cut over to the right to make towards Finchley. You get to Golders Green tube station at quarter to two. A man will be waiting outside with a half-ton van, bearing the name 'Edwards Bros., Greengrocers, Hampstead.' He will drive you along the road for a hundred yards. Then take the wheel from him. He will show you which way to go. Stop the van when he tells you to, pull up, but leave the engine running, and have the van pointed towards Highgate. As soon as you see the other car, start to move, but don't travel at more than walking pace.

"Tommy will jump out of the one car and climb into your van through the back. Drive on towards Highgate. You'll meet plenty of cars coming the other way—by then the chase will be in full cry. If you are stopped tell them that the car passed you not more than fifty yards down the road, travelling at a terrific pace. If anyone attempts to look into your van—bump them, and don't be too delicate about it. When you turn to the right carry on until you can turn off towards Hampstead. Run down Haverstock Hill towards Chalk Farm, and then the man with you will tell you what to do.

"This is a big chance for you, Strange. Do you think you can manage it?"

"I don't see any reason why I can't. At any rate, I'll do everything you've told me to do, and if things go wrong it won't be my fault."

"You can't be fairer than that. This is going to put you in easy street within twenty-four hours if you can manage it. There's another job tomorrow, but whether you get a chance at that one depends upon whether you pull this stroke this afternoon. If you get Tommy all clear you collect five hundred, and if the job tomorrow is pulled without a hitch you can go away on holiday with five thou in your pocket. That's a bit tempting, isn't it?"

Mick rubbed his hands as though inordinately pleased.

"It certainly sounds like heavy coin, Mr Clason. Anything else?"

"Yes. As soon as you leave here get round the second-hand clothes stalls on the back streets and buy yourself an old coat, a muffler, and a cap. You wouldn't look right driving a van in those togs. That's all."

"Do you want me to telephone you when all is clear?"

"Yes, but at my home tonight. Not here. Good morning."

They shook hands at the door, and Mick walked through the swing gate of the outer office. As he reached the door it was suddenly swung open, and the lady from the inquiry office ushered another man into the room.

The two men looked at each other, both a little surprised, and nodded without speaking.

The newcomer was Alibi Delaney!

Cardby had plenty to think about as he looked for the old clothes stall. But much of his anxiety had passed. Now he was definitely on the right track. Had he met Maddick yet? That was the problem!

# 14

## TOMMY KANE ESCAPES

When Mick alighted from the tube train at Golders Green he extracted a crumpled Woodbine packet from the greasy blue serge waistcoat and struck a match. On his head was a cap, the peak bent out of all pretence of shape, the dirt on the cover so thick that it was almost impossible to determine the original colour of the cap. The coat and waistcoat were old, shiny and slightly too tight for Cardby. The sleeves gripped him under the arms with the force of a vice. At each moment he was afraid they would split. His own trousers had been discarded for a pair of worn, once grey, flannel trousers. Round his neck was a black silk muffler. The whole outfit had cost four shillings, and certainly was not worth one. Outside Mick drew in a deep breath of air and looked round. On the other side of the bridge stood a van.

The name was right— "Edwards Bros., Greengrocers, Hampstead."

The back of the van was open, and a board some eighteen inches high prevented anything from falling out. Inside the van Mick could see sacks of potatoes, cabbages, baskets of fruit, parsnips—all the stock-in-trade of the greengrocer. Maddick had arranged the affair properly.

In the driver's seat sat an undersized man of indeterminate age, but probably nearer fifty than forty. His cap was pushed to the back of his head, and he had not had a shave for a couple of days. Mick didn't speak to him as he climbed into the seat. The driver immediately started the van moving. When he did speak he kept his eyes turned on the road.

"Everything O.K.?"

"Absolutely. Go ahead."

"No change in the instructions anywhere?"

"None at all."

"Then slide under me and take this wheel."

The van was pulled to the side of the road while they changed seats. At the end of another five minutes the strangely silent man spoke.

"Turn right here, and then first left."

Mick might just as well have sat at the side of a corpse. The man sat still, without animation, without any excitement, without any show of enthusiasm. And he sucked at a foul pipe, twisting his head occasionally to spit a stream of tobacco juice into the road.

"Turn right again, and the second on the left."

"All fixed up inside?" asked Cardby, throwing his head backwards to indicate the inside of the van.

"Yes, he can get behind the potato sacks."

For another quarter of a mile they trailed on in silence.

"Turn right again, and pull up at the side of the fourth lamp-post."

As the van stopped a nearby clock chimed two. They had ample time. Cardby produced another Woodbine. He looked about him.

"It'd be a bit awkward, matey," he said, "if a policeman came round the corner just when he was making the changeover, wouldn't it?"

The man spat another mouthful into the road and stared ahead.

"The cop don't come down this road until twenty-one minutes past two."

Maddick, thought Mick, certainly had a flair for organisation. The engine was ticking quietly—a fact that filled Mick with some surprise. Such smoothness was hardly to be expected in a tradesman's van.

"Nice bit of work you've got under the bonnet," he said. "She's very lively and picks up well. What is it?"

"We pulled the Chev. engine out," replied the man laconically, "and fitted her out with another engine. She'll do seventy with this load up, and when she's empty I've done better than eighty with her."

"Very useful. I reckon you know the roads round here like the back of your hand?"

"Pretty well. I've driven this van round them twice a day for the last four days—just to get the lie of the land and get people used to seeing me. They don't take any notice of me now."

Again there was an interval of silence. Their eyes peered ahead.

"Here she comes!" said Mick, pressing his lever into gear and raising his foot from the clutch.

A hundred yards away a car had lurched round the bend at a dangerous angle and straightened out before slowing down. Mick saw the driver and the man at his side. In the back of the car sat two other men. As the van passed the car both were travelling at about seven miles an hour. A moment later Mick heard the rising whine of the other engine, and his companion touched him on the shoulder.

"All right," he said. "You can carry on. He's inside."

They had not travelled more than twenty or thirty yards when another car tore round the corner and pulled up with screeching brakes.

"Car passed you?" shouted a policeman, standing on the footboard at the side of the driver.

"Yes," bawled Mick, "five seconds ago. Driving like a madman. Straight on."

The van ambled on steadily. Before they reached the corner two more cars flashed round the bend, both containing policemen. Evidently the officers had poured out of the police station to commandeer the first cars that passed. Again the question was shouted and answered.

"Turn right," ordered the man, and Mick swung the van into a quiet side road. For three minutes ley proceeded without anything further being said. Mick, by now, was marvelling at the simplicity of the whole affair. At the cross-roads at the bottom of the street the policeman on point duty stopped them.

"Have you seen a black and cream touring car anywhere up the road?"

"Aye," replied Mick. "It passed us a mile back with all the policemen in London chasing after it. The driver'll be killed before they catch him. Damn near hit my van he did."

"All right. If you see it again tell the first policeman you can get hold of."

They turned down Hampstead Lane and attracted no attention as the van dropped from the heights and commenced the descent to Chalk Farm. They were half-way down Haverstock when Mick was again told to turn to the right, then left, then right again. He progressed slowly after this, Mick turning and twisting as he was instructed. In the distance behind them they heard the continued clang of a bell.

"Flying Squad's out," said Mick.

"Turn to the left here," was the only reply.

After another few minutes the man gave his final instructions.

"Turn to the right at the bottom and then run along for another hundred yards. You'll see a sign out showing Mercy Bros., Garage. Turn in there, and as far as I know that'll be the end of our job."

"Not been a very tough one after all, has it?"

"Might have been a damn sight worse," replied the man, ejecting another stream of juice as the van left the road and turned through the double doors into the garage. Immediately the van arrived in the centre of the small floor space two men rolled the doors together and the lights were turned on. Mick dropped from the driving seat and stretched himself. Then he felt for his cigarettes and looked round the garage for a moment.

A man slid from the back flap of the van and rubbed his hands. Mick looked at him curiously. So this was Tommy Kane, the star of the Maddick galaxy? The escapee was short and slim. Nature had intended him for a jockey rather than a safe-breaker. His face was white and pinched, his nose hooked, the lips thin and pale, the chin pointed. His eyes were watery, the colour a limpid blue. Cardby looked at Kane's hands. They explained a lot. The fingers were long and thin, the hands pale and delicately veined.

"Thanks," said Tommy. "I reckon I've got a good chance now."

While the safe-breaker disappeared into an inner office, another man took his seat at the wheel of the van, turned it in the garage, and the doors were swung back as the greengrocery load once more took to the street. Mick heard the final instruction.

"Be sure to keep round Highgate way."

The young man, uncertain of the next move, walked round the garage. His former companion sat down on a spare wheel and pulled at his pipe. In the corner stood a large limousine. Mick was examining it when he heard his name called.

"Hey, you. Get into these."

The man handed over a chauffeur's uniform, complete with cap and black tie. Five minutes afterwards, when Mick had completed the change, Tommy Kane appeared again. But in the interval he had effected a transformation. The blue suit, grey trilby hat, blue shirt and collar had gone. Now he was dressed in a black coat and vest, striped trousers, white shirt and collar, silver and black check tie, and patent leather shoes. On his head was a hard hat, his hands were covered by chamois leather gloves. From the breast pocket peeped a white silk handkerchief, and in his mouth was a large cigar.

"Your name," said Tommy, grinning, "is Harvey. My name is Mr Raymond Perrin. You're my chauffeur, I'm an insurance broker. I live at 'The Withies' between High Ongar and Writtle. That's where you're taking me now. In case you don't know the road I'll tell you the way. Run down into Camden Town, along Seven Sisters Road, and Tottenham High Road, and past Tottenham Hale Station until you come to Woodford Green. Then go through Epping, North Weald Bassett, High Ongar, and you'll find ' The Withies' about a mile farther along the road on the right-hand side. All O.K.?"

"Yes, sir," said Mick, touching his uniform cap and winking.

It took some time to turn the huge limousine, but at half-past three they were on the way, and at four o'clock they had left London behind. Not long afterwards they passed through High Ongar.

"The Withies" could not be seen from the road. Mick slid out of the driving seat and opened the entrance gate. On the right stood a disused lodge, and the drive had not been weeded for months. Tufts of grass showed among the gravel and soil, and the laurels on either side of the drive had grown over so that at times the leaves brushed the sides of the car. The house stood about three hundred yards away from the road, a low-built, rambling place, screened round with trees. There were signs of green damp on the outer walls, and only one thing indicated that the house was not deserted—smoke spiralled into the still sky from two chimney stacks.

As the car drew to a standstill the enormous front door of the house opened. On either side of the porch were huge pillars, ending in a flat balcony below a central bedroom window. The door was oak, blackened by the passage of time, furnished with a knocker in the form of a lion's head. Beside the door was an old-fashioned bell chain.

The opener of the door did not appear. Kane jumped out of the car, and pointed to a decrepit garage at the end of the drive.

"Dump the car in there," he said, "and then follow me into the house."

Cardby left the car and sauntered along the drive, examining the house more closely. On two floors, it covered a large amount of ground. Facing it was a lawn—or what had been a lawn. The grass was rough and coarse, rising in ungainly tufts. On either side of the grass were beech trees, and at the end of the lawn another row of trees blocked the view—fir trees, dense and black against the sky. The drive ended in front of the house apparently the original builder had burked the expense of a horseshoe approach.

The front door was still open when Cardby arrived on the steps, and he walked through into a large, bare hall. There was no furniture, and no covering on the floor. On the right were three doors, opening off the hall, on the left were two. Facing him was a staircase about ten feet wide. This, after rising to a height of eighteen or twenty feet, turned sharply to the right and left.

Cardby looked round for signs of life. There was no one in sight. So he lit a cigarette and commenced to whistle. A door on his right opened about six inches, and a hand beckoned to him. Mick walked forward.

There were four people in the room.

Tommy Kane stood near the sideboard with a whisky glass in his hand. Mariel, otherwise Kathleen, otherwise Eleanora, sat on an ingle seat near the fireplace. She wore a heavy fur coat, and her face was white. On the opposite side of the fireplace stood Clancy, the erstwhile "Gribble." On the edge of the oak refectory table sat Alibi Delaney.

"Here we are again," said Mick, throwing his leather gauntlet gloves on the table. "All good friends and jolly good company.

Welcome home, Mr Thomas Kane. We're glad to have you with us in the old ancestral domain. And are you the only one who can have a drink?"

The woman waved her hand towards the sideboard, and Mick took a bottle of beer. There was a curious atmosphere in the room, an air of tension.

Clancy filled glasses for all of them except Mick.

"Here's to tomorrow," he said.

The five people raised their drinks to the toast. Mick gulped some of his beer without knowing anything about the toast. He knew he'd learn before long.

"Did you have any trouble?" asked Mariel.

"Not a bit, my dear. Everything went on greased wheels, didn't it?"

"Not a hitch," said Tommy Kane. There was another uncomfortable period of silence. They all started when the telephone bell rang. Mariel jumped from her seat and crossed to the instrument standing on a small table near the window.

"Hallo," she called. ". . . Yes, speaking. . . Yes, he's here. Tommy, come over and have a word. It's the boss."

The strain eased, although all looked uncomfortable. Even Kane had lost some of his nonchalance as he picked up the telephone.

"Kane here. . . Yes, absolutely O.K. . . You will? . . . We'll be seeing you then? . . . That's good. . . Yes, all I want. . . What do you say? . . . Oh, him. . . Yes, he's here too. Want to speak to him? . . . All right. Hey, come over here and have a word with the boss—you, I mean."

Mick strolled across the floor leisurely. Once and for all he had a chance to show Maddick's satellites that his nerves were steady, that he cared for no man, that even Maddick held no threat for him. There might come a time when such an impression among them would help him out of a difficulty.

People would not be anxious to oppose a man who had the nerve and effrontery to oppose Maddick.

"Pete here," he said.

"Good boy," commented Maddick. "I just wanna tell you that you handled that job in style. There'll be a good time coming to you, Borden."

"When's it coming?"

"Don't get impatient. After tomorrow you'll sit pretty—I told you that before. Just sit on your feet and keep them warm until you hear from me."

"Hell! Maddick, that's a tough break to give me after I've finished your job for you. This place is like a mortuary, and my little playmates aren't busting with merriment. What about me having an evening off for a change?"

"So you can pack your skin with booze, walk around with some jane, and talk yourself into trouble? Not for me, big boy. You just sit tight."

"Wait a minute, Maddick. You've only borrowed me, you know. I've still got a bit of a say. I'll go luny sitting in a dump like this waiting for things to happen. Or I'll get nerves and then I'll be no good to you."

"Get an earful of this, Borden. I've told you to stay where you are; what I say goes. Understand that?"

"There's a difference between understanding it and agreeing with it. I'm damned if I'm going to live here like a hermit for you or for anybody else."

"Does the little boy wanna hit the bright lights then? I'm not going to tell you again. I'll be along myself tonight, and I want all of you in that house when I come. If anybody isn't there it's going to be more than unhealthy for them. Just another thing to cheer you up, Borden. I'm bringing someone down with me to keep you company. So sing your blues away, big boy. When you see your new playmate you'll be glad you stayed. But if you should happen to walk out you're not likely to see anything else in this world after

I've found you. I'll be along about seven. Don't get too much to drink. You'll want all the nerve you've got tomorrow."

Mick waited until he heard the receiver click down at the other end. Then he spoke with some irritation.

"All right, Maddick, you can have it your own way for the moment, but you're not going to have me running round your coat-tails for ever."

He replaced the phone on the table, and turned to look at the others. All were gaping. Even Mariel was startled.

"If that isn't the cat's whiskers," said Clancy. "I never thought I'd live to the day when I'd hear somebody brown off the boss."

"Hell," said Mick, "if you were a man, Clancy, instead of an imitation you'd talk for yourself occasionally instead of acting as a 'yes man'."

"Maybe," remarked Delaney, "we've got more sense than you've got."

"Or less guts," retorted Mick. He felt no anger. But he wanted to let them know where he stood. Alibi shuffled his feet and drew nearer. His powerful hands were at his sides, and he was balanced on the balls of his feet. Mick had seen men stand like that too many times to mistake the meaning of the pose. He looked at Delaney quizzically, the cigarette still in the corner of his mouth.

"Are you trying to tell me in a backhand way that I've got no guts?"

Alibi had lowered his voice and his hands moved restlessly. Mick held one hand on his hip, the other touched the edge of the table. They stared at each other.

"Not exactly, Delaney. I was only suggesting that if you've got two thoughts in your head about the value of self-respect you wouldn't spend your life as a doormat."

Alibi's right fist came up in an arc, his shoulder bent to take the impact of the punch, his feet swivelled to throw his weight into the swing. Cardby moved his head, slowly it seemed, but quick enough to miss the bony fist by an inch. His own hand started low down, from the hip, and Delaney moved too late. He saw a sheet of red, a blinding flash of light, a stream of comets, and then—nothing.

The others had not moved. Mick sucked his knuckles reflectively before he stepped forward and moved Delaney's head from its resting-place against the wainscot. Then he picked the big man up in his arms, laid him in an easy-chair, and rubbed some soda water over his face. Alibi's eyes flickered and his body trembled.

"Sorry I hurt you," said Mick, "but I didn't think you'd lose your temper like that. Feeling better now?"

The man struggled into a sitting position. His eyes glared.

"Before I'm through with you," he said, "you'll pay for that one smack until you'll be sorry that God gave you fists."

"That'll be something for me to look forward to. Now let's stop arguing and turn to something a bit more sensible. Is there any grub in this house, or have you only got a few items of furniture."

"If you want some you'd better look around for it," said Clancy.

"Hospitable lot of folks, aren't you?" said Mick. Then he emptied his glass of beer and left the room.

"Thought you were a muscle man, Delaney," said Tommy Kane sarcastically.

"I didn't know he was going to take me unawares, did I?"

"Why didn't you? He seemed to have a pretty good idea about what you intended to do. If I were you, lad, I'd keep away from that youth. He carries too many guns for you. And there's something else that you might think about too. Pete is very popular with Maddick, and it might be asking for trouble to upset him."

In the meantime Cardby found the entrance to the domestic quarters and wandered from room to room. The place was old and rambling, and one stone-flagged room led down a step into another one. In vain he looked for the larder. In one of the kitchens he noticed a door in the corner, bolted from the outside. On a shelf at the side of the door was a flashlamp. Curious, the youngster unbolted the door and swung it back. Before him was a flight of steps, only the first four or five treads visible. They vanished into complete darkness.

Mick took the lamp and started on a tour of investigation. After all, he thought, if they do find me rambling about I can say that I'm as much entitled to roam around as they are.

The walls flanking the steps had once been whitewashed. Now they were smeared with heavy dust and covered in all the angles with filmy cobwebs. The stairs took a turn to the left after a short descent and finished at the commencement of a long passage. Cardby turned the light on the walls. There were four doors—two on each side. The two doors nearest to him were open. Mick looked inside, but the huge cellars were empty. He passed to the farther doors.

The one on the right was fastened, but not locked, and Cardby lifted the latch. Here again the room was empty, except for a few rats that scampered away as the light flickered round the wails and ceiling. In none of the cellars so far had there been a window. All were built well below ground level, and there was apparently no attempt at ventilation. The ground was damp, moisture seeping through the ill-fitting flagstones. In the air was a heavy, musty smell.

Mick crossed the narrow passage and stood before the third door. A massive key was in the lock, and the key was turned.

He swung it round with an effort. The lock was old and worn, probably corroded as a result of the damp atmosphere. Again he swung his light round the room and saw nothing. This seemed to be the smallest of the cellars. He was turning to go when he imagined that some noise had come from inside the room.

Slipping his automatic from his pocket he stepped through the doorway and turned the light slowly over the floor area. Suddenly the light stopped moving. The yellow circle was covering an object in the corner.

Cardby moved nearer and turned his torch down-wards. Then he heard a groan. The object was the figure of a man lying on the bare flagstones!

He bent down and touched the man on the shoulder. The figure moved, groaning again, and Mick pointed the beam on his face. He shuddered.

The hair was long and matted, lying across the forehead in dank pieces. The face was ghastly white, the jaws sunken. Once the man opened his eyes—eyes full of terror. His skin was covered by a heavy growth of hair. Above the right eye was a black bruise as big as a tennis ball. As the light moved again Mick saw the manacles on the man's wrists, fastened to a chain and the chain fastened to a stanchion in the wall. The legs were chained to an iron loop on the floor.

"Who are you?" he asked, shaking the man gently by the shoulder.

The prisoner blinked his eyes when Mick turned the light away.

"Who are you? What's your name?"

When the man spoke his voice was trembling and feeble, even the effort of speaking a few words seemed to exhaust him.

"I—I'm Caudry," he whispered. "Detective Caudry, Scotland Yard."

Mick shuddered and his eyes grew moist. He patted the man softly.

# 15

## MICK MAKES ARRANGEMENTS

Good God! This man lying on the floor was weary and old, bent and weak, his energy sapped, his spirit broken. And Mick knew that Detective-Constable Caudry of New Scotland Yard was not yet thirty! He stood, irresolute, wondering what to say. What could one say to a man who had left his youth, his health and his strength behind him in a few weeks become a human wreck?

"Listen to me, Caudry," he said at last. "Can you hear me?"

The man twisted a little on the floor and nodded.

"I'm not one of the Maddick crowd, but I'm supposed to be, and I'm going to get you out of this. But you'll have to stick it for another few hours. The first chance I get I'll come down to you again and get you out of it. Keep your heart up, laddie, you'll soon be all right again. And remember that you haven't spoken to me and don't know me."

Caudry's dirt-lined, unshaven face drew up into an attempted smile. Mick admired him for the effort.

"That's good," he whispered. "Thanks very much."

"So long for the moment, Caudry. Keep your pecker up. I'll see that you're all right."

"Thanks." Caudry was exhausted again.

Cardby relocked the door and returned upstairs. No one, apparently, had followed him from the drawing-room. The youngster's emotions were boiling over. He knew that in that way lay danger. What he wanted was brain and common sense, not emotion and temper. But it was ten minutes before he could trust himself to return to the others and continue with his part. It would have been so much more simple to break into action, violent, bloody action.

"Are all you folks slimming, or are you on a health diet?" he asked. "I've walked all round the damned place until I'm tired, and I can't find enough to feed a mouse. Where is the grub, if any?"

"You certainly didn't expect to find it in the cellar, did you?" asked Alibi maliciously.

"I did not. What's the joke at the back of that?"

"If you weren't looking for food what did you go into the cellar for?"

"And who told you that I've been underground?"

"Your coat is enough to tell all of us. Why, man, you're smothered with dust and cobwebs."

"That's not surprising, Delaney. Show me a place in this blasted place where you don't get covered with filth. It hasn't been cleaned since the Conqueror came to England. In any case, suppose I do want to look around downstairs, or upstairs either, for that matter, what have you got to say about it? Are you running this show or is Maddick?"

"How would you like me to tell Maddick that you've been exploring round the cellars?"

"I'd be delighted. In fact, if it would please you at all, I'll save you the trouble by telling him myself. But if I do I'll take the chance of mentioning a few more complaints about you that wouldn't help you any. If I were in your place, Delaney, I'd pipe low. You're not made of the right stuff to act as a big-timer. You've got above yourself, my lad, and the altitude's got into your head."

"All right, smarty. We'll see who laughs last out of this lot."

"It'll be me, Alibi, because you couldn't do anything that would stop me laughing. I'm made that way. Every time I look at you I want to laugh."

"Then you'd better get on with your laughing before my turn comes."

"All right. Suppose, just as a joke, one of you tells me where I can lay my hands on a bit of food."

"Come along," said Mariel, "I'll show you. I think the farther you and Delaney keep away from each other the better it will be for all of us."

She lead the way across the hall into a dining-room. There, in one of the sideboard cupboards she found some cold ham and bread.

"Don't look after your guests too well, do you, Mariel?"

"You're getting what the rest of us have. We don't live in this dump. Why, until this morning, I don't think any of us have been here for three or four days."

Mick thought of the young detective in the cellar. Poor devil!

"Are you going to have some with me?" he asked, and the girl nodded.

They sat down together at the gloomy oak table. Mick looked round.

"The place wasn't altogether furnished for comfort," he said.

"You're right. But it suits us all O.K. Maddick saw it advertised two or three months ago as partly furnished. It belongs to a man who has gone out to the Malay States, so we took it for a term of six months. I don't know why Maddick wanted it. We have hardly used it at all."

"Are you in on the big push tomorrow?"

"Nobody knows. All we've been told is that the job is big. What it is, where it is, and who is going to pull it we don't know. That's why Maddick is coming down tonight."

"Bit risky, isn't it, for him to come down here himself?"

"I should worry," said Mariel, taking another piece of ham. "You won't see him, and I'm sure the others won't. Some folks say 'See Naples and die.' I feel more inclined to say, 'See Maddick and die.' One look at him is the best short-cut to a cemetery I know of."

"There's one thing puzzling me, Mariel, and you won't be giving away any secrets by telling me. Are there any Yanks in our crowd?"

"I've never met any. If there are a few they don't count or I'd have known them. That's why I know that Maddick must think something of you. I don't work with small-timers. I was staggered when he put me in harness with a man who'd only been with us for a week."

"Never mind, it wasn't our fault that we made a mess of it."

"I'd like to know who squealed. I could plug them with pleasure."

Mick raised his eyebrows and looked at the girl. She had spoken of murder quite casually, but she meant it. Beneath the angel face and sympathetic eyes was something hard and callous. Cardby, at that moment, thought that, as a prisoner, he would rather be in the hands of Alibi Delaney than this girl with the handsome face and charming smile.

"What's the procedure when Maddick gets down here?"

"I don't know. He's never been here before when we've been here. I imagine he'll telephone before he arrives, giving instructions."

"There are times, Mariel, when all this hocus-pocus and mystery business gets on my nerves. I've always worked above-board before, and I don't mind telling you that it's a damn sight more comfortable than working for a man nobody knows."

"I should worry," said the girl. "The pay's good, and the risks are not too big. You don't know a good thing when you see one."

## MICK MAKES ARRANGEMENTS

"Have you ever been inside, Mariel?"

"Not me. Only the mugs take the trips. The first policeman to catch me will deserve promotion. I've been on this game now for four years, and I've never been anywhere near a pinch."

"And I," said Mick, lying with calm assurance, "was in the game for six years before I realised that no matter how smart you are your luck won't hold out for ever. It isn't skill that counts in the long run, Mariel, in our game. It's a question as to whether the luck holds out."

"That's what you say. I call it brains—not luck. Every small-timer who gets in front of the jury goes down with a moan about the bad luck he's had. The clever ones don't rely on luck. They count it out."

"Do they? Suppose that at the Mead reception that Gribble girl had taken it into her head to grab you by the wrist when the lights went down? Would that have been bad luck?"

"It would—for her. I don't go to affairs like that without some sort of preparation."

"You mean you'd got a gun?"

"Good God, No! How would one expect to get away with firing a gun in a crowded room. I'd got something in my handbag that is more useful than a gun—and you can't miss with it. She'd have felt a slight pain in the arm and she'd have been dead before I got out of the house."

"Sounds neat. What had you got?"

"Just a hypodermic needle full of prussic acid, and you can't cure that at a reception. You may get rid of an ordinary poison with your emetics, but my speciality stays put until the corpse is ready. The only thing to do when I've introduced myself to 'em is to wash their stomach out with sodium thiosulphate, shove the strongest ammonia you can get under their nostrils, use more sal volatile than you've ever seen before, and give a hypodermic injection of atropine. And if you've got all the stuff handy it's an even money bet that the person dies before you can start work. That's what would have happened to the Gribble girl. Would you call that luck?"

"The judge would call it murder."

"What's one murder more or less?"

"Nothing like being philosophic about it. You were talking a moment ago as though you have had a professional training as a chemist or a doctor. Where did you pick all that stuff up?"

"Through being fascinated by the Borgias when I was a callow girl. I've dabbled in poisons ever since."

"Pleasant habit. I hope you don't try an experiment on me."

"I won't until you need it."

"That's reassuring, Mariel. Thank you very much. Shall we join the others or continue the talk?"

"What about a spot of air? I feel like a stroll."

"That'll suit me. Do you know your way around here?"

"We can walk round the grounds. There's plenty of space."

They unbolted the back door and passed through to a flagged yard. Day was dying and shadows were skimming the ground. Beyond the yard was a derelict garden, weeds growing everywhere, and the paths untidy. They passed through the garden, opened a swing gate and walked over a paddock. At the end was a wood, stretching black against the skyline for more than a mile. The temperature had dropped and the air was thin.

"I've lost all my enthusiasm for this stroll," said Mariel. "I'm heading for somewhere warm. Come along."

"Just one thing," remarked Mick, as they turned round. "If you see another row brewing between Alibi and me, you might step into the gap as peacemaker. I don't want to waste my time rowing with him."

"Don't worry about him, Pete. All he says is hot air. He's about as dangerous as a tame mouse. But take my tip and don't fall out with Clancy. He isn't much to look at, but he's as bad as Maddick when he starts. I know something about him, and I'm telling you in time. So far you're all right, since he doesn't like Delaney. That smack you handed him probably pleased Clan. But don't bank on the fact that he's a friend of yours."

"A bit changeable, is he?"

"More than that. He's very awkward to handle, Pete."

"You seem to know a lot about him."

"I ought to. He's my husband!"

"Congratulations. But why tell me all this?"

"Only because one of these days I might want a helping hand from you, and then you can remember that I've given you a bit of advice."

"That's surprising, Mariel. I thought you were sitting on top of the world in this crowd."

"Think again. There's nobody working for Maddick who knows where they stand for more than an hour at a time."

"How pleasant."

When they returned to the house Kane was asleep, Clancy sat reading a paper, and Delaney was staring out of the window. They ignored the entry of the girl and Mick. Minutes dragged by on leaden feet. Cardby yawned and stretched himself. He wanted action.

Then the telephone bell rang, and Clancy waved Delaney to one side as he walked over to the phone.

All that could be heard by those in the room was the constant flow of "Yes," "Yes," "Yes" that came from Clancy. The conversation, or perhaps it would be more accurate to say monologue, lasted for three or four minutes. Finally, when he replaced the receiver, Clancy shook Kane by the shoulder and roused him.

"Wake up," he said, "you've all got to listen to this."

Tommy rubbed his eyes, and Clancy stood with his back to the fire.

"That was Maddick on the telephone," commenced Clancy unnecessarily. "He'll be here at eight o'clock, and he's told me what we've got to do. But he wants me to say this before I tell you— anyone who disobeys these instructions will say farewell to this life—and quickly. At eight o'clock he'll arrive by car. Everyone must then be in this room. Under no circumstance must anyone go to the front door. He has the key and will let himself in. This door must be shut, and as soon as we hear the car arrive we've got to turn out the light. Maddick will then stand in the hall and talk to us.

"When he's finished, and we've heard the car go down the drive, we can turn on the light. That's all."

"Wait a minute," said Delaney. "We can easily walk into trouble that way. If it's dark everywhere and we can't see him when he's talking to us, how will we know that it's Maddick?"

"I forgot that part of it. You'll know it's him by two things. Firstly, he'll sound the hooter twice when he arrives outside the front door, and secondly, he'll know all our names. That's enough."

"And what do we do after he's left?" asked Mick.

"How the hell do I know until he tells us what we've got to do?"

"That's sensible. What do we do until he arrives?"

"Sit down and play with your fingers."

"I think not, Clancy. I'm tired of sitting still. I'm going to have a walk in the grounds."

"You'll never come back here alive if you do. What do you think we are to let you wander round while we're waiting for Maddick to arrive? Do you think he's going to drive right into trouble? You'll stay here."

"All right. I don't mind. What about a drink?"

# 16

## CONFERENCE AT THE YARD

"It seems to me," said Sir Wynnard Salter, "that we are making no substantial progress."

"Rome wasn't built in a day," replied Cardby, a red flush showing on his thick neck. "The boy's in the right place to get the stuff, and he daren't hurry. You'll hear from him when the time comes to take some action. You can't expect him to get on the telephone to us with every pettifogging thing he hears about, can you?"

"I would like to know what progress is being made, Cardby."

"So would we all. But we've got to wait and see. You can't say that we've done nothing so far. The boy did give us the tip about that robbery at the Mead reception."

"I know, but he didn't tell us anything about them rescuing Kane, the safe-breaker, did he?"

"I should imagine he was too busy helping Kane to escape to give a thought to us. I think, Sir Wynnard, you'd be more fair if you thought the matter over from the boy's point of view. The probability is that he knows where Kane has hidden and can put his hand on him at any time. That being so, he'd have sense enough to give Maddick a bit more rope. In any case, who is Tommy Kane compared with Maddick?"

"I know, I know," said the Assistant Commissioner irritably. "That's what I get all the time. Just one string of excuses after each other. It's time that something was done."

"Something will be done," said the Chief Constable, "when we know what it is that wants doing. At the moment I think it would be madness to take any step that would cut across young Cardby's path. That boy is our trump card and we've got to play him for all he's worth."

"There's one thing I must mention," said Cardby. "You can bet on it as a certainty that when my lad sends for us it will be a hurry call. So when that message comes through I think we should answer it as strongly as we can. What I suggest is that Inspector Hall should not, during the next few days, cruise more than a mile away from here, and that the rest of us should leave a message telling where we are at any time when we go out. When the time comes—if it does come—to round up Maddick we'll need the best men we've got, and I'm thinking the net will have to be thrown farther than you think."

"Is there nothing, then, that we can do except sit here and wait?"

"I've got one small job that I want to do myself, but I don't know whether it's going to help at all."

"Well, what is it?"

"I'm going to see Mr Newall, the solicitor, of 45a Chancery Lane."

"What's he got to do with it?"

"That's exactly what I want to know. Maybe nothing, but I'm not ready to bet that he's a gilded innocent."

"Be careful, Cardby, you know that handling solicitors is playing with fire. What have you got against him?"

"Nothing. I only want to ask a few questions."

"I think," said the Chief Constable, "that before you take any steps in that direction you ought to tell us something about it."

"All right. I will. It doesn't need me to tell you what sort of defence the ordinary man gets when he comes in front of the judge. A few of 'em take a dock brief, some of them plunge to the extent of perhaps three or five guineas for counsel, and only one in every thousand pays more than twenty guineas. We all know that. Taking the safe-breaker, con man, or forger as typical cases, you can say that their defence would average out at between ten and twenty guineas for the barrister. Probably I'm overestimating. Now let's take the few instances when Maddick's men have got into the dock.

"Solly Steinmann had Stewart Read, K.C., when he was charged at the Old Bailey with long-firm fraud. That brief was marked at a hundred and twenty guineas. When I put Phil Kell in the dock he had Conway Addison to defend him, and that cost two hundred. Little Ponty Moules was defended by Nigel Travis, K.C., and that cost sixty guineas. Betsy Wade was looked after by Stewart Read, for a consideration of eighty-five, when we raided her four clubs, and only this week Arch Redfern was defended by Conway Addison. That was a heavy brief. Add to that the fact that Tommy Kane was represented, even before the justices, by Nigel Travis, and you'll see that money's no object."

"We all know that," exclaimed Sir Wynnard irritably; "but what's this got to do with Newall?"

"Plenty. It's just occurred to me that the counsel keep on changing, but the solicitor never changes. In every case we've handled the defence has been looked after by Newall. He is the one who arranges everything, the man who briefs counsel. Don't you think it's time that someone said a few words to him? Look here, if I walked out now and knocked off one of Maddick's men he would be represented in court tomorrow morning, and Newall would be responsible for the defence."

"Are you sure about this?" asked the Assistant Commissioner.

"Positive. I've been working on it for two days."

"Is it your suggestion, then, that this man Newall might be Maddick?"

"I'm not prepared to go as far as that, although it seems more than likely. At any rate, if he isn't Maddick, he's very near to him, and must know a lot about what's going on."

"In that case I certainly think you must have a talk to him."

"I'll walk along then. We've got nothing to gain by sitting here for another hour talking round and round the bush."

On his way out Cardby met Sergeant Gribble.

"Hallo, misery," he said. "What's your latest trouble?"

"I'll be glad when my pension rolls nearer home. I'm fed up with this job. How's Mick going on?"

"Ask me another one. I haven't heard from him. How did the girl like her bit of detective work the other evening?"

"Splendid. She wants some more of it. Seems to have got into her blood, but I told her that it was the world's worst job. She nearly landed Mick into a fine mess."

"I bet he cursed her. That's the worst of women, Gribble. They always try to do things too thoroughly. It's a good job they didn't know each other or the cat might have been out of the bag properly."

"Aye. Well, I'll get along with some work. Just knocked a couple of blokes off for a job of arson. For a change they've got nothing to do with Maddick."

"That should encourage you. It means you've got a chance of getting them convicted. I'm off to invade the portals of the law."

Inspector Cardby did not go directly to Chancery Lane. Instead he stopped first at the office of a friend—Mason Grey, a middle-aged barrister, with no money and a long tongue. He found him in his chambers.

"Got a warrant?" asked Grey.

"No. Just dropped in to ask you a few questions. Mind breaking a few thousand professional rules?"

"Not a bit, so long as you're tactful. What is it?"

"I'm anxious to get your idea about a few men in your own line of business. Mark you, I know nothing against them, but it would help me to know just how they stand and what sort of name they have."

"I might be able to help you. Seeing that I get briefs at the rate of ten a year I have plenty of time to listen to gossip."

"Well, what do you know about Newall, Montague Newall, of Newall and Gibbs, Chancery. Or, alternately, as they say in your cursed line of life, what do you know about the firm as a whole?"

Grey stuffed his pipe and lit it before he answered.

"Funny firm. They handle criminal cases and taxation. Not long ago they were very small fry, but they've pulled up no end lately. There's no one doing criminal stuff who isn't only too glad to be in with them. And I know for a fact that Snow, the silk, makes best part of eight thousand a year doing paper work for them—income tax, super tax, property tax, and all that stuff. They've made a good name, and their money is good."

"Anything known against them?"

"I haven't heard of anything."

"How did they come to take on criminal work?"

"Ask me another. At one time they never touched it. Then, all of a sudden, they were quite a power in the land. Most of the really big briefs at the Old Bailey pass through their hands. They touch nothing that's small."

"Know anything about Stewart Read?"

"He's a different proposition. What's wrong, Cardby?"

"Nothing that I know of at the moment. Do you know him?"

"I can't give him the best of characters. As a junior he always knew a bit more about the criminal classes than the next man. Said his hobby was criminology. Used to walk round looking for crime. But what did him at the Bar was the knowledge that he's been touting for years. He had feelers out in all sorts of places, and whenever a man got into trouble they soon met someone who told them to go to Read."

"That's one of the unforgivable sins, isn't it?"

"It is. He's done quite well out of it, though. I don't think he's making the money now that he used to make as a junior. But hundreds have found that out after they've taken silk. A hundred guineas on the brief is very nice, but if they only come once a month, and as a junior you used to get ten guineas every day or two, you're apt to notice the difference. You won't find a single member of the Bar ready to say a good word about him."

"Bad luck for Read. Now, what about Conway Addison?"

"One doesn't hear a lot about him. He went out to India a long time ago, and made most of his money practising there. When he came back to England he found his feet and handled a few decent cases. Now he just does enough to keep the wolf a comfortable distance from the door. He's a mean old devil too. Puts five bob down on a subscription list and that sort of thing. I was told he lives in a frowsty three-room flat somewhere in Bloomsbury, but I don't know whether that's true."

"And now we finish the list with Nigel Travis."

"He was going great guns when he was stopped in his stride. You may remember the case. Travis was making best part of twenty thousand a year when he was cited as co-respondent in the Egley divorce case, and after that he slumped and slumped. I doubt whether he is making three thousand now, but he still lives at a fair pace. Perhaps he had saved some from his palmy days."

"Thanks very much, Grey. You're a walking 'Who's Who' of the Bar. See you again soon."

Cardby made his way across the road to Chancery Lane. There, at 45a, he sent in a card to Mr Montague Newall. He did not have to wait for long. The gentleman was disengaged and would see him.

## CONFERENCE AT THE YARD

The Yard man disliked Newall from the first glance. The feeling was mutual, although the solicitor smiled genially.

"It isn't often we have you gentlemen down this way. What can I do?"

"Quite a lot, I hope. Am I right in saying that you have acted for the defence in the cases of Tommy Kane, Arch Redfern, Solly Steinmann, Phil Kell, and a few others?"

"Yes, all you have mentioned have been clients of mine."

"Have you formed any view as to whether those men were working for themselves and by themselves?"

"I think I know what you mean. The answer is ' No.'"

"Why do you say that?"

"Because in not one case have I had my instructions from them."

"That's exactly why I came to see you. How does it come about that you have represented all these men?"

"A man of your experience, inspector, should know that I can't answer that question. There are rules, you know, very definite rules, governing matters discussed between solicitor and client."

"Don't misunderstand me, Mr Newall. I am not asking you to detail for me any discussion you may have had with your clients. I am asking you to tell me how the instructions reached you."

"My answer would be the same in that case."

"Hardly. You have told me that in no case have you received the instructions from your client."

"That, inspector, is the argument of a sophist."

"Maybe. I don't want to prolong this matter, Mr Newall. Would you mind telling me from whence came your instructions?"

"I have told you before that I am not free to give that information."

"In that case I must ask you to come with me to New Scotland Yard. The matter is quite important, and if you desire it the question will be asked again in the presence of the Public Prosecutor—or even the Attorney General, if you like. And to make matters more happy for you we will invite the chairman of your committee to attend in order that he can advise you upon matters of professional etiquette."

Newall laid his fountain pen on the desk and stared hard at Cardby. Some of his assurance had gone. The inspector took advantage of the pause to hammer home his point.

"I am not asking you to convey to me any single matter that would affect the confidence existing between yourself and the men for whom you acted. All I want to know is this : Who gave you your instructions?"

The solicitor thought for a while and licked his dry lips.

"As a matter of fact," he said, "it is a very curious story."

"All the more reason why I'd like to hear it without causing you the inconvenience of going to the Yard."

"The story goes back to a date nearly fourteen months ago. What I am telling you now, inspector, is, of course, strictly confidential. At that time affairs here were not going too well. It is true that we have always had a fair connection since we specialise in questions concerning taxation, but the general business had fallen. In fact, I had become quite worried about matters. Then one morning I received a letter. I think it would save time if I showed that document to you."

Newall rose from his chair and crossed the floor to the steel filing cabinets. After a search lasting five minutes he extracted a file and returned to the desk. He handed a letter across to Cardby.

The notepaper was white, common foolscap size. There was no address at the top, no signature at the bottom. It read:

"You have an opportunity of acquiring the best client a solicitor could have. Whether you succeed in persuading this client that you are a fit person to undertake his business depends upon the manner in which you could fulfil the following instructions!

"All instructions would be sent anonymously, and would have to be followed without the slightest deviation. No questions must be raised on your part, and any attempt to unveil the anonymity of the sender would instantly result in the cancellation of any agreement. In no instance would the client on whose behalf you acted be acquainted with the manner in which your instructions were received.

"If you could undertake to keep these rigidly, I, on my part, can assure you of business that would amount to three thousand a year. To give you confidence in this proposition, I may add that I am prepared to place three thousand pounds to the credit of your account as an advance against work to be done.

"Should you feel that you can keep such an agreement, please insert an announcement in the personal column of *The Times*, commencing with the letter M, and signing yourself Lex. If such an announcement does not appear within four days this offer is closed."

"Now," said Newall, "when I got that note I thought it was either a poor practical joke or the effort of a lunatic. But for the sake of paying for one advertisement I decided to see what would happen. If you turn to the back of the letter you will see the notice that was published in *The Times*."

Cardby turned the sheet of paper over. He read:

"M.—Am willing to accept all conditions.— Lex."

"And what happened after you inserted this, Mr Newall?"

"Something even more surprising. A man came into the office and handed a parcel to one of the clerks, telling him that it was important and that it was to be given to me immediately. Inside that parcel was three thousand pounds in one-pound notes. I won't tell you what I thought!"

"And after that you acted for this mysterious individual?"

"I did. I couldn't afford to ignore a sum of money like that. And, Inspector, from that day to this I have not been asked to do a single thing that could not have been done quite properly by any solicitor in the kingdom. All along I have been looking for snags, and so far I haven't found one."

"Have you handled anything other than criminal cases?"

"Yes, quite a lot of taxation matters."

"I think all that remains is for you to tell me how those instructions came to you."

"The simplest way of answering that is to show you one of the messages I got. That will explain everything since there is no sort of variation among them. I have all of them in this file. I'll find one."

He handed Cardby four sheets of foolscap tied together at the corners with red tape.

"Before I look at this," said the inspector, "tell me how these messages come into your possession."

"In all sorts of ways. Some have been delivered at my private house by district messenger, some have been sent here by post—the postmark has always been W.—others have been handed in to the office by men who have left without giving a name."

The inspector looked at the document before him and read::

"At 7.20 p.m. last night Phillip Kell, a fitter, of 354 Malin Street, Vauxhall, was arrested by Chief Detective-Inspector Cardby, of New Scotland Yard, and charged with receiving stolen property— to wit, seven steel engraving plates. He made no answer to the charge. This morning Kell will appear at Bow Street. The police will ask for a remand for seven days. Do not oppose the application. Later, talk to Kell, and formulate some line of defence. Brief Stewart Read to appear for him. In the course of your inquiries you will find that information valuable to the defence will be given by the following persons.

"Amy Myers, tailoress, 14 Grampion Street, Stepney.

"Horace Charles Webb, machine turner, 56 Maiden Road, Camberwell.

"Percy Scholer, paper merchant, Ford's Yard, Lewisham.

"Samuel Farris, decorator, 4 Coulson Avenue, Brixton.

"Interview these people and prepare their statements for Stewart Read. Further instructions will follow."

The further pages were filled with the further instructions that had come to Newall as the days went by. Cardby smiled ironically. He remembered only too well that Kell was acquitted. Now he knew why. The case for the defence was saturated with perjury. The whole of the evidence was framed.

The inspector spent half an hour reading through the instructions in case after case. Each set orders, each piece of information, was placed in logical array. Not a word was wasted, every telling point for the defence was elaborated and strengthened. And in each case the 'unknown client' had specified his own counsel. In certain cases he even stipulated the fees to be paid.

"Very interesting," said Cardby. "Do you mean to tell me that after receiving all these instructions you don't know who sends them?"

"I do not. Perhaps I could have found out if I had tried, but you must remember what he said— that any attempt to unveil his anonymity would lose me the work. I don't intend to lose that three thousand."

"I take it that you have had a second payment of the same amount?"

"Yes, it was handed over in the same way two months ago."

"Have you any idea who this person might be?"

"I haven't even stopped to guess. Even that might lose me the money."

"Naturally, Mr Newall, you know that you are acting for a criminal?"

"So is any man who takes the defence in a criminal charge— unless the person charged is not guilty."

"But in these cases you're only taking the instructions of the person behind the accused man. You realise that you are the legal representative of an organised gang?"

"I told you, inspector, that so far I haven't even guessed, and I most certainly don't intend to start now."

"In that case, Mr Newall, it only remains for me to say two things. In the first place, watch your step. In the second place, forget that this interview has taken place between us. Good afternoon."

# 17

## MADDICK GIVES INSTRUCTIONS

The stillness at "The Withies" was unnerving all of them. Even Mick was fidgeting restlessly. He would have welcomed anything that promised action. But the quiescence continued. They felt that zero hour had come. That this was the lull before the storm. Tempers were short, nerves ragged. Outside, the rain had started to patter down, and the incessant beating of the drops on the large windows only helped to increase the uncomfortable air of tension. Cardby paced the room until Clancy scowled at him and told him to stop "prowling like a lion."

Tommy Kane sat with his feet on the table, smoking cigarette after cigarette with quick, nervous puffs. Mariel held a pencil in her hand and was bent over a crossword puzzle, but for twenty minutes or more she had not put down a single word. Delaney sat with a frown on his face, looking up occasionally to glare at Mick.

"Five minutes to eight," said Kane. "We haven't long to wait now, thank God. I don't mind the quiet when I'm working on a job, but it's getting on my nerves tonight. I feel every minute as though someone's going to plonk a hand on my shoulder and say ' Just step this way with me.' All of you look as though you're waiting for a death sentence."

"This game doesn't suit me," said Mick. "I'd rather pull ten strokes tonight than move around this room looking at you lot. What'n hell is the matter with you all? The police aren't here yet, are they?"

"We don't like that sorta joke," said Clancy. "Stow it."

"Don't stop anybody talking," interrupted Mariel. "I'd rather listen to nursery rhymes than sit here among all you dumb folks."

"Ssh! Ssh!" whispered Clancy. "Is that a car?"

Not a sound was made in the room. Above the beat of the rain they heard the squelch of gravel as it was flung from under the wheels of a car. Clancy dashed across the room and pressed his hand on the electric light switch. It is said that the deprivation of sight heightens the sense of hearing. Those in the room found that that was so.

Mick noted the change in the hum of the engine as the driver changed down to take the bend in the drive. Then again came the squelch of gravel, and the lights of the car passed over the windows in a sudden flare and vanished again. The wheels crunched as they drew to a stop. Those in the room, tensed and nervous, heard a door slam; then a key was thrust into a lock, and they heard the door shut and footsteps in the hall. The handle of the inside door creaked as it turned. They knew, without being able to see, that someone stood on the threshold.

"Is everything O.K., Clancy?" asked the man in the doorway.

"Yes. Who is that?"

"This is Maddick. Answer to your names. Is Delaney there?"

"Yes," said Alibi.

"And Pete Borden?"

"Yes."

"And Kane?"

"Yes."

"And Mariel?"

"Yes."

"And nobody else?"

"No," said the woman, "there is nobody else."

"All right. Delaney, you're standing too near to this door. Move away a bit. Mariel, come away from that window. Just in case of accidents, I'd better tell you that I'm holding a gun in my hand, and the first person to move will stop one. All stay where you are. If I hear a move I'm going to shoot first and ask questions afterwards."

Mick was puzzled. Maddick, since he had last heard him, had changed his accent. Here was no trace of the American tone, no suspicion of the transatlantic phraseology. The speech was clipped and incisive. Obviously Maddick meant every word he said.

"I have told all of you," continued Maddick, "that if we are successful tomorrow there will be no further need for any of us to work. All will acquire sufficient money on which to retire. It does not necessarily follow that the organisation will be disbanded entirely. It is my intention to continue the work nominally—engaging in enough business to preserve the form of the organisation in case it is ever wanted again. But, to all intents and purposes, we will sever our connection with each other after tomorrow."

Those in the room made no sound. Mick stared towards the doorway, but could see nothing. It seemed to him that the space on the threshold was darker than its surroundings, but even this might have been imagination.

"Now that I have explained that matter," proceeded Maddick, "I can tell you what is to be done. Tomorrow the Royal Society of Lapidaries hold their first exhibition at Crescent House, King Street, off St. James Street. The jewels to be shown are valued at rather more than a million and a quarter. I want those jewels. Some of them are unsaleable; on those we can receive money—I can arrange this—from a certain insurance assessor.

The others I can dispose of. In fact, I have already made the tentative arrangements.

"To give you some encouragement I will mention that each man taking part in the affair will receive enough to provide for his needs until he dies. The lowest paid will receive a few thousand, while those whom I consider to bear the brunt of the work will receive between ten and fifteen thousand each. Such sums of money are worth a risk, aren't they?"

"They certainly are," said Clancy.

"The arrangements have been made," said Maddick, "and if they are followed with intelligence and daring, I can see no reason why all should not be well. These jewels have come from all over the world. Many have been lent by various crowned heads, many by Indian maharajahs. The last consignment arrived in this country yesterday. It was not possible to keep things of such value in any ordinary place, so the entire exhibits have been placed at a safe deposit in Bedford Street, Strand.

"The arrangement made is that at eight o'clock tomorrow morning, when the roads are comparatively empty, a van will stop at the safe deposit, the jewels will be loaded, driven to King Street, and then arranged on the stands in time for the opening of the show at ten o'clock. It is my intention to take those jewels while they are in transit. If you follow me carefully you will see that it can be done.

"At the side of the driver will sit a uniformed constable. Inside the van there will be two more uniformed men. The door of the van will be locked. The driver will turn into Chandos Street, across Trafalgar Square, and down Pall Mall. The attack must be commenced as the driver slows down to turn into St. James Square.

"Clancy and Delaney will have a car standing at the curb in Pall Mall. You must be there at five minutes to eight. The van should arrive ten minutes later. On the doorstep of this house you will find, after I have gone, a gun the like of which you

## MADDICK GIVES INSTRUCTIONS

may not have seen before. It is a gas gun. I have already loaded it. I want you, Clancy, to take your sights very carefully when the van comes in sight and aim to hit the top of the woodwork above the driver's head. Do not hit either the driver or the policeman. The gun is loaded with carbonic oxide. As soon as the shell explodes the two men will lose consciousness.

"Drive the car to the side of the van and take both the policeman and the driver out—dropping them into the back seats. Then beat it as fast as you can go. I don't care in which direction you travel. As soon as you come to a quiet street, and there is nobody watching you, dump the two men on the pavement and drive round for a while. Then make your way back here before the afternoon is out. The car you will use will be waiting for you at the corner of Hertford Street and Down Street—a grey saloon. Now that's your end of the job, and if you can do it—I won't be blaming you if things go wrong.

"The most important part of your job is to get the men out of the van and into the car as quickly as possible. Is there any question you would like to ask?"

"Has the gun got the ordinary trigger and ordinary sights?" asked Clan.

"Yes, exactly the same to fire as a rifle. Don't forget to hit the roof."

"Are we supposed to dump the car anywhere on our way back?"

"Certainly. You don't think I'd let you come here in it, do you?"

"And we pick up another anywhere we like?"

"You can take your pick of ten thousand any day."

"All right, sir. That's all O.K."

"Good. Now you can have your instructions, Kane, and this time you'll have to do a job a bit off your own line. You can drive a car?"

"Sure."

"Then go at quarter to eight tomorrow morning to the Crosby Garage in Greet Portland Street and tell them that you've come for Mr Hunt's car. They'll hand over a four-seater saloon in maroon. At first glance it'll look like an ordinary car to you. But it isn't. I've had it specially fitted up for this job. Under the dashboard, to the left of the engine switch, you'll find a button. When you press that a bell starts ringing, and it will ring until you depress the button. Make a note of that. Then, above your head, you will see a small box. Place your hand at the back of that and pull it down. The front of the box will then face the windscreen. At the side of the box is a switch. Turn that on. You will then be showing the blue letters, M.P., in front of the car, and your bell will be ringing. In short, you'll be a Flying Squad car.

"Don't touch either of those things until later. Cruise from Great Portland Street along to Bedford Street and have a look at the van and the men while they're loading the jewellery. As soon as the van starts off follow it. When you see that Clancy and Delaney have done their work, and the van starts off again, follow it. I'll jump from there to Borden's job and then I'll come back and tell you the rest of your work, Kane."

Mick had been wondering for five minutes what his job was to be. There didn't seem much left to do.

"Borden, you must stand at the corner of Carlton Gardens. Be there at five minutes to eight. A few yards away you will see Clancy and Alibi. Watch their work and give them a hand if they get stuck. But the very second they start to get the men out of the van jump into the driving seat and start away. You must wear old clothes—something like those you wore at Highgate this afternoon.

"Drive the car into Cleveland Row at the side of St. James Place. In front of you, in the Row, you will see a furniture van. There will be four long planks leading from the road to the inside of the pantechnicon. The double doors will be wide open. Drive the van straight up the planks, and into the van. Immediately you do that the doors will be closed, and the van will back out into St. James Street. You will stay inside the van until everything is over in case things go wrong at the last minute. That's your job. All clear?"

"Sounds like a gilt to me," said Mick easily.

"Don't get too confident, Borden. This is an important job. Now I come back to you, Kane. Follow the van until it turns into Cleveland Row. Then wait until it comes out. By that time a hue and cry will be on. It will be your job to see that the van gets through. Switch on your M.P. and set the bell going when the van gets near Piccadilly Circus. Swerve in front of the van and ask the constable on point whether he's seen a Morris commercial van pass. He'll say ' No,' so you pass through Shaftesbury Avenue and carry on until you get to New Oxford Street. If you find that the warning hasn't got that far, turn your light off and stop the bell. But if it has got there, just ask what you did at Piccadilly Circus.

"Of course, the furniture van will follow you, and you should make the way easy for it. The police are so used to seeing stolen things fly in front of a squad car that they won't contemplate the villain of the piece following in the wake of the police car. That's our trump card. The van will cut down Bloomsbury Street into Gower Street and run along into Euston. Once the van has got by Euston Station you can leave it, Kane. Is all that clear?"

"Yes. I only use the sign and the bell when the warning has passed me?"

"That's right. And now we come to you, Mariel. You've got a job that will suit you well. At five minutes to eight tomorrow morning you must walk into Cleveland Row. There you will see the furniture van. Climb inside and hide behind one of the doors, and as soon as Borden drives the van inside, shut the doors behind him. Under a piece of sacking in the front right-hand corner of the van you will find a cylinder—a gas cylinder—full of arseniurretted hydrogen. Insert the mouth of the tube in the keyhole of the van door and give the two policemen a taste of the gas. But be very careful not to get any of it yourself.

"Later, when the pantechnicon stops, you can make your way back here with Borden. How will that job suit you?"

"All right. You don't want the policemen killed, do you?"

"I don't think so, although it doesn't matter very much. Just give them enough to put them out of action for a couple of hours."

"And what do we do with them afterwards?"

"I'm not leaving that job to you. You have got nothing to do when that van stops but return home."

"There's one thing I'd like to ask you," said Mick. "Since we've all got to be in the West End shortly after half-past seven, how do we get from here to town?"

"A Daimler will arrive here at six o'clock. That's for Tommy Kane, Delaney and Clancy. Half an hour later you can take the car out of the garage and drive Mariel into town. Leave the car outside the National Gallery. Maybe by breakfast time the police will have handed it back to the owner. I don't want to stay longer than I can help, but I want to be certain that everything is all clear. Any questions before I go?"

"When will we know how things have gone off?" asked Clancy.

"Tomorrow night. I will come here at eight o'clock—just as I did tonight—and you must do exactly as you have done. All that I said about this visit will apply then. By the way, who is looking after the cellar?"

"I am," said Delaney. "Any instructions?"

"How is he?"

"None too good."

## MADDICK GIVES INSTRUCTIONS

"Give him a meal and a drink. We'll see him off tomorrow night. By the way, once more, I've got a companion for him. I told you on the phone, Borden, that I'd bring a friend of yours along with me. When I've gone, and you've heard the car pass down the drive, walk into the hall. You'll find your prisoner there. Put her down in the cellar with the other invalid. You can look after her, and see that Delaney doesn't get jealous! Goodnight to all of you. The best of luck tomorrow."

The door slammed, then they heard the outer door close. Immediately the car engine hummed, the gear was pushed into place, and they heard the crunch of gravel as the car started down the drive. A minute later, as the sound of the car dimmed until it hummed in the distance, Clancy walked over to the light switch. Everyone blinked as the lights glared.

Mick was white-faced. He feared the worst. Mariel laughed at him.

"You look like a corpse," she said.

"It's only excitement," he replied, struggling to appear casual. "I'll have a look at the present Maddick left for me."

Cardby walked into the hall and turned on the light.

Standing against the front door was Miss Mavis Gribble!

The girl was handcuffed on her right wrist, and the other cuff was fastened on the iron bar across the door. She wore a tweed coat and no hat. Her face was white, but the eyes were courageous, the manner firm.

# 18

## MICK BUSIES HIMSELF

The others crowded behind Cardby and stood in the doorway of the room. The girl stared at them unflinchingly. Mick was struggling to hide the flood of fears running through him.

"Good evening," he said, with a mock bow. "So we meet again, Miss Gribble?"

"Unfortunately, yes."

"Not a bad-looking kid," said Alibi, moving forward.

Mick placed a hand on the man's shoulder. His eyes narrowed.

"Hold your horses," he said softly. "This is my pigeon."

"Any harm in me having a look at her?" asked Deianey nastily.

"No, so long as you keep your distance. Have you seen enough?"

"Seems very fond of his lady friend," remarked Mariel, eyeing the girl critically. "Where'd you meet her, Pete?"

"At the Mead reception. She is Sergeant Gribble's daughter."

"Is that so? I could do her a lot of good."

"Why don't you start with yourself?" asked Mavis steadily.

"You'll have to knock some of the sauce out of her, Pete," said Kane. "They're always better when you've treated 'em rough for a while."

Cardby looked at the eager faces surrounding him and decided that a stand must be made. Things were looking ugly.

"Listen, you folks," he said. "Maddick promised me that he'd turn this girl over to me. He's kept his word. You all heard him say that I was in charge of her. That ought to end the matter for you. This is my business, and the first person who butts into it will get more than they want. Any of you feel like arguing about it?"

The three men and the woman looked at him intently, as though determining whether he was serious. But the set of his jaw, the hard light in his eyes convinced them. They stood back.

"Hell!" said Kane; "we don't want to stand here arguing about a bit of skirt. Let's get back into the warm."

He led the way, and the others followed him, Delaney turning at the door to have a last look. He winked at the girl and shut the door.

"The first thing to do," said Mick, "is to unfasten you from that door."

"That's easy. The key is against that door near your feet."

Mavis was strangely quiet while Mick unlocked the handcuffs. She rubbed the red weal on her wrist to restore the circulation. Mick was silent. A thousand ideas were running through his brain — each of them discarded as impracticable.

"Come with me," he said in an unnecessarily loud voice, "and don't try any monkey tricks or you'll be sorry."

The girl looked at him contemptuously and followed him into the back of the house. He took the flashlamp from the shelf and led the way into the cellar, Mavis shuddering as the first breath of dank air struck her nostrils. He unlocked the door of one of the empty rooms and stood on one side while she entered. The girl stifled her terror when she saw the green, damp, flagged floor, the lichen growing on the walls, the lack of ventilation, the absence of any seat. She turned to Mick.

"What exactly do you think you're going to gain by keeping me here?"

Cardby walked over to the door, looked along the passage and returned, turning the key in the door from the inside.

"Listen to me," he said softly. "I can't stay for more than a minute, so I'll explain to you later. I am with you. Do you understand? I am not one of Maddick's men. I am working for the Yard."

"That sounds very probable," said the girl scornfully. "Is that why you were at the Mead reception—helping to steal the necklace?"

Cardby gestured with impatience and touched the girl on the shoulder. She shrank away from him until her back touched the wall.

"For God's sake, listen," he pleaded, "and don't talk until I've done. I am with you, and I'll see that no harm comes to you. Young Caudry, of the Yard, is in the next cellar. I'm going to help him too. I can't do anything for either of you at the moment. You'll have to wait until later, when the others have bedded down for the night. Then I'll come along and tell you all about it. In the meantime, I'll see that no one else comes to you. I can't do more than that yet. I am going to lock the door from the outside, and I will carry the key in my pocket so that you will be left alone. Don't lose your nerve, Miss Gribble. Just bank on me, and I'll do the very best I can for you."

The girl stared at him. She didn't believe him. But there was an earnestness in his tone, a sincerity in his manner that puzzled her. In any case, she reflected, she could lose nothing by accepting any offer of help. Things could not be worse than they were.

"All right," she said, "I'll wait until you come down again. Then I will hear what you've got to say."

"Thank you, Miss Gribble. I won't let you down. Keep walking round this cellar. It's too damp to sit down in."

Cardby locked the door, pocketed the key and returned to the room upstairs. Mariel looked at him quizzically.

"And how is the little turtle dove?"

"Safely fastened away until Maddick decides what is to be done with her. Can't you folks think of something else for a change? I would have thought that your programme tomorrow would have given you enough to think about without troubling about this chit of a girl."

"What about yourself?" asked Delaney.

"My job doesn't need much thought. It's a sitter."

"Well," said Mariel, "whatever you folks are going to do I neither know nor care, but if I've got to start getting up at God knows what time in the morning I'm going to bed now. Happy dreams, everyone."

"I think I'll fade away too," said Clancy, and the two left the room together. Mick yawned and walked over to the box at the side of the fire. He threw two big logs on to the blaze and settled down in an easy chair.

"I'll kip here. Nothing like an odd spot of fire."

"What are you going to do?" asked Delaney. His voice was menacing.

"I'm going to have a drink and a rest for a while. Then I'm going down to the cellar to see that everything's all right. What are you going to do, Alibi?"

"I was thinking of doing whatever you do."

"Then you've got another think coming to you, I aim to be by myself tonight, and since my nerves are a bit jumpy, and my temper isn't in the best of condition it's going to be dangerous to follow me round."

"Suppose I don't trust you alone in that cellar?"

"Then the obvious thing for you to do is to telephone Maddick and tell him why you don't trust me, why I shouldn't be in charge of that girl, why I shouldn't take part in the job tomorrow, and why I should be under lock and key with the other two. Go on, grab the phone and make yourself busy. I'm not stopping you—I'm inviting you."

Delaney thought matters over for a minute. He knew he was beaten. But he surrendered with ill grace.

"Have it your own way," he said, "but if you pull any slick stuff I'll bore a hole through you."

"If you get the chance. What are you going to do about that feed for your man in the cellar? Have you forgotten what Maddick said?"

"Damn the man in the cellar. Since he's going to be bumped off in a few hours what's the good of giving him good grub and drink?"

"Don't trouble yourself. I'll do it for you. I'd rather go to that trouble than have Maddick learn that it hasn't been done."

"Please yourself. If you're mug enough to do it—carry on."

Mick turned his back on Delaney and poured out a drink of whisky and a glass of beer. The former he gave to Alibi, the latter he took himself. When he had drained the glass, he walked into the other room and cut some ham sandwiches, returning again to take an empty glass. This, without showing Alibi, he filled to the top with spirit.

"I'll pop down now and see how they're going on," he said. "See you soon. I'll give your love to the man below."

Delaney nodded drowsily and placed a cushion under his head. When Mick left the room he had settled down to sleep.

There was no sound in the house as the youngster made his way to the head of the cellar steps, took the torch and descended. First he went to Caudry's cell. The man was still huddled on the floor, apparently asleep. Mick shook his shoulder.

"Pull yourself together," he said. "I've come back as I told you I would. Hold your head up and sip some of this whisky. It should do you a bit of good. Carry on, I'll hold the glass. Don't take too much, since you've had nothing to eat for a while. That's better. Now try one of these ham sandwiches, but only have one. Your stomach's bound to be weak. When you've finished that you can have another drink of Scotch and another sandwich, but take your time with the food. If you eat it quickly you'll get most damnable indigestion."

Caudry raised himself sufficiently to drink some of the whisky. Then he held the sandwich in his manacled hands and commenced to eat.

"I'll be back with you in a minute," said Mick. "I've left another sandwich at the side of you."

He walked out of the cellar and passed to the one next door, took the key out of his pocket and opened the door. The girl was standing against the wall in the far corner.

"Here I am," said Mick, trying to speak lightly. "I thought you might be hungry by now, so I brought something for you to eat. Before you have it, take a drink of this whisky. Don't say ' No.' I'm only giving it to you because it's so cold down here, and this spirit should thaw you a bit."

Mavis looked at the glass and shook her head.

"Think it's drugged?" asked Mick. "I'll show you that it isn't by taking some myself." He swallowed a mouthful and shuddered, pulling a wry face. "Ugh! I forgot it was neat. Never mind, it will do you good. Try it."

She took one small sip, then another.

"Certainly is warming," she said. Her active brain was trying to fashion pattern out of chaos. Could she believe this man?

"I think you'd better get one of these sandwiches now, miss."

She took one and commenced to eat ravenously.

"You," he said, "are Miss Gribble. Tell me, is that really true?"

"Of course it is. We're not all liars."

"Have you ever heard of Chief Detective-Inspector Cardby?"

"Naturally. I've heard daddy mention him very, very often."

"Have you ever heard whether Cardby has any children?"

"Yes, he has a son."

"That, Miss Gribble, is me !"

"And that," retorted the girl emphatically, "I do not believe."

"I know it sounds impossible," said Mick, "but I think I can convince you. It will take me a few minutes, but since I can't help you unless you trust me, you'll have to believe me."

He told the girl of his work during the past days, detailed everything, spoke of his father and of the work at Scotland Yard, told her why she was sent to the Mead reception, and how he told his father of the planned robbery. At last he finished and asked appealingly:

"Surely you believe me now?"

"It doesn't sound like the sort of tale one would make up," said Mavis reluctantly. "Have you ever met my father?"

"Yes, once at the Metropolitan Police Sports— three years ago. That was only about three months after he'd been promoted."

"That's true enough. Could you describe him to me."

The girl nodded as she heard the description.

"All right," she said. "I believe you. What are you going to do?"

"You are the one who can finish all this business, Miss Gribble. In the morning, early, we are all leaving this house to do a job in the West End. You and Caudry will have the place to yourselves. I've thought out a simple way of catching all of them—Maddick included. When I leave you in a few minutes I'm going to leave this key with you, and you must lock the door from the inside. Have you got a wrist watch?"

"Yes."

"Good. Don't do anything until seven o'clock tomorrow morning. Then telephone my father. Tell him, first of all, that a robbery is to take place in Pall Mall just after eight, and then under no circumstance must the thieves be arrested. Tell him to pass the word round to the Flying Squad that any furniture van seen proceeding along St. James Street, Piccadilly Circus, Shaftesbury Avenue, Bloomsbury Street, Gower Street and Euston way must be allowed to pass and must not, upon any consideration, be followed. Is that all plain?"

"Yes, I can remember that."

"Good. Then tell him that if he has time he should convey the same message to the policemen on duty on that route. The van must not be stopped and no arrests must be made. That is the most important item. Now we come to what should be the finish of everything. This house is 'Withies' and it's just outside High Ongar. The house stands back from the road. I want at least twenty Yard men here at eight o'clock tomorrow night. Two of them can hide behind the hedge facing the main gate. Four of them can get behind the bushes along the drive. Two more can watch the sides of the house, and two will be wanted at the back. There is a wood at the back of the house that will need four men to look after it.

"Above all, these men must get into position so that they are neither seen nor suspected. At eight o'clock a car will drive to the front door of the house. In that car will be Maddick. As soon as he gets inside the house, I want my father, your father and three or four men to rush the house. All the folks inside will be armed, and tell them to take the woman's handbag away from her instantly. If you can give those instructions in detail and get my father to understand them all, we'll wipe up the whole of this crowd. Is everything clear?"

"Yes, I think so. Anything else?"

"Three further things. They must arrange for some heavy car to come along the road at three or four minutes past eight. That car must be placed to block the entrance to the drive. There is only one gateway. The other thing is that since the house will be in complete darkness, they will want to bring powerful lamps, and, lastly, if you hear two quick knocks on this door, you'll know it's me. Open the door instantly and give me the key. If they knew that you had the key it would be the end for all of us. By the way, before I forget, the telephone is in the last room on the left in the hall."

"Suppose there is someone in the house?"

"Have you ever used a gun?"

"No, never in my life."

"Well, here's one, and I hope you won't have to use it. Just lift this safety catch here and pull the trigger. The gun will do the rest."

"Do you mean that I would have to shoot them?"

"Surely. But be sure to drag the body somewhere where it wouldn't be found when we come back."

"But you'll want this gun yourself, won't you?"

"No, thanks. There isn't any sense in carrying only one gun when you're expecting that every minute it'll be taken from you. Just one other thing. Caudry is in the next cell. When the coast is clear you'll find a file on the top of the gas stove in the kitchen. Go into his place and file those manacles off him. I'll handcuff you now to this ring on the wall. Here's the key. Keep it in your pocket so that you can unlock yourself. For the love of God don't make any mistakes or we'll all be dead before the night is out. Good luck, Miss Gribble, and may all go well."

"I'll do my very best," replied the girl. Mick left her.

# 19

## THE PALL MALL HOLD-UP

Cardby gave the other prisoner another drink of whisky and a couple of sandwiches, told him what was going to happen and walked upstairs.

There he settled down to a fitful sleep, and when he woke the grey shreds of dawn light were showing through the window. The grass was heavy with dew and a sullen sky looked full of rain. Mick had grown cold, and he paced the room, swinging his arms. This woke both Kane and Alibi, and they cursed him as they rubbed their eyes. The fire had gone out.

"What time is it?" asked Kane. Mick looked at his watch.

"Twenty-five past five. You've got just over half an hour. Better run upstairs and wake the others."

The safe-breaker strolled out of the room, and Delaney followed him. Cardby washed in the kitchen, drying himself, in the absence of a towel, on his handkerchief. When he returned to the room Mariel and Clancy were there. They took breakfast together.

"How're your prisoners?" inquired the woman.

"Haven't seen 'em for about five hours, but the last time I peeped at 'em they were all right. Everybody feeling fit for the job?"

"I'm not," said Kane. "My head aches, I've got cramp, my nerves are all on edge and I'm cold."

"Have a spot of whisky in your tea," said Clancy. "That's what I'm going to do. Pass the bottle, Alibi."

"Looks as though we'd better get some refills," said Mick as he emptied the last drop from the bottle into his cup. "I don't fancy sitting here for hours later in the day without a drink."

"I wonder who'll be back first," remarked Kane.

"Alibi and I," said Clancy. "Our job finishes first."

At exactly six o'clock a car zoomed along the drive and stopped outside the front door. Taxi Long was driving. Two minutes later the car backed on the drive and turned towards the gates. In the back were Clancy, Delaney and Kane.

"That's the start of that," said Mariel, watching the back of the car through the window. "Tell me, Pete, if everything pans out right today, are you going to leave the racket for good?"

"It's hard to say. I haven't found out yet whether I've got it in my blood or not. I sometimes think that a quiet little flat and an innocent round of amusement might be better than sitting back for the rest of my life waiting for the cops to come. What do you say, Mariel?"

"I couldn't give it up now, whatever I was worth. I couldn't get a thrill out of living honestly. I suppose I'm what the judges call a confirmed criminal. Still, it's a merry life while it lasts."

"That's true. But the luck won't hold out for ever."

"When my luck stops I'll stop."

"You're too fond of life, my girl, to take your own away."

"Am I? You show me the prospect of doing a stretch and see whether I'll live to do it. No, Pete, life is only good while you get what you can out of it. But when it turns sour in the mouth, like Dead Sea fruit, it's better to say 'goodbye to all that,' and stage a fade-out."

"You're not exactly cheering me up this morning, Mariel."

"Sorry. I've got the horrors, I think. I feel trouble in my bones. They must have dipped me in witches' water when I was a kid. I get all sorts of hunches, and they usually play out right. I've got one now. There's trouble coming along in large quantities, and it won't be long before it arrives. You watch your step, Pete, and remember what I say."

"Cheer up, Mariel." Mick felt some tinge of sorrow for the girl. "Don't forget you've got your husband to live for."

She laughed mirthlessly and stared at her polished nails.

"He's something to live for, believe me. If he saw me dying under the wheels of a bus his only thought would be that he might not easily find another woman who'd fit in so well with his scheme of things."

"We'll stop this talk before we both start crying. Run along up to your room and get your coat and hat while I give those folks in the cellar another look to make sure that everything is all right."

Cardby ran down the steps and knocked twice at Miss Gribble's door. He waited for a time until she unfastened the cuff and came across the floor. As she opened the door, she slid the key into his hand.

"All right," he said, "I just popped down to tell you that in ten minutes the coast will be clear and you can get on with the job. Come straight back here as soon as you have finished and unfasten Caudry."

He slipped into the other room to give the man a last reassuring pat on the back. When he reached the hall Mariel was waiting for him, her hat and coat on.

Mick opened the front door. The air was bitterly cold and rain had begun to fall.

"Stand here for a moment in the dry while I get the car out of the garage. I say, though, have you got the front door key?"

"No, one of the others must have taken it."

"Let's hope they get back before we do."

Cardby manœuvred the big car out of the garage. He still wore the chauffeur's clothes from the day before. It was easy for Maddick to give his instructions. But how was he to get some old clothes at this time in the morning? The engine was cold, and Mick opened the choke. The woman stepped into the back of the car.

"If we get stopped," said Mick, "you are Mrs Rodney Mawley, and I am Simms, your chauffeur. Everything O.K.?"

The woman nodded and pulled a fur rug over her legs. Mick eased the clutch and the great limousine moved forward down the drive. A nearby clock struck the half-hour. The road was deserted. The youngster returned to the driving seat after closing the gate to the drive behind him. Then the car quickly gathered speed, and by the time they had left High Ongar behind the powerful engine was purring smoothly. At Seven Sisters Station Mick swung left-handed, and he drove steadily until he saw Finsbury Park on his right. He turned again to drop through Highbury and Islington, past the Angel Station and so through to Holborn.

Then he coasted along slowly. It was twenty-five to eight. He dropped Mariel at the corner of Shaftesbury Avenue, raised his cap obsequiously, and drove down into Trafalgar Square. There he left the car in front of the National Gallery and strolled over to the coffee stall on the far corner of the square. At ten minutes to eight, having eaten two "hot dogs" and drunk a cup of coffee, he sauntered along towards Pall Mall. He was fifty or sixty yards away from the entrance to St. James Square when he saw the grey two-seater pulled up at the curb. Delaney and Clancy were already in position.

Mick paced the pavement aimlessly. But the look of unconcern on his face was not representing the state of his mind. Now that the chase was nearing a close the strain and stress of the previous days was beginning to tell on him. He felt drawn and tired. Question after question filed through his

# THE PALL MALL HOLD-UP

head—without finding answers. Had Miss Gribble telephoned to his father? Had she given the message correctly? Would his father have had time to warn the Flying Squad and the police? Would Maddick make any last-minute change in the plans? Was Caudry free by now? What would happen at eight o'clock? Suppose there was someone in the house when he left!

The streets were not crowded. The rush had ceased. Those who were due at business at eight had arrived. Those—and they represented nine out of every ten—who were not due until nine had not started. The time could not have suited Maddick better. Big Ben boomed out eight times. Now things were due to happen at any moment. Mick crossed to the right-hand side of the Mall. He assumed that the van would be on the turn before it stopped. Then he felt shivers run down his spine as another thought flashed across his mind. Suppose the driver lost consciousness so quickly that he had not time to stop the van! Suppose the van careered into a shop front or a wall and was put out of action! That would finish everything. All the good work would be undone. Mick would have to start his troubles all over again.

He looked towards Trafalgar Square and saw a van coming towards him. This was it! There could be no doubt about it. A uniformed policeman sat at the side of the driver. Mick stuck his hands in his pockets and waited. From out of the corner of his eye he could see Clancy levering the gun from underneath the dashboard. When the van was twenty yards away the muzzle of the gun protruded an inch through the lowered window. Clancy was taking aim.

Plop!

Mick heard the dull explosion, heard the smack as something hit the van. Then the van wheeled towards the pavement and the driver dropped over the wheel. The engine was dying away as the man's foot came off the accelerator, but only twelve feet separated the bonnet from a lamp-post. The policeman had sunk in his seat. Clancy and Delaney were already out of their car, dashing across the street.

Cardby leapt for the running-board, pushed the driver away from the wheel and tugged at the handbrake. The van stopped with a jerk, the engine spluttered and died. Two cars came round the corner from St. James Street, but the drivers had not seen them. All they saw was a van on one side of the road, a car on the other, two men walking across the street, and another man standing on the footboard, talking to the driver of the van. So they went past.

The policeman was hurriedly dragged to the car, and before the driver had been lifted out, Mick had the engine going again. Delaney had not reached the car when the van pulled away. Behind him Mick heard a shout. He pressed his foot on the pedal and kept straight on. Swerving into Cleveland Row, he saw the furniture van in front of him. The doors yawned open, and there were two twenty-foot planks on each side, leading from the road into the van. Behind him Mick heard the imprisoned policemen thundering on the cover of the van. He changed down to first gear and prodded the accelerator. The engine roared, lurched forward, the wheels gripped the planks. Mick waited until his front wheels were on the lip of the pantechnicon. Then he slammed down his clutch and applied the hand-brake. The van came to a standstill with the bonnet about a foot away from the front of the van. Instantly all was dark.

The clamour of the policemen became more and more noticeable. Mick felt the van lurch as he dropped down from the driving seat. They were on their way—where to, he did not know.

"Mariel," he called softly, "are you there?"

"Here," came the reply, and the girl turned on a torch.

She stood near the doors at the back of the van. At his feet was a cylinder, equipped with a valve and a piece of steel-ribboned tubing. He heard the crash of gears as the engine was put into reverse. Then the van started forward again. The policemen continued to shout. To add to the din, Cardby heard the muffled peal of a bell, jangling without a stop. The noise drew nearer, passed them, and ebbed away. Kane was doing his stuff!

"Let's quieten these swine," said the girl, seizing the cylinder. "Get hold of this torch while I see how we can fit the tube in the lock."

"Wait one second," said Mick. "You hold this torch while I do the job."

"Not likely. Maddick told me to do it."

"You told me, Mariel, that you had studied poisons. Do you know anything at all about arseniuretted hydrogen?"

Before the girl could answer the van stopped, and the two stood breathless, fearing every moment that the doors of the van would be flung open. It seemed to them that those in the roadway must hear the shouts of the imprisoned constables. But nothing happened. The van rumbled on its way.

"Hold that light while I do the job," insisted the girl.

"You haven't answered my question. Do you know anything about this gas? Have you ever used it before?"

"No, but I'll soon find out something about it."

"That's where you're wrong, my girl. You won't."

"And why not?"

"Because I won't let you. Give me that cylinder."

"I'm going to turn the juice on those two flat-feet."

"Talk sense, Mariel. This morning you were saying that you'd never live to take a lagging. If you turn that gas on you won't get a lagging. They'll wake you up early one morning and the chaplain will ask you if you've got anything to say before you pass away. Then you'll take a short walk and that'll be the end of you. It can't be very pretty to swing on a rope, can it?"

"But I'm only going to put 'em out for a while."

"Don't you believe it. If you haven't handled that stuff before you'll kill them as dead as doornails. I don't know much about poisons, but I can tell you something about this one. Even when it's diluted down to 0.02 p.c. this stuff is deadly. Hand me that cylinder. I'm not tender-hearted, but I think too much of my skin to start committing murders."

Again the van stopped and they waited apprehensively. It moved on.

"I'll give them one whiff," said Mick. "Hold that light."

Mariel gave up the argument and held the torch. Cardby peered into the keyhole. There was no key in the lock. The driver or the policeman on the front of the van must have locked the door from the outside and placed the key in his pocket. He inserted the mouth of the tubing and gave the wheel a half-turn. The men continued to bellow and beat the sides of the van with their fists. He turned the wheel a little more. The cries died away. Then there was silence.

Mick placed the cylinder on the floor and stuffed his handkerchief into the keyhole.

"We don't want that stuff to seep back to us," he explained. Adding, "God! I hope I haven't given 'em too much. . . We ought to be in Gower Street by now. I wonder where the hell they're taking us to?"

"I neither know nor care. Let's sit down on these sacks in the corner and make ourselves a bit comfortable."

Mick produced his cigarettes and they smoked in silence. Later he turned the torch on the face of his watch.

"Half-past eight," he said. "Let's see if we can work things out a bit. This van started on the road at about seven minutes past the hour and it has stopped four times. Reckoning each stop at two minutes we've been on the road for a quarter of an hour. That should place us between two and three miles away from

Pall Mall. If he has headed Euston way, he should be on the other side of Euston Road... Who is driving?"

"Don't know. I didn't look. I simply climbed into the van without seeing anyone, and the next thing I knew was that you arrived."

The van stopped twice again, obviously in traffic, but each time it moved on. Mick was beginning to feel more comfortable. Now it did seem that Miss Gribble had got through to his father. He prayed that all the remaining events of the day would pass off also without hitch. But he didn't persuade himself that they would. It seemed certain that before the day was out blood would be shed—and he felt reasonably sure that some of his own would be among it.

Mariel snuggled against him and held his arm. He felt uncomfortable. Of course, he was doing what was right. That much he knew. But that didn't alter the fact that he was a betrayer. It wasn't even as though he held a proper place in the Force. That would alter his feelings a bit. As he smoked he wondered what would happen to the woman at his side. She was too much of an orchid to last in gaol. He couldn't imagine her spending years among coarse companions, attired in the rough garments of a woman convict.

There came no sound from the inside of the smaller van. The gas had done its work. Mick only hoped that it hadn't done its work too effectively. He had incurred sufficiently into crime without adding murder to the list. He turned the light on his watch again. It was ten minutes to nine. Outside the van he could hear the thunder of traffic.

"How much farther are we going?" he asked.

"God knows," said the woman. "I could sleep. The jolting of this van is making me tired."

"Then go to sleep. There's nothing to stop you."

Her head sank against his arm, and within a few minutes he heard her gentle breathing. She was asleep. Mick slipped his hand into his coat pocket and patted the automatic. Then he let his head slide against the doors of the van and shut his eyes.

It was five minutes past nine when the van stopped. Cardby opened his eyes and heard the voices outside the doors of the van. He shook his companion and drew her to her feet. With one arm round her and the other hand in his right pocket, he stood waiting for the doors to open.

The iron bar across the doors fell with a slam, and Mick put his foot into the near-side door. It swung open, and his eyes blinked as they met the light. The van was backed against a door set in the wall of a high building. The base of the door was level with the floor of the van—about four feet above the ground. A flap had been let down from the door, and three men stood staring inside the van. Mick had not met any of them before. All wore white aprons and were middle-aged.

"Everything all right?" asked one of them.

"Yes," replied Mick, stepping on to the flap. He looked round him. They were in a narrow yard with a towering warehouse on either side. He heard a voice from the side of the van, and the driver appeared round the corner. Mick looked at him curiously, certain that he had met the man before. He gasped when he identified him. For the driver, with his dirty cap pulled over one ear, his greasy coat, shiny trousers and general appearance of slovenliness, was the immaculate Mr Clason of Crosby House!

He grinned at Mick and the girl.

"Enjoy your ride?" he asked. "How are the policemen."

"We enjoyed the ride," said Mick; "but I don't think they know whether they've enjoyed it or not. They don't know a lot about it."

"Good... We'll have to hurry now and get this stuff unloaded. Open the back of the van and we'll make a start."

"I can't. The door's locked and there's no key."

"We can soon fix that. What's the door made of—wood or metal?"

"Metal. Feels to me like steel."

"George," said Clason to one of the aproned Workmen, "bring me one of the small acetylene blowers."

The command started Mick on another train of thought. That was a strange request to make. Was this the headquarter store of the Maddick ging? But however unusual the request might have been the blower was soon found and Clason climbed into the van. A minute later there was a roar and the tongue of blue flame shot out and licked round the lock. The steel was thin and the acetylene gas cut through it like a knife cutting through a piece of cheese. When the lock had been cut out Mick placed a piece of sacking round his hand, grabbed the opening, and pulled the doors open. Only the front of the van was stacked with goods— hundreds of small leather cases and wooden boxes. Near the doors lay the two policemen, inert.

"Move the cops," said Clason, "then we can get at the stuff."

As Cardby seized the first man by the wrist to take him on his shoulder he felt the pulse and sighed with relief. The beat was faint but discernible.

"Wait a minute," said Clason, "there's no need to have them inside. Joe, come over here and take these cops into your van."

By the side of the pantechnicon stood a ten-hundredweight van, and a man came out from the driving seat and took the unconscious policeman as Mick lowered him. Then the second policeman was passed to the smaller van. He, too, was alive, Mick noted with satisfaction.

"All clear, Joe," said Clason. "Take 'em anywhere you like where it's lonely and dump 'em at the roadside. Go ahead."

The work of unloading the van did not take more than ten minutes. Clason sighed with satisfaction when the last armful of packages was taken into the warehouse. Mick and Mariel stood in the furniture van, awaiting further instructions.

"There's nothing else for you two to do now," said Clason. "I'll look after these two vans. The best thing you can do is to make your way back to the 'Withies' as quietly as you can. I'll be seeing you tonight."

"Are you coming down then?" inquired Mariel.

"Yes, we're coming down together." He did not mention whom he meant by "we." They all knew.

"Before we go," said Mick, "you might tell us where we are."

"That's easy enough. When you come to the end of the yard turn to the left and take the second on the right, and first on the left. Then you're in City Road. You can find your own way from there."

So the van had not passed behind Euston after all! It was just another deception on Maddick's part. Mick waved his hand to them all and helped the woman to the ground. They walked along the rough cobbles to the entrance. As they passed under the arch at the end of the passage Mick noticed the enamel plate on the wall bearing the name Tilson's Yard.

"How shall we get back?" he asked.

"Let's have some decent grub somewhere before we go. I'm hungry."

"That'll suit me. Could you amuse yourself for half an hour while I call at New Street and collect a suit? I don't intend to walk around all day looking like a chauffeur."

"I'll take a cab to my place and meet you at half-past eleven outside the front entrance to the Criterion Theatre."

"Splendid. Hi!" Mick caught the eye of a roaming taxi-man, told him to drive to Haymarket, and they both climbed in. It was five minutes past ten. As they entered the West End they saw the screaming placards:

"MILLION POUND JEWEL ROBBERY."
"AMAZING DAYLIGHT HOLD-UP."
"DAYLIGHT BANDITS STEAL MILLION
POUND JEWELS."

Mariel pointed to them and smiled.

"Don't you feel important, Pete? You're getting as much publicity as an aspiring débutante."

"I'd rather have more of the money and less of the publicity."

"Where are you going to take me to lunch?"

"Oh, we'll find some quiet spot. Seeing that the police may still remember my face I don't aim to sit in any crowded restaurant."

"I wonder what happened to Tommy Kane?"

"He'll be heading back for the 'Withies' by now— so will the others."

Mick did not add that he would like to have been back there himself. It was not a comforting thought to think that the three men were there with Mavis Gribble.

# 20

# THE YARD MAKES ARRANGEMENTS

"You really think," asked Sir Wynnard, "that the whole of this message you received is genuine?"

Cardby rapped his knuckles on the table. Even his large stock of patience was petering out.

"Of course it is. You don't suppose the girl would telephone me for fun, do you? You don't think she'd vanish and leave her mother and father half-frantic with worry in order to pass along false information, do you?"

"Now, now, Cardby. This is no time for arguments."

"I know that all right."

"What we want to know is what you suggest doing."

"The first thing I did was to tell Hall that the robbery should not be interfered with. He looked after that part of it, and his men saw that the way was made clear for the furniture van."

"Surely that was taking an enormous risk?"

"My point of view is simple. We here know nothing about what is going on. My son knows everything about it. His instruction on that point was very emphatic, and there must have been a good reason for his message. I think we can assume that he knows where the jewels are, and he is certain that they can be recovered. The Chief Constable and I have had a long talk this morning about the remainder of the message, and we have decided to go beyond the instructions. If this job is to be done at all it must be done thoroughly. We've waited for this chance for more than a year, and we may never have such an opportunity again."

"You'd better tell me what you intend doing."

"I'll tell you—if the others don't mind me speaking for them—what each of us will do. In the first place, before I start, you'll be glad to hear that we've got a plan of the 'Withies,' showing the house and grounds in detail, from the London agents who handled the property when it was to let. The present occupier took the place under the name of Gurlie Mather, and said he was a retired tea planter. We've worked out all the arrangements with the plan before us.

"Inspector Hall will take two cars, with eight men, arriving in Epping at eight o'clock. He will proceed from there to the ' Withies.' He will take one of the cars along the drive to the house. The other will be left to patrol the stretch of road in front of the house. Hall will adopt his own course when he arrives at the door—depending entirely upon the circumstances existing when he arrives. That ends his job.

"Inspector Finch, of the squad, will patrol the road leading from Brentford to Chelmsford, commencing at quarter to eight and finishing at nine o'clock. That will prevent any getaway on that stretch.

"Murphy will take another car and, for the same space of time as Finch, will patrol the road—it covers two and a half miles—from Writtle to Chelmsford. That will block every exit from the house by road.

"Inspector Reeves will take four men, all coming from different directions, and walk to the house, arriving in the grounds at about ten minutes to eight. They will hide themselves behind the trees and bushes on the front lawn, and in the gardens, and hold themselves ready to help in any emergency that might arise. Their biggest job will be to get into the grounds, one by one, without arousing any suspicion.

"Chief Constable Cross is taking charge of the back of the house. He has himself picked six men to patrol the wood at the end of the paddock, and he will have with him another four men. I am setting my watch with the chief's, and at exactly four minutes after eight o'clock he will gain entrance to the house through the back.

"On either side of the house are fields. Sergeant Miller is taking two men to guard the one field, and Sergeant Poison is doing the same in the other field. So that the house will be entirely cut off on all sides, and the roads will be adequately guarded.

"That only leaves my part of the job. I leave Epping at five minutes to eight, planning to arrive at the house three or four minutes after the hour. With me will be Sergeant Gribble, Sergeant Main, and Constables Wilbur and Perry. We will drive straight to the house, gain entrance, and, if all goes well, make the arrests. That just about completes the programme."

"Don't you think the chief should go with you instead of making his own way in from the back of the house?"

"No, Sir Wynnard," said Cross. "Cardby explained his position to me, and I agree with him entirely. He says, and it is true, that the two people facing more danger than anyone else are his son and Gribble's daughter. That being so he thinks it only right that he and Gribble should be the first people in the house. After all, they have got more than the mere arrests to think about."

"Yes, I can see that, Cross. Very well. I think the arrangements are most adequate. Let us hope that everything goes off as it has been planned. If you want any more assistance you've only got to let me know, and I'll do whatever I can for you."

"That's all there is to be said, so we'll adjourn," said Cardby.

# THE YARD MAKES ARRANGEMENTS

"Just one thing," said Sir Wynnard. "Please telephone me at my private house immediately you have completed the work."

"I will," said Cross, and the men left the room together.

Gribble was waiting in Cardby's room to hear the story. The sergeant, always pale and worried, was now restless and nervy. There were heavy lines on his forehead, and the blue patches under his eyes showed a sleepless night.

"All set," said Cardby, touching Gribble's shoulder. The two men, whose constant arguments were regarded by the Yard as a prize joke, looked at each other with understanding. This was not the first tight corner they had faced without a tremor, but for the first time in their careers they were fighting for something more than law and order.

"Come and have a drink, Gribble, and cheer yourself up a bit. Everything is going to be all right. By this time tomorrow you'll have Mavis back with you, and Mick will be with me, and Maddick will be where he ought to have been a year ago."

"I hope to God you're a true prophet."

"We'll only have ourselves to blame if anything happens to either of them. They've done all they can, and it's up to us to show the kids that even the old 'uns can do a bit occasionally."

They walked out into Whitehall and turned towards the Strand.

"If anything happens to either of those kids," said Gribble, "you'll never put Maddick into the dock."

"Why not, my lad?"

"Because I'll put him into the mortuary. I'll shoot hell out of him."

Cardby slapped him gently on the back.

"No, you won't," he said softly, "because I'll be the first to find out whether the kids are all right or not, and I'll be carrying a gun tonight."

In the public house they raised their glasses.

"Damnation to Maddick," said Cardby. They both drank.

# 21

## MADDICK ARRIVES!

It was six o'clock when Mick and Mariel boarded the bus in Epping and started on the road to the "Withies." They had lunched and visited a cinema. Throughout the afternoon Cardby had been worried, more worried than he had ever been in his life, but he had to remain with the woman, had to show that on his part there was no eagerness to return.

They walked up the drive through a fine drizzle of rain. A light showed in the window at the right of the front door.

"Better scout round before we knock," said Mick, "just in case anything is wrong. I think I could see through the edge of that blind. Come off the gravel on to the grass."

At the turn in the drive the youngster walked over the flower bed beneath the window and peered through the space at the edge of the blind. Clancy, Kane and Delaney were sitting at the table. They were playing cards, and at the side of each of them was a pile of silver. Mick walked on and knocked at the door. After an interval of waiting Kane slid back the bolt and turned the key.

"All O.K.?" he inquired.

"Absolutely. How did you lot go on?"

"Like taking eggs from a blind woman. Never had an easier job in my life. Seen the scream in the papers?"

"Yes, I read two of them coming down in the train."

"That business of the squad car seems to have beaten them properly. When it comes to bright ideas Maddick certainly does take the palm. We lads are just having a game of cards. Like to make a fourth?"

"In a minute. Before I do anything else I want to have a look in the cellar and make sure that all is as it should be. See you in a minute."

"Hey, you," shouted Delaney from the inner room, "what was the big idea of walking out with that key in your pocket?"

Mick walked into the room and stood, with his hands on his hips, eyeing the other man. For a few seconds his eyes were fixed in their stare and he made no attempt to speak. Finally, when he spoke, the tone was clipped.

"I took that key," he said slowly, "because I thought it would save you a damn good thrashing by stopping you getting into that cellar. I knew a low skunk like you, Delaney, would try to do behind my back what you wouldn't do when I was here. Now you know why I took the key."

Delaney went white, and his fists clenched until the knuckles showed white against the red skin. Kane touched Mick on the shoulder.

"Don't start any more rows, big boy. After tonight we won't be seeing each other any more, so we may as well end up peaceable."

"You're talking sense, Tommy," said Cardby. "I'll have that game of cards with you in a couple of minutes."

Mick slipped across the hall and cut some ham and bread. Then he hurriedly descended to the cellar. Two taps brought Miss Gribble to the door. He took the key in his hand and handed her the food.

"Everything go off all right?" he asked.

"Yes, I telephoned your father, told him all you said and filed the shackles off Caudry. I got him another drink and something to eat, and he's walked some of the stiffness off. You'll find him a lot better now."

"How do you feel yourself?"

"As though I could do with some air—otherwise all right."

"Good. I won't stay with you now. In two hours' time your troubles should be over. I'll pop in and have a look at Caudry."

The young detective had certainly improved. He was standing, although shaky, against the wall. He even attempted a smile when he saw Mick.

"Don't stand there," said Cardby hurriedly. "If anyone came in quickly it'd give the whole game away. Get down on the floor whether you like it or not, and lie as though you are still manacled. We can't afford to take any risks now. Got anything in the way of a weapon?"

"Yes, the girl gave me a hammer, but I couldn't hit very hard with it. I feel as though I've got no strength in my arm."

"Never mind. Stay quiet until eight o'clock— you'll hear plenty of noise then. Until then, lie down. Here's a bit of grub for you. Stay quiet."

Mick walked upstairs again and joined the others. They were playing pontoon, and he took his seat at the table without any great enthusiasm. What little interest he had in the game vanished when he found that both Kane and Delaney were cheating shamelessly. He lost three or four pounds and then threw his hand in.

"I've had enough of it," he said. "You three carry on by yourselves."

But as he rose from the table the game was suddenly interrupted by the jingling of the telephone bell. Clancy answered the call. The person at the other end was in a hurry, for within a minute Clancy replaced the receiver.

"Just a little change in the proceedings," he said. "That was Maddick on the telephone. He's coming at quarter-past seven instead of eight o'clock."

Mick turned to the sideboard to hide the sudden pallor that crept into his cheeks. His hand shook as he poured out a drink of whisky. God! Now everything was wrong; Maddick would go on and on. All the risk, all the work had been for nothing. By half-past seven the man would have been and gone. And half an hour later the police would arrive to find an empty house — empty except for two bodies — the corpses of Mavis Gribble and young Caudry. He swallowed the drink and glanced casually at the clock. It was five minutes to seven — too late to do anything.

By now all the forces from the Yard would be on their way. It was impossible to get in touch with them. This was the end of everything. Maddick was bringing Clason with him. That would make six of them. Too big a handful for one man!

He had to do something — and quickly. But what? His brain was seething. He could think of no way out. The finger on the bronze clock moved round to three minutes after the hour. Mick sat on the edge of the table and hummed. There were twelve minutes left. What could one do in twelve minutes?

Still whistling, he walked out of the room and ran down to the cellar, opening the door to the girl's prison.

"Listen," he said, clutching her by the arm. "Maddick is coming at quarter-past seven instead of eight o'clock. Something has got to be done quickly. Give me that gun and lock yourself in from the inside. Here's the key. Just sit tight and refuse to open the door to anyone unless you are sure it's me."

The girl handed over the gun and grasped the key without speaking. Cardby dashed into the next-door cellar.

"Caudry, do you feel well enough to take part in a scrap?"

"I'm as weak as a kitten."

"Are you strong enough to fire a gun?"

"Sure. I could do that."

"Then grab this one. I'm going to let you out of here. As soon as you get into the kitchen make your way through the back door, round the side of the house and through to the front drive. But, for God's sake, keep under cover all the way. Hide somewhere behind a pillar or a bush when Maddick's car comes up the drive. He's due here in five minutes now. Let him go into the house, but don't let him come out. Do you follow? Your job is to stop him driving away in his car. I don't care if you have to shoot him to stop him—Maddick has *not* got to leave this place. If he leaves the car with no one in it try and put it out of action. Do your damnedest, Caudry. Come along."

The way was clear when they reached the top steps, and Mick waited until Caudry shut the back door behind him. Then, resuming his flippant whistle, he strolled along the hall and walked into the room.

"This is a hell of a place," he said, when he noticed them staring at him. "I've been all over the house looking for something better than ham and dry bread and can't find any grub at all. Are you folks bedding down for a long fast?"

"But you had some grub in town," said Mariel.

"I know all about that. It so happens that that was six hours ago, and my stomach reads the riot act every three hours. Isn't there anything to eat in the place?"

"Don't bother about that now," said Clancy. "The boss will be here in a minute, and you'll have to be in this room when he arrives. Stop your moaning and have a bit of patience. You're no worse off than the rest of us. Look at the time, and you talking about food."

It was thirteen minutes after seven!

"Pour me out a drink, Pete," said Kane. "I can do with one."

Pete was dashing soda into the glass when he suddenly stopped. His keen ears had caught the sound of wheels crunching on the drive. A second later the sound was heard by everyone in the room. Cardby handed the drink to Kane before Clancy switched off the light. As soon as the room was dark he moved nearer to the door, leaning on the edge of the sideboard seven or eight feet away from the place where he expected Maddick to stand. He had only one remaining chance. Whatever the risk might be Maddick must be delayed. He must not leave the house until the police arrived. That meant detaining him for three-quarters of an hour. Mick did not fancy the prospect.

He eased the gun from his hip-pocket and moved it to his right-hand coat pocket. His finger was on the trigger, the safety catch was off.

The car slid to a stop, and then they heard the key in the lock and the wheeze of unoiled springs as the door opened. Mick heard the sounds gratefully. Caudry, at any rate, had not been discovered.

All his nerves were tensed when he heard the lock click on the inside door, and he heard the wood scrape the carpet as the door opened. But although he stared towards the opening, he could see nothing.

"Are you all there?" asked Maddick. Once again there was no trace of an American accent. The voice was deep pitched and vibrant.

One after the other they answered to their names as they had done on the previous evening.

"Borden," said Maddick, "stand away from this door unless you want to meet a sudden death. I want more breathing space, and I'm holding a gun in my hand."

"Sorry," said Mick, moving backwards. His finger was still on the trigger, and he had decided definitely that even in the dark he could hit the man in the doorway so that he would never rise again.

"That's better. You folks did your job well. That's all I'm going to say about that. Tomorrow morning you'll all get what's coming to you. I want you to stay here tonight, and then you will all be paid out together. Now we'll turn to one or two other things that I want to mention. After tomorrow we never meet again. If you want to run on with the same game you can. But you won't have me at the back of you, and if you accept my advice you'll get out while the going is good. Each of you will own a fair sum of money. But that's your concern, not mine.

"I have run my course and I'm satisfied. I have organised my last job. After today there will be no more Maddick. Is all that quite clear to you?"

Cardby saw a chance to speak—to delay the man's departure.

"Wait a minute," he said. "Before you make up your mind so definitely, I know a job that could be done that would be as good as the one today, and just as easy. I've had my eye on it each year for the past three years, and with your organisation we could get away with it easily."

"You won't tempt me," said Maddick, "but what is it?"

"The Wensbury Loan Club is paying out in three days' time. They'll have about four hundred and twenty thousand quid in their office, and the safe would be child's play for Tommy Kane. They've only got two night watchmen in the offices. It'd be the easiest thing you ever did."

"Where are their offices?"

"Corporation Street, Birmingham. The safe is on the ground floor, third room on the left as you go in. I know all about it. I nosed round that job for weeks and couldn't do it single-handed. Why not handle it and finish up with a grand slam?"

"Sounds too good to be true, Borden, but I'll think it over and let you know. Have any of you got any complaints before I go on to another matter? I don't want any of you to feel dissatisfied."

"Let's do this job that Pete was talking about," said Kane eagerly, and Mick could have shaken hands with the man gratefully.

"I have told you that I will consider it. That's enough."

"But Tommy could handle that safe like opening a sardine tin," said Mick to help things along.

## MADDICK ARRIVES!

"Be quiet! I am going to ask you all a question now, and anyone who lies to me will suffer for it. Is there one of you in this room who knows who I am?"

For a moment they were all quiet.

"I haven't the slightest idea," said Delaney, and the others hurried to plead equal ignorance.

"That is good. Now, I have been thinking today about those two people we have in the cellar. I do not think we can risk letting them free. That being so, I intend to dispose of them tonight. I take it that you have looked after them carefully?"

"I have looked after the girl," said Mick. "The man had nothing to do with me."

"Is the man all right, Delaney?"

"Yes, sir. I've looked after him."

"Then perhaps you two had better go downstairs and bring them up—unless you would prefer to do the job down there and save us the trouble."

Mick was between the devil and the deep sea. Which course should he take? The decision was taken out of his hands.

"We'll see 'em off in the cellar," said Alibi.

"All right. Don't move for a moment. I do not intend that you should walk past me. I am going into the room opposite while you attend to them. You can then return to this room."

"You want to be careful, sir," said Clancy; "Borden is a bit sweet on that girl."

"Borden," replied Maddick coldly, "has enough sense to know that if he played any trick with me he wouldn't live another five minutes."

The clock struck the half-hour. Mick was becoming desperate.

"It isn't that I'm sweet on the girl," he said, "it's only that I'm a bit sensible, and I don't agree with having her bumped off. It wouldn't be like an ordinary bumping off, and if you'd only stop to think about it you'd see what was going to happen. You'd never get away with it, never."

"We haven't got room for yellow folks," said Maddick.

"And you know damned well that I'm not yellow. If you dose that girl with lead you'll turn England upside down, and it won't be any good to us if you give us a hundred thou apiece. We won't live to enjoy it."

"Borden, you're talking too much. Whatever I say goes. And I say that we can't turn this girl loose. She's too dangerous. If you feel squeamish about it you can settle the man, and leave the girl to Delaney."

What was going to happen when they found that Caudry had gone? That was the most worrying thought in Mick's mind.

"Wouldn't it be better," he asked, "to clear out of here and leave them where they are? At any rate, they'd probably be dead before they were found, and by then we'd all be out of the danger zone."

"The girl is going to be bumped off tonight. So is the man. You two get downstairs and make a start on the job. I'm not going to stay here all night. And when you come back, Borden, there's another word or two waiting for you that won't be nice to hear."

"Then let's be hearing what it is."

"It's only this—that I've got a man in the car outside who saw you in Pall Mall this morning and he says that your name isn't Borden."

"Have you heard any more funny stories today?"

"Lay off being saucy. It won't pay you. This man says he can't swear about it until he's had another good look at you. So I brought him along. Before I go tonight he's going to give you the once over. If he is right, and you've been double-crossing, there'll be three bodies in the cellar instead of two."

"Is that so?" Mick tried hard to sound flippant. "And who is this guy with the bad eyesight and big imagination?"

"A very good friend of ours, a man who has helped us quite a lot. All that interests me is that I'd trust him in preference to trusting you."

"Thank you. And what's his name?"

"We know him as Lolly Morrison. But he might be known to you better as ex-Detective-Inspector Collier, formerly of New Scotland Yard!"

Cardby gasped. This was the end of the trail. Collier had often called at his house before he retired on pension. He had known Mick since he was ten or twelve years of age—had seen him as recently as two months before. Of course, the man would recognise him. Then the balloon would go up and hell would be let loose.

"Never heard of him in my life. Who does he say I am?"

"So far he hasn't told me. He says he'll let me know when he's had a good look at you."

"Right, I hope he enjoys it. When I've done that job in the cellar he can look at me for an hour if he wants to. Are you ready, Alibi?"

"Count ten before you start," said Maddick. "I'm crossing over to the other room."

The door slammed. The lights went up. Alibi and Mick left the room.

## 22

## MANY THINGS HAPPEN

The two men walked down the hall, shoulder to shoulder. Delaney was watching his companion out of the corner of his eye. They said nothing until they reached the kitchen, and took the torch from the shelf.

"You're going first," said Alibi. "I don't fancy having you at the back of me. Go on. I'll carry the torch."

"Getting the jumps a bit, aren't you?"

"No, but I heard what Maddick said about you double-crossing, and I'm going to see that you don't do it on me. Let me tell you, smarty, that if you're going to be bumped off later in the evening, I'm the one who is going to have the pleasure of doing it."

"That's something for you to look forward to. Shine the light on these steps. I don't want to break my neck going down."

Mick was trying to remember whether he had locked the door after letting Caudry out. He couldn't remember. He knew that at his back, not three feet away, was a revolver. Delaney had taken it from his pocket when they reached the kitchen. Mick kept his hands in his jacket pockets. He, too, had a finger on the trigger.

At the foot of the steps he waited until Alibi joined him. Then again they paced shoulder to shoulder as they advanced to the cellars.

"We'll take the man first," said Delaney.

"Suits me." Mick was relieved. If the girl had been chosen first it would soon have been known that she held the key to the cell.

He was still more encouraged when he saw that the door to the other cellar was locked. Delaney nodded to the key.

"Turn that," he said, "and you can use your right hand to do it."

"Can I? Well, I'm not going to, Delaney. Why you've got a drop on me I don't know, but if you think I'm going to take my mitt off my gun while you hold yours, you've got another think coming to you. I'll open the door with my left hand, thank you, or not at all."

Delaney looked down at his companion's coat and saw the circular bulge where the nozzle of the gun was pressed against the cloth. Mick put his foot into the door after turning the key.

"Let's step inside," he said. "You'll have to go first, since you've got the light. Carry on, and I'll follow you."

Delaney looked at him suspiciously and walked through the opening. He swung the light round inside the cell and then turned quickly on his heels.

"What the—" he started, but never completed the sentence.

Cardby took his hand off the gun and gripped Delaney round the throat. The man gurgled and dropped his gun as the pressure increased. But Alibi was no weakling. He bucked and bent, wriggled and twisted all over the flagged floor, fighting with his hands to loosen the grip. Mick set his teeth and held on. Delaney swung suddenly, and Mick's head crashed against the wall, sending a blinding pain through his head and bringing tears to his eyes. For a second his grip relaxed.

Delaney didn't wait for another chance. Wheeling quickly, he struck home with both fists into the pit of Cardby's stomach and followed this with a savage kick that numbed his leg. Mick heard the breathing near him, and struck, only to miss.

The torch had fallen to the ground and they were battling in the dark. Delaney edged towards the door and Mick dived for his knees. Both of them crashed to the floor. There they wrestled and clawed like madmen. Mick felt the blood spurt on his face where Delaney's nails had savaged a deep track. Then he felt the jar on his knuckles as his fist met solid flesh. Alibi groaned and flayed desperately with both hands. One of them caught Mick under the eye, another one cut his nostril. Then his fingers smarted again as they pounded on the man's mouth. His hand was being lacerated on his opponent's teeth.

Delaney threw himself to the left and Mick went with him. Over and over they rolled, panting, cursing and fighting. Cardby slid from under the man and stood waiting for him to get up. He saw the man rising like a dim shadow. The bulk loomed in front of him. Cardby peered through the mask of blood. He had been gashed over his right eyelid and the blood was streaming into his eye.

Then he balanced himself on the balls of his feet, drew back his hand and let it go again with every ounce of his strength behind it. The jar of the impact staggered him. He heard a dull crash as Delaney's head struck the wall on the far side of the cellar. Then all was still.

Getting down on his hands and knees he searched for the torch, praying that it had survived the smash. He was in luck. It had fallen on one of the steel rings set in the wall, and that had broken its impact when it struck the floor. He turned on the light and looked at Alibi. The man was hopelessly unconscious, his face smothered with blood, his lips cut and sagging over gums where teeth had been and were not. Mick looked at his clothes. They were badly blood-splashed. That meant that he dare not go upstairs again!

He looked at his watch. It was quarter to eight. Suddenly he picked up Delaney's revolver and fired it. The crash of the report filled his ears, the sound bellied round and round the cellar.

Acrid smoke filled the air. He dashed out of the cellar, stopping to lock the door behind him. Then he pulled his own gun out of his pocket and walked towards the steps—a gun in each hand.

God! If he could only keep Maddick and the crowd in the house for another quarter of an hour!

There came the sound of hurrying feet at the stairhead.

"Maddick wants to know what in hell you're playing at down there," shouted Clancy. "He doesn't aim to wait all night for you. Get the job done and slip out of it."

"It's this damn fool Delaney," shouted Mick. "I can't do anything with him. He's chawing to the girl instead of getting on with it. Trying to make himself look smart, I suppose."

"I'll make him look smart, blast him," cried Clancy, and Mick heard the rattle of his feet as he came tearing down the steps. The youngster slid to the side of the wall where the stairs debouched into the cellar. He changed his guns over, holding the revolver in his right hand. Clancy shot into the passage from the bottom stair. But he did not get far.

Mick raised his arm and the butt of the heavy gun fell on the back of the man's skull with a crash. Clancy twirled like a top, flung his arms into the air, and pitched face downwards on the stones.

Without hesitating Cardby pocketed the guns and seized the man by the shoulders. Then he dragged him along to the cell occupied by Alibi, unlocked the door and threw him in, fastening the door again.

Walking back towards the stairs, he raised his gun again and fired. He waited intently. Once more he heard feet pounding along the passage upstairs. Kane called from the top of the stairs!

"Have you all gone mad down there? What the hell are you doing? If you don't get out of it pretty slick Maddick'll be keeping you all there for good. Come on, he's waiting to go."

"Delaney's gone crazy," said Mick. "He started fighting with me and then Clancy came down to help me out, and Delaney's plugged him. Clancy stopped a slug in the ribs, and I can't get Delaney out of the girl's cellar. It's terrible, Tommy, come on down and let's see if we can settle him."

The safe-breaker walked unsuspectingly into the trap. A minute later he lay on the floor beside Clancy and Delaney. This time Mick took the guns from them. So now he held one in each hand and one in each pocket! He was sure now that Maddick would wait no longer. He must have smelt a mouse. The man was much too wily to fall into a trap similar to those laid for Clancy and Kane. The youngster wondered where Caudry was—what he was doing. A lot depended on that kid now, and he was barely strong enough to stand on his feet.

Mick turned out the torch and slid it into a trouser pocket. He did not want to walk around in darkness, but at least he had the pleasure of knowing that if he could see no one they, at any rate, could not see him. Without a sound he made his way to the head of the steps.

He stood for a few seconds outside the kitchen door. Which way should he go? If Maddick walked out through the front door Caudry would have him. Mick decided that his best plan was to remain in the house, guarding the exit at the rear. At any minute he expected to hear Mariel's voice raised, to hear the strong tones of Maddick issuing instructions, to see the front door burst open, and Clason and Collier tear into the house with guns in their hands.

But Mick wiped the blood off his face and grinned. He had something to smile about. The girl was safe. Caudry was free. He had Maddick within a few yards of him, and, above all, he had come to the showdown in a blaze of action. But it wasn't over yet—not by a long way.

He heard the door open on the left of the hall. That would be Mariel. Then soft footsteps sounded, coming towards him. He drew back into the kitchen, hiding at the back of the door.

The woman passed within two feet of him. He held his breath. What would she do?

He heard the swish of her clothes, smelt the perfume as she stood near him. Crossing the kitchen she opened the door leading to the cellar and stood silent. No noise came from below.

Cardby could see her dim outline. A faint light was filtering through the dirty windows of the kitchen. He might not get another chance like this. Quickly he slid a gun into his pocket and took a large silk handkerchief from his breast pocket. On tiptoe he moved forward. When he was a yard away from the woman she spun round—too late. The handkerchief was stuffed over her mouth, and Mick seized her by the waist with his other arm and swung her off her feet. She kicked and wriggled as he started down the stairs with her. Twice she almost tore herself loose, but Mick tightened his grip. Should he tap the woman behind the ear with the gun? That would help things a lot. But he wouldn't do that.

He was carrying her towards the far cellar when he heard a sound that brought him to a standstill. He knew, without thinking, what he had heard, and his heart sank. He dropped the woman to the floor, but before he could turn she sprang at him, clutching him from behind. He felt agonising pain as her pointed nails dug into his neck and scraped his throat.

Spinning round, he flung the woman into a corner. Then, deciding that the time for squeams had gone, he walked over and struck her on the skull with the butt of the revolver.

As the woman sank to the floor, unconscious, he darted up the steps two at a time. But when he reached the door he knew that his worst fears were realised. Maddick, hearing the struggle as he took the woman into the cellar, had dashed from the front room to bolt the cellar door from the outside!

Cardby placed the two guns on the step and examined the other pair, looking for the heaviest weapon. He chose a .38. Without bothering to turn on the torch he fumbled until he found the lock. Then he balanced the gun over a fork made by his fingers and fired into the lock. He heard the blinding crash, the scream as the bullet tore through the wood and steel. He shook the door. The lock had gone. Only the bolts remained. He emptied the gun on them, firing twice into the top bolt and three times into the bottom one before the door gave way.

He dashed into the passage. The front door was wide open. Without pausing, he leapt down the steps expecting to find that the car—and Maddick—had gone.

But the car was still outside the door. Clason sat at the driving wheel, holding his hands in the air. By his side sat ex-Inspector Collier, and in the back of the car Mick saw the snarling face of Andy from New Street. Young Caudry stood with one foot on the board of the car and the gun in his hand was surprisingly steady.

"He's gone through the back, Cardby," he said, without turning his head. "He can't be more than a hundred yards away. Beat it."

Mick waited no longer. In twenty strides he passed through the house. The door opening on to the yard was yawning, and he jumped down the three steps, sliding a couple of yards on the rough stones before he regained balance. He put one of the guns into his pocket. He could run better with a free hand.

He knew that any fool could pick him off as he hurried from the house.

# 23

## MICK MEETS MADDICK

He could see more clearly now that he was in the open. The darkness in the house was much more dense, and his eyes were now picking up outlines that would ordinarily be invisible. The rain was now tumbling down, and he heard the continuous splash as it cascaded off the roof through the worn gutterings. Which way did Maddick go? That was the question.

Running through the garden, dodging along the criss-cross paths, peering behind bushes and into derelict summerhouses, Mick could see no trace of the man. He stood against the railing dividing the garden from the paddock when a neighbouring clock pealed eight strokes. Hell, what a lot had happened in half an hour!

Running wildly, he got half-way across the paddock, and then saw the wood looming up before him. He remembered that the men from the Yard would be in position there. He need not bother about that part of the hunt. And the front of the house was well guarded. But somewhere between the house and the wood Maddick had gone to earth — and Mick meant to find him. He spun round and ran back towards the gardens, vaulting the rails to save the time needed to find the gate. Now he ignored the paths. What did it matter to him if he trampled all over the grounds.

He thought as he ran. Maddick could not have got to the wood during the brief time he had left the house. He would not go round to the front of the house, knowing that in that way lay danger. It all came back to one thing—he must be in one of the outhouses or hidden in the garden.

This was no time to consider risks, thought Cardby, and he turned on the torch, running in the wake of the yellow pencil of light. From the front of the house he heard the roar of motors. The Yard had arrived!

Mick passed through the garden and commenced another search of the outhouses. One by one he examined them carefully, but all four were empty. Disconsolate, he turned to one of the side-paths and started walking towards the paddock again. Then he came to a stop.

Before him, tucked away in the corner of the garden was a small two-storeyed cottage—obviously built for the use of a gardener. In itself there was nothing remarkable about that.

But Mick had seen a glint of light in one of the downstairs windows. The flicker had been momentary. For a second he had thought that it might have come from his torch, but, brief time though the light shone, he was able to note that only the window was lit, that there was no spread of light on the surrounding wall. That meant, beyond all question, that the light had been flashed *inside* the cottage.

Cardby turned out his torch and put it away. Then he examined his own automatic to ensure that there should be no mistake. He stepped off the path and paced slowly along through the soil of a long flower-bed. Each few yards he had to pass farther into the garden to avoid a bush. But all the time his eyes were fixed on the cottage windows. He saw no more light. Yet the earlier flash could not have been imagination.

The rain eased down, and a crescent moon sailed from behind a thick cloud, silvering the garden. Now he could see the cottage clearly. It had not been used for years—so much was obvious with the first glance. Not one of the windows had preserved all its panes. The brickwork was mouldering and there were slates missing from the roof. Even the front door was twisted at an angle, lying drunkenly on a broken hinge. Behind the cottage a spinney of trees rose against the blue-black sky.

He slowed down again and examined the place for a minute before going nearer. Curiously enough, it had not occurred to him to wait until help arrived. During the past few minutes the issue between himself and Maddick seemed to have become acutely personal.

Ten feet away from the entrance to the cottage Mick stepped back on to the path. Behind him he heard the clamour of voices. But inside the cottage all was quiet.

He walked forward and touched the door with his left hand. It swung inwards and then swung out again. The top hinge had corroded and the action of the one joint had given the door a back-lash. Again he pushed the door, and this time he pressed his body against it and jumped inside the room. His feet struck something lying on the floor and he pitched to the ground.

The gun flew from his hand and he heard it slide across the floor. He placed his hands on the stone flags and raised his head. At that moment he heard a sound behind him and swerved to one side. But he was too late.

Something struck him at the back of the head, a world of stars exploded before his eyes, then he felt himself falling, falling . . .

A film of red waved before his eyes like an undulating belt. He moved his head slightly. The effort sent a stab of pain through him. His head felt useless, heavy, too heavy for his neck to bear the weight. And he felt sick. He turned and tried to move his arms. He could not. In some distant way he thought they were broken. He moved his wrists again. No, he was wrong, his arms were bound. Thoughts came to him slowly, very slowly. He felt a pain in his right leg and twisted, trying to get into a more comfortable position. But he couldn't move his legs. They, too, were bound. The slightest effort wearied him, brought sweat to his face. He tried to think. What had happened? What had he done? Had Delaney hit him? What had happened in the cellar?

Recollection came back to him with a flash of memory. Now he recalled falling inside the cottage. And Maddick had hit him. Where was he now? He would not open his eyes until he had thought a little. Better to play possum for a while. Surely his father would soon appear. They were not more than fifty yards from the house. A search party would arrive at any minute. In his head came a succession of buzzes, and then thumps that jarred him.

He heard a movement near him, and then a sharp pain ran through his leg. He flinched.

"Come along," said a voice. "Stop shamming. You've come round."

Mick knew that further dissimulation would gain nothing for him. His eyelids felt heavy as he raised them.

Before him stood Mr Conway Addison, K.C.!

"Permit me," he said, bowing, "to introduce you to Maddick."

So this was the end of the trail. The hunt had ended the wrong way round. He had set out to find Maddick. Now Maddick had found him!

"I'm delighted to meet you," said Mick, opening his bruised and bloody lips in a grin. If the end had to come there was no sense in squealing; he had played his hand and apparently lost.

"You're a very impetuous young man," remarked Maddick casually, as though reproving a small boy.

"And you," replied Cardby, "are a very foolish old man to think that you could get away with your game for ever."

The man didn't answer and Mick looked round the room. He was astonished. The place was about twelve feet square, and the walls were draped with silk-fashioned hangings. An electric light hung from the ceiling, shaded by an alabaster bowl. An electric fire glowed in the corner and a Chinese rug covered the floor. In the corner facing Mick was a silk-covered divan, and before the fire was an easy chair. Two bookcases filled the walls. His eyes turned upwards. The ceiling was panelled with polished pine boards.

Maddick saw tne look of mystification and smiled tolerantly.

"Don't puzzle your brain. I'll tell you where you are. You're under the cottage. I arranged this place weeks ago. Quite comfortable, isn't it?"

"Absolutely. How long do you imagine you're going to stay here?"

"Only for a few days—just until it's convenient to remove. Of course, you understand that when I move you will have to be left behind?"

"Naturally. I'd hate to think that you might encumber yourself by taking me as excess luggage."

"So would I. Seeing that there's no animosity between us, I don't mind revealing a secret to you. Do you see that cylinder standing on the top of the bookshelf? That's full of carbon dioxide. When I leave I will shut the door behind me after I've turned on the tap to give you the contents of the cylinder. The room, let me assure you, is almost airtight and quite sound proof."

"Why not put me out of the way now?"

"For two reasons. In the first place, I want someone to talk to. In the second place, I would hate to live here with a corpse until the time comes for me to leave. It isn't that I have any sympathy for you—just that in all things I consider myself."

They were silent for a time. The room was deadly quiet. Addison lit a cigarette and sat down on the arm of the chair. He had taken off his outdoor clothes. Now he wore a neatly-cut dinner suit, and the change of clothes and surroundings made him look younger.

"You're a wonderful optimist," said Mick. "How do you think you're going to get out of the country?"

Why should I get out of the country?"

"Because I am not the only person who knows who Maddick is."

"You're lying. Who else do you say knows?"

"I wouldn't bore you with the list of names. Certainly Chief Constable Cross knows, and Chief Inspector Cardby, and Chief Inspector Hall, and more of the men from the Yard."

"I don't believe you."

"You need not. It doesn't matter to me one way or another. Of course, one further trouble you'll have to face is that you'll gain nothing by the robbery you staged this morning. The police have already taken the jewellery away from the warehouse. Just too bad, isn't it?"

Addison puffed at his cigarette and watched the spirals circle to the ceiling.

"You were too young for the job," he said, "much too young. It was like sending a three-year-old into the bull-ring. They ought to have known that you never had a chance."

"Why say that? You haven't won all the tricks just because you're alive and I'm going to die. Your gang is busted, you've got none of your money, you can't return to your home or your chambers, and so far, the police have arrested Clason, Delaney, Clancy, Mariel, Andy, Tommy Kane, the men at the warehouse, Taxi Long and another score of your assistants. If you get away with your life—and I'm sure you won't—

you'll be on the run till the day you die. Just think that over, Addison."

"I've thought all that over. You've been a great nuisance, young man. By the way, now that we are friendly, you might let me know your name."

"Certainly. I am Michael Cardby, the son of Chief Inspector Cardby."

"Well, well, well," said Addison, "so that's why Collier thought he knew you? Pity you've got to die. You'd have made a good policeman."

"I was just thinking that there might have been a day when you were a good barrister. What started you on this game?"

"It's a long story, my lad, and one that would probably tire you."

"I don't think so. After all, we've got to pass the time away somehow. Before you begin just do one small thing for me. Grab one of those cushions from the divan and shove it under my head. The bump is aching, and the floor isn't improving it."

"Of course I will. That gun-butt fell on you quite heavily, Cardby. For a moment I thought you were dead. You certainly came a purler over that log in the doorway. Hold your head up. There you are!"

"That's better. Now you can start on the story. We've got plenty of time. Would you like to give me a cigarette before you begin?"

"Certainly."

The men were treating each other with mock courtesy.

"If I wander from what I'm saying, just stop me. I don't mind telling you all I know. Again, I'm doing it for my own satisfaction—not for yours. I have never told anyone before, and it might ease my feelings to talk a bit. Then, again, I'll get a certain amount of pleasure out of giving you information that you want, knowing with each sentence that you'll be aching at the thought that you'll never live to tell the story. That'll be a sweet bit of the revenge. Make yourself comfortable."

"I feel quite pampered. Now let's hear all about it."

"I'll have to start with a time three years or more ago."

# 24

## MADDICK'S STORY

"When I came back from India I had come to the end of my money, and I had no name at the English Bar," said Maddick, as though lecturing. "For a time things were very difficult. Then I had a brief to defend Phillips, the man who held up the Midland Bank at Lomney and got away with four thousand pounds. During our consultations he told me where he had cached the money. He got three years. While he was serving his time I took the money. That's what started me.

"You can imagine that I was worrying about the time when he came out. For months I wondered what I could do when he found that I had taken his money. At last I decided that I might as well go the whole hog. I was already a robber; I might as well be a murderer. So I met him coming out of Dartmoor and told him that I would drive him to the place where he had left the money. He never got there. I killed him en route and dumped the body in the Hampshire Avon with a couple of good weights on the legs. To this day I have heard nothing about it being recovered."

The man confessed the murder quite light-heartedly. There was no trace of remorse detectable in his speech, no sympathy for the dead man.

"Things were still bad at the Bar," he continued, "and I thought some money might be made in other channels.

After my one experiment with crime it didn't seem to me to be difficult. So I sat in my chambers for weeks and months, considering ways and means. I did not intend to undertake the committal of crimes myself. It was my ambition to build up an organisation on a grand scale.

"First of all, I had to get the men. That was easy, particularly since my work called me into the courts often. Whenever I came in contact with a man of exceptional brilliance in his own line of crime I got into touch with him through indirect channels and recruited him. I had a little capital by me, and I used that to pay the men during the time when I was making my complete arrangements. I saw at that stage that the big secret of success is to dovetail the work among a number of men and let no man know anything of the business in hand beyond the piece of work apportioned to him.

"It was necessary for me to organise distributing channels. I did all that thoroughly. My jewellery was sold to the old firm of Taylor and Co. of Covent Garden. I bought that firm through a nominee from the liquidators, and the police never realised that it had changed hands. Then I founded a firm called Merediths, Limited, in Leadenhall Street, and they handled all cash I received. Why shouldn't they? They were, and are, recognised foreign exchange brokers. I had no trouble at all in disposing of any of the stuff I got hold of. The only important thing was to prevent the parties concerned discovering who ran these affairs. I think I may claim that as a counsel learned in the law I know enough of nominee practice to use every device possible."

Addison paused to light another cigarette.

"So much for the stuff I had to sell. But then, again, I had to create some establishment to act as a barrier between me and those who worked for me. It took me a long time to consider that matter. Finally I formed the Regent Income Tax Agency. Such businesses receive all sorts of callers in large numbers; it

# MADDICK'S STORY

would act as an adequate shield. Of course, I didn't mean to bluff the whole way. That would have been dangerous. As a matter of fact, Cardby, that agency did an enormous amount of genuine work. I had a crack income tax man in my chambers, and he gave them advice, and Newall, a solicitor, did a lot of work for the agency. Clason was just the figurehead, and he was the only person in the whole crowd who knew me.

"I could trust him. He's my brother. Am I boring you?"

"Not a bit. Most interesting recital. Carry on."

"When I wanted anything done I would inform Clason, and he'd pass out the information through the Regent Income Tax Agency. Likewise, when he wanted me to learn something, he would ask for a legal opinion upon some matter affecting one of his clients. In that way I could keep my finger on everything without being seen. You would never have checked the phone calls that I made—I never discussed anything other than legal matters from my house or my chambers.

"Well, Cardby, as time went on I found that I didn't have to look round for recruits. Those who already worked for me were only too anxious to get their pals into the crowd. All I did was to look around and pick upon anyone who looked bright. That's why I picked on you and sent that solicitor along to defend you. But I ought to have smelled a rat when you got out of Brixton. I was taken off my balance for a minute and thought it was further proof of your cleverness. That's why I was glad to have you as a recruit.

"Of course, as time went on I found that more and more money was needed to pay all those working for me. Perhaps you won't believe me when I tell you that I've paid out as much as three hundred thousand pounds in the one year. But it's a fact. I took over houses in the West End and in the suburbs so that I'd know where the men were when they were wanted, and that added to the expense. That's why, reluctantly, I had to utilise the houses for anything that would bring in money."

"I don't see why a thief and a murderer should be squeamish."

"Perhaps you don't. But I have always contended that a murderer can still be a moralist. I'm one myself. Now you know, broadly, how everything was done. The police troubled us from time to time, but they were never near enough to the truth to cause me anxiety. If they employed narks we soon found out, and they went the way of all flesh."

"What happened to Caudry then? Why didn't you murder him?"

"Because the information we were getting about the Yard wasn't altogether new, since Collier has been away for a year, and we thought that Caudry might pass on some useful information. But he was very, very obstinate. We couldn't do anything with him at all. That's why, tonight, I decided to put him out of the way."

"And what about Miss Gribble?"

"That was really more bravado than anything else. When I knew that the Yard had employed her I thought I would give them a scare so that they wouldn't repeat the dose. I telephoned to her asking her to meet her father outside the Marble Arch at five o'clock. The rest was easy."

"Did you really mean to kill her?"

"Certainly. I daren't let her go after I'd taken her, and I imagined that if they discovered her body they would not be quite so enthusiastic about employing amateurs."

"What made you agree to talk to me that night at Hobart Place?"

"I really thought myself that a squeal had been put in, and I wanted to see if you knew anything about it. That place I took furnished for six months and installed Clancy and his wife—she's Clason's daughter, by the way—my niece. I had a microphone rigged up in the lounge so that I could hear what was said, and that phone you talked to me on only had a ten-foot wire."

"You seem to have arranged things very nicely. A moment ago you told me that Mariel was your niece. Do you mean that she didn't know you?"

"She knew me as her uncle, but not as Maddick."

"What's the next item on the agenda?"

"I feel very, very tired. I'm getting old, Cardby, and I can't keep long hours as I used to. I'm afraid you'll have to have an artificial sleep. I don't think you can wriggle loose, but you're such an enterprising young man that I daren't trust you. I think if I give you just one prick of morphia I can sleep quite safely."

"I don't think you'll have to bother about it," said Mick drowsily. "I can hardly keep my eyes open."

His head was swimming and he breathed more deeply. Addison rose from the arm of the chair and quickly sat down again. His eyes fluttered and closed, and, with an effort, he opened them again. There was a heavy, sweet smell in the air. He looked round curiously and started towards Mick. His legs were shaky and a weight pressed on his head.

Cardby lay still, his face pale, his breathing stertorous.

Twice Maddick made an attempt to reach the small cabinet in the corner of the room. Then, with a last glance at Mick, he abandoned the attempt and staggered towards the divan. The air was heavy, the pungent smell increasing. Addison lay on the divan and tried to marshal his wits. What was happening? What was wrong?

But his bemused brain wasn't equal to the occasion, and he fell back on the cushions with a weary sigh.

There was no sound in the room except for the deep breathing of the two men. They were not sleeping.

They were both unconscious!

# 25

## THE RESCUE

At eight o'clock the night was filled with sound and light. A squad car tore up the drive to the "Withies" and stopped with a jerk a few feet away from the front door, the bonnet nearly touching the radiator of another car. Five men jumped out, Inspector Cardby at the head.

Caudry pointed to the men in the car and gasped out his story. He was wan and trembling, almost at the end of his resources.

"Reeves!" shouted Cardby, and the inspector came running across the lawn with a man at his side.

"Take charge of these men. You say, Caudry, that Maddick ran out through the back and my boy ran after him?"

"That's right, sir, and all the others are fastened in the cellar."

"Then get down to the gate as well as you can and tell Inspector Hall when he comes to go straight down to the cellar and take charge of the folks. Then you'd better rest in one of the cars. Come on, Gribble."

The men rushed through the house into the yard and through the garden. They stopped in the paddock, meeting the Chief Constable as he led his men to the house.

"Seen two men running?" asked Cardby.

"No. We've come right through from the wood and haven't seen anyone. What's happened?"

"We've got everybody but Maddick. He ran through the back with Mick chasing him. Spread out and we'll search the grounds. They can't have got to the wood, and there are men in the fields on both sides of the house. We'll find 'em somewhere in the garden." Cardby didn't say what he feared— that they would find two corpses.

As they spread out, a man came running down the path.

"Thought you'd like to know," he shouted to Gribble, "that your girl is all right. She was in the cellar."

"Thank you," bawled Gribble, and went on with his search. Footprints were found, followed for a few yards, and then abandoned. Ten minutes went by without any tangible find. Then Cardby heard a man call to him from the far side of the garden.

"Just a minute, inspector."

The stout man covered the ground with a speed amazing for a man of his bulk. He found the caller on a side-path.

The man flashed his torch on the garden bed at the side of the path. There were deep prints in the wet soil.

"Someone stepped off the path here," he said.

"Look, sir. They kept moving round these bushes."

The moon had retired again and the night was black. Cardby raised his torch and saw the cottage in front of him.

Slipping his hand into his pocket he drew a gun. After all his service with the Yard this was the second time in his life that the inspector had carried one. By now Cross and Gribble had joined him, together with four or five men.

"Keep quiet," whispered Cardby, as he led the way. He followed the footmarks until he was within three yards of the broken door. Then they stopped.

"This is where someone stepped on to the path again," he said. "They must have made straight for the door. Let's walk in, but for the love of God, keep quiet."

They advanced on tiptoe. Gribble held back the door while Cardby shone his torch round the room. His eye caught a glimpse of two things that took the colour from his face. Against the wall, on the far side of the room, was an automatic. At his feet was a plank, so placed that anyone entering the room must fall over it.

He stepped over the plank, beckoning to the others to stay outside for a moment. Then he picked up the gun and his lips tightened. It was Mick's automatic. His light stabbed the floor and he saw something else. On the stone flag some three feet away from the gun were splashes of blood. He looked round the room. Obviously it had not been used for some time. The plank was the only article to be seen. There were cracks in the flagged floor, and the fireplace had fallen away from the wall. Windows were missing and streaks of green damp showed on the walls.

He stared at the floor and then walked through into the kitchen at the back. He saw the broken sink, an old boiler—there was nothing else in the room. The back door was open. Beyond was a small plot of uncultivated ground—then the hedge surrounding a field. He returned to the front room and made his way towards the worn stairs in the corner. They were worm-eaten and looked dangerous. Cardby decided that some lighter man could make the ascent with less risk. He called Gribble, and the thin man vanished to return a couple of minutes later.

"Two empty rooms that haven't been used for years—that's all."

The men walked outside and joined the others. They retired down the path for a conference.

"Maddick got to that cottage first," said Cardby, "and the lad went in after him. There's no doubt about that. And there's no doubt about the fact that they're not far away. Maddick couldn't get far himself—let alone carry a man like Mick for a distance with him."

# THE RESCUE

"Then where the devil are they? "asked Cross, bewildered.

Cardby did not reply. Instead he ran over to the hedge and called to the sergeant in the field.

"Seen anyone go by this way?"

"No, sir. Not a sign."

The inspector returned to the path before the cottage and examined the footprints again.

"There's something very funny about this," he said, as he straightened up. "I know it sounds impossible, but I reckon they're somewhere in that cottage. These tracks go one way, but there are no marks leading away from the house. Where could they be?"

"Is there a cellar?" asked Cross.

"Damn it," said Cardby. "I never thought of that. I'll have another look round. You folks can wait here."

He examined the ground floor of the cottage again, but could find no cellar. Gribble was walking round the outside walls, flashing his torch here and there in an endeavour to pick up a clue. At the back of the house he saw a small grid covering a drain. The pipe leading to the drain had broken off short about four feet above the ground. Gribble was walking away when he slipped, his feet sliding on a mass of dead leaves.

Mick knew nothing about that fall. But it saved his life!

The sergeant's head struck the wall and he slid to the ground, his face turning towards the cottage. When he came to rest his face was over the grid. For a second he lay, trying to gather his senses. Then he rose to his feet. It was when he was walking away that a presentiment came to him, a thought that some valuable experience had just been his. He stood still, trying to place his thoughts. He walked back to the grid. What had attracted his attention?

He knelt on the soil and bent over the grid. Immediately he knew what had occurred to him.

The air coming from the grid was warm!

He placed his hand over the opening. Then he sniffed.

Gribble scrambled to his feet and hurried back to the other men.

"Is there a man among you who doesn't smoke? "he asked.

"I don't," said one of the detectives.

"Then come over here with me... Put your nose over that grid. Tell me, can you smell anything?"

"Yes, tobacco smoke."

"You're sure?"

"Positive."

"Right. That will do."

Gribble found Cardby at his elbow and he led the inspector away.

"There's a room under that cottage," he said. "The grid there is used as a ventilator, and the air coming through is warm. Besides, there's someone smoking down there. What shall we do?"

"Get some crowbars and bust the place in," said Cross.

"No, you don't," asserted Cardby quickly. "If Maddick is down there with my lad you can bet that the boy is out of action. Maddick knows that he's going to swing in any case if we catch him, so another murder won't make any difference. He knows by now that the lad has caused all this trouble. If we break in like that the first thing Maddick will do is to kill the boy. Then probably he'll turn the gun on himself. We'll have to think out something better than that. Let's get away from this place for a bit. Two of you men can stay here and keep an eye on things."

The inspector led the way to the house. Sweat stood in beads on his face, and his forehead was wrinkled with worry.

All the prisoners stood in the front room, surrounded by police. Mavis Gribble dashed towards her father, swinging her arms round his neck. Cardby turned away. The greeting brought a lump into his throat. He was glad—more than

## THE RESCUE

glad—that Gribble had got his daughter back safely. But what about Mick? He was not the only one through whose mind that question was running. The girl, agitated and pale, was plying her father with questions about young Cardby. Her only answer was a gloomy shake of the head. Tears came to her eyes and she walked away.

Still thinking, the inspector left the men and walked up the stairs, wandering aimlessly from bedroom to bedroom, turning on lights and looking round without particular interest. He ascended to the second floor. There he opened a door facing the stairs and turned on the light. His brows wrinkled and his eyes were staring.

The room contained nothing but cylinders and bottles. Cardby, in spite of his oft-repeated pleas of ignorance, was no fool. He walked over to the first cylinder and turned it on. Then he sniffed. There was no chance of mistaking that foul odour—it was sulphuretted hydrogen. He tried another and coughed violently—it was hydrochloric acid gas, the next was bromine, and the next chlorine. He turned his attention to the bottles. As he smelt the first, his eyes sparkled and he stroked his chin.

The bottle contained nearly a gallon of ether.

He lifted the bottle and walked downstairs, meeting Gribble and Cross in the hall. They stared at the bottle.

"We've got to do something soon," he said, "so we may as well take a risk as sit back and do nothing. Send the men round to find a few crowbars. This is a bottle of ether. I'm going to pour the whole lot down that ventilating drain. That should put both of them to sleep. We'll wait for a couple of minutes after that before we rip up the floor. Hurry up and get those crowbars."

The men soon found two bars in the gardener's shed, and a few minutes later Cardby knelt at the side of the grid with the bottle in his hands. As a precaution he had soaked a handkerchief in cold water and tied it round his nostrils.

At first he allowed the colourless liquid to trickle down the drain. But after a few seconds he gave the bottle a more exaggerated tilt, and within two minutes the whole of the ether had gone. The sickly, sweet smell hung round the drain, and the inspector was glad to back away. They waited for a time in the garden before entering the cottage.

Four men held torches while Cardby and Gribble took the crowbars. The inspector selected a stone bearing a wide crack down the centre and threw his sixteen stone on the bar. The stone came up and was lifted out place. Then he and Gribble moved the next stone. Below was solid earth. Cardby took a spade and dug until the perspiration poured off him. He got down to a depth of two feet before his spade struck something solid. He turned the light downwards. His spade had struck wooden planks!

He took a pocket-knife from one of the men and cut a space between two of the boards big enough to insert the tip of the crowbar. Within a minute there was a crash as the wood gave way, and a beam of light shot through the opening into the cottage. The inspector slipped to his hands and knees and peered through the space. He was smiling when he stood upright. For below him Mick was lying on the floor, and Conway Addison—the inspector had seen him too often at the Old Bailey to forget his face—was lying on the divan. Both were unconscious.

"Gribble," said Cardby, "get your gun out of your pocket and point it at Maddick's heart while we make room enough to drop down. If he moves, tell him you've got the drop on him. And if he continues to move let him have it."

Ten minutes later the men hauled two limp forms through the opening in the floor into the cottage. Their most difficult task was to lift Cardby back into the room.

Outside in the air they unfastened Mick's arms and legs. Maddick was placed on the stone floor. His gun had been taken from him, his wrists were fastened in handcuffs, his ankles were also shackled, and a length of rope fastened the two pairs of bracelets together. They were taking no chances.

Mick was the first to recover, and his awakening was certainly pleasant. He opened his eyes to find Mavis Gribble bending over him. He smiled.

"Oh!" she said, and patted his face. "I'm so glad that you've come round. I was so worried. Are you feeling better, Mick?"

"Splendid, Mavis," he said, adding; "but if you leave me I'll be liable to go on again. Just stay where you are."

Addison came round in the front room. He stared in amazement at his shackles, looked at the group of men round him.

"Good evening," he said. "I am afraid I've caused you some inconvenience."

"Nothing worth mentioning," replied Cardby senior. "We had to smash the floor of your cottage, that's all."

"How careless of me not to have left instructions for you. The whole of that fireplace could be moved. There's a ladder at the back of it. How is my young friend, Cardby?"

"Do you mean my son?"

"Of course. Congratulations, you've bred a useful lad."

"Come along," said the Chief Constable, "we'll get you into the car. I'll charge you when we get to the Yard."

"It'll take half an hour to read them out, won't it?" asked Addison coolly. "I'm ready whenever you are."

Cardby and Gribble walked into the other room.

"Come along you two," said the inspector. "We're moving off."

"You are," said Mick, sitting up. "But we're not going with you. I feel fine now, and a slow drive will do me all the good in the world. I'll take Maddick's car and escort Mavis home. Then I'll come along to the Yard and tell you all you want to know. If you allow an hour for going home, another hour for thinking things over, and then half an hour to the Yard, that'll be about right. I'll be there then."

"A good policeman," said Cardby senior, "always thinks of his duty first."

"I'm not a policeman yet. Shut the door, dad, there's a draught."

# A fan of Sherlock Holmes?
# Then meet Solar Pons

The original fan fiction from the great August Derleth—the Sherlock Holmes of Praed Street.

"the best substitutes for Sherlock Holmes known."
– Vincent Starrett

"an excellent series of adventures in detection in their own right." – *The Chicago Tribune*

For more details and a full list of titles:
visit https://www.hachetteindia.com/home/yellowbacks